a strange and brilliant light

ELI LEE

Jo Fletcher
BOOKS

First published in Great Britain in 2021
This paperback edition published in 2022 by

Jo Fletcher Books
an imprint of
Quercus Editions Ltd
Carmelite House
50 Victoria Embankment
London EC4Y 0DZ

An Hachette UK company

A CIP catalogue record for this book is available
from the British Library

PB ISBN 978 1 52940 774 7

10 9 8 7 6 5 4 3 2 1

Typeset by CC Book Production
Printed and bound in Great Britain by Clays Ltd, Elcograf S.p.A.

MIX
Paper from
responsible sources
FSC® C104740

Papers used by Jo Fletcher Books are from well-managed forests
and other responsible sources.

Praise for *A Strange and Brilliant Light*

'Mind-bending'
Carole Stivers, bestselling author of *The Mother Code*

'Wonderfully written, putting a human face on the complex
prospect of work in the age of AI and what it means to be alive'
Nina Lyon, author of *Uprooted: On the Trail of the Green Man*

'A disquieting take on Big Tech's plans for the future of work'
Gwyneth Jones, author of *Bold As Love*,
winner of the Arthur C. Clarke Award

'Important ideas are wrapped in an absorbing,
character-driven novel that's also a thought-provoking
consideration of the ways we might cope with something
that is already happening all around us'
Lisa Tuttle, *The Guardian*

'Smoothly written'
Financial Times

'Lee gives the reader a massive amount to ponder as well
as delivering a brilliantly written and absorbing story
about some very real people'
Blue Book Balloon

'A slickly written and enjoyable novel'
SFcrowsnest

'A thoughtful, interior-focused story . . .
like Ishiguro's *Klara and the Sun*'
SFX Magazine

'A beautifully written, thought-provoking novel'
Muse's Book Journal

For my mother

PROLOGUE

One Year Earlier – Lal

Lal was starting to realise that even when you got what you wanted, there was something more to want. When she was very young what she wanted most was ice cream from Popotops. She didn't get it often, but on special occasions – her and Janetta's birthdays, and at the end of summer – their father would drive them to Conaus Square and she'd run through the glass doors into the café and excitedly announce her order. Coffee fudge, chocolate, banana marshmallow. Caramel sauce, cookie crumbs and chocolate chunks. For a moment she was in heaven, but all too soon her want would irrepressibly return – more, again, now.

There had been Popotops adverts on television back then, the screen filling with soft snowy spirals of white, rising to a perfect peak. She'd been rapt, begging her parents to take her there more often so she could stand in line between the cherry-topped tables and gaze at the bright silver coffee machine and banks of ice cream and shelves of cake and pie. Her father said that when she was eight, she actually lay down on the floor and screamed for it. He'd done an impression on the living-room carpet, fifteen years later. *Take me to Popotops!* he'd squealed in a high-pitched voice, writhing like an untrained puppy. *Take me to Popotops!*

Now she sat in her office at the back of the café, surrounded by boxes of tiny pink tubs and flimsy spoons and waffle cones. She'd invested a lot of time in becoming manager, including three years on the shop floor, standing, smiling and serving. It was the first time she'd sensed her own worth, and this wasn't something she'd ever felt before. Before had only been the wishing. She still gorged herself on ice cream with her friends who worked there, after hours when they were closing up, in their uniform of red baseball caps and white tunics with *Popotops* scrawled across the front. But she was capable, she seemed to love hard work, and when she became manager she was momentarily fulfilled, even if it was within the smallest world, just a chain café in a sleepy city on the western coast.

Today she was attending a conference at Tekna, the corporation that had acquired Popotops two years ago. It was the first time store managers had been asked to join, and she'd shut her office door as if to make a point – that she alone had been invited somewhere special. She could hear Rose and Van chat to customers outside or barge down the corridor to the storeroom. Van whistled or sang to himself. Rose was quieter, beyond the occasional box thudding to the floor and a sharp *Fuck!*

She drew the blinds over the single high window and in the gloom her screen awoke to show an empty stage; then the view changed, panning to the rows of Tekna managers and executives in the audience. They were waiting for something not just to start, but to *happen*, their faces alert, their bodies upright and expectant. They were five hundred miles south in Mejira, and she could see how pleased and proud they were to be there. She tried to picture herself actually there, sitting amongst them.

Suddenly the camera panned to a stark bone of spotlight and a woman appeared beneath it. She looked a lot like Lal. She had the same round cheeks, button nose, and plump lips, but on this woman they were sculpted more perfectly – the cheeks and nose more innocent, the lips plumper and fuller. She had the same short brown hair, too, except hers gave off a golden shimmer. Her eyes were placid and gentle, where Lal's were full of want, and she was thinner, too, in a way that someone full of want could never be. As she stood spotlit and alone, surrounded by darkness, a wild applause erupted before her. That elite audience, those managers and executives, came to life. There was whooping and cheering and the thunder of feet on the floor, pounding out approval. Lal was seized with an envy so intense that for a moment she couldn't breathe. She wasn't sure if she wanted to be the woman or the audience, but it didn't matter – she simply felt that old, pulsing need, a sense she deserved more than what she'd got, more than her soft body and her ordinary brains, more than being the waitress and then being the boss.

When she was younger she had not been promising, had not distinguished herself at all. At home she begged for attention, jealous of her older sister's intelligence and ease, but beyond this she was not memorable, nor did she try to be. There was a photo at someone else's birthday party, a few years before the carpet tantrum, in which all the other kids sat together with heaped bowls of cake and ice cream. Lal didn't have one – she'd been forgotten – and she was open-mouthed and helpless, frozen in time with this look of lack.

On-screen, meanwhile, the woman stood motionless, her hands cupped together, her face preternaturally calm. A man in a leather jacket strode onstage a moment later and came to stand beside her. Lal knew who he was – Uhli Ranh, Tekna's CTO, in charge of technology for all its brands, Popotops included. He looked under-slept, rumpled, and utterly in command of himself. He scanned the audience with a wide grin and basked in their applause. For a moment his gaze rested on the camera, on the store managers sitting in their poky offices all over the country, and then he turned to the woman beside him.

'They want to meet you.'

Lal's office grew darker, as if the sun had disappeared completely, and she focused on the woman's eyes, so bright they seemed lit from within. The woman stared straight ahead and minutely opened her mouth, and the audience went still.

'Hello, I'm Karina,' she said warmly. 'How can I help you?'

For this, she received a standing ovation. She continued to smile, fluttering her eyelashes, and Lal peered more closely. Her neck, she realised, was tilting at an angle that looked a touch too far down and a little too much to the left. She scanned the audience, her smile at halfmast now, and when her eyes came to rest again on the camera this time Lal saw it – the absence in them, the gentleness that had shaded not into something remote, not an unwillingness to connect, but instead had given way to a total vacancy. And then Lal understood. She was an aut.

'One day,' the aut said, still smiling, 'I will be just like you.'

After the applause had died down, Uhli Ranh took over. He was proud and bullish onstage. 'Karina here is a humanoid aut,' he told the crowd, 'a prototype, the first of her kind. To start with, we're putting her on the front line at Popotops, and then we're going to take her global.'

He looked at her affectionately, and the audience's whistles and claps and cries of joy continued. Lal took a picture of the aut and sent it to her sister. She was curious to see what she'd say – would she recognise what it was? The answer lit her phone up straight away; of course she did. You couldn't get around Janetta – she knew everything already. But then she asked if it was conscious.

What a strange question. Lal had no idea.

The door opened a crack. 'Sorry to interrupt,' Rose said, coming in. 'I need some Alti Bay.'

Lal didn't respond except for pulling her chair close to the desk so Rose could step past and plunder the coffee stores in the corner. The aut left the stage with a beatific smile and Ranh held out a black oval, as small as a seashell, in his palm.

'In a few months,' he said, eyeing them all knowingly, 'these server auts will be standard in every store across Iolra. Want to see how they work?'

Rose tore open a box behind her so Lal couldn't hear the answer, but Ranh lowered his palm to someone in the front row. 'Go on, ask it for a coffee.'

The woman said something and the aut flickered enigmatically blue.

'You think it got that?' Ranh said.

The audience was mesmerised. A tiny drone buzzed into view from the wings and deposited a coffee into the woman's hands.

'Great,' said Rose miserably.

'Shhh—'

'How can you lap this up? That aut is going to take our jobs.'

'Please, Rose—'

Behind her Rose was staring at the screen, balancing several bags of beans against her chest. Ranh was explaining that the server aut scanned your body and tracked wherever your payment device was – no need for you to do a thing.

'That's a horrendous privacy breach,' Rose said. 'Is he for real?'

'Can you please get out?'

They could talk to each other like this because they'd been best friends almost all their lives. Lal could give Rose a pleading stare and they'd both know it wasn't about her being left alone to do anything managerial, it was purely about her weakness for Tekna. It was common knowledge that Lal was in love with the company, while Rose hated it. But she decided to push the seniority angle anyway.

'This is for managers, Rose – you're not supposed to be here.'

But Rose didn't move, and she didn't take her eyes off the screen. Lal returned to it, too, to see Uhli Ranh standing with his hands on his hips, watching a small white cylinder do nothing. The top of a strawberry milkshake began to emerge slowly from it, then the rest of it too, as if from the depths of the earth. He handed it to a man in the audience, the broad, delighted grin never leaving his face.

Lal knew what this was doing to Rose. She could feel the heat of her anger, heard her breathing more loudly, prepared herself for recriminations. She imagined her spitting her wrath at Ranh, throwing bags of beans at the screen, boxes of spoons and cones. She turned and moved in front of the screen as if to shield those faraway executives from her friend.

But Rose was stunned. Her lower lip dropped and her face had taken on a greenish hue and she didn't say a word.

Lal said defensively, 'I told you – this is for managers only.'

Rose looked at her, dismayed, grabbed a stack of napkins and left. Lal almost flinched from the ice in her wake. Then she remembered Janetta's baffling question and quickly responded.

Back on the screen, amid the applause, an image of the Mejira skyline appeared, a horizon of chrome and glitter and glass, and at the centre was the Tekna Tower, vaulting into the clouds. After this there was a video on the origins of Tekna. Its founder had been an orphan, his parents killed in the Second Yalin War. He'd owned an integrated steel mill and diversified into shipbuilding, car manufacturing, retail and entertainment.

Watching this, Lal's eyes brightened. She thought of her years of want, her childish cravings when Popotops meant just scoops of thick sweetness, the weight of desire fulfilled. She was boxed in now by the very same thing, trapped in this world of her youth.

Outside, she heard the familiar cadences of Rose and Van talking, louder and more quickly than usual, Rose probably complaining about the auts she'd just seen. Lal blocked it out and focused on the screen. It appeared to her like gold, and her surroundings as a dull reproach. She wanted to put her hands through it, reach out to what was there – she wanted to disappear into it and enter that other world.

One Year Earlier – Rose

It had turned into a beautiful day. Rose was glad of it, because it meant her brother's barbecue could go ahead. She was in the mood for cracking open a beer or two in Naji's big, messy garden and chatting to his mates and not really having to think about anything too much. It had been a long time since her brother had decided to have people over, and while she knew it was partly because his girlfriend, Hela, was pregnant, and they wanted to celebrate it, she also knew that there was something symbolic about him finally opening his house up to guests again.

She had a day off, and before the rain had cleared and they knew the barbecue was going ahead, she hadn't known what to do with all that time on her hands. She had thought she would try to do some studying, or maybe see Lal, but she'd woken up depressed, so it was good she'd been given her orders for the day. There was a chance otherwise – quite a large chance – that she'd have ended up getting stoned and sitting in her room and thinking about things, or *not* thinking about things, just staring out of her window for hours at the block opposite. Her mum would have come in, she would have told her to go away; her brother Yash would have tried too, and although she liked his company, she'd have told him to go away as well. Now, though, they were all leaving together at two on the dot, all walking around to Naji's to spend the afternoon with his mates.

In the kitchen, her mum and Yash had made piles of sandwiches and her brother was wrapping them while her mum finished the washing-up.

'They look really nice.' Rose reached for a roll, but her brother slapped her hand away.

'Get off!'

Rose held her hands up. 'Sorrysorrysorry.'

'You can eat them when we get there.'

'Okay, okay,' she said, sloping over to her mother and resting her head on her shoulder.

Her mother wiped her hands on a towel, gave Rose a hug, and kissed her on the forehead. 'Come on, love, we'll have a nice afternoon.'

Rose stayed a moment longer, allowing the hug she'd asked for, then jerked away and, folding her arms, went back to her bedroom, fell onto her bed and exhaled.

They'd moved to this small flat a year ago and Rose's room was so close to the kitchen that they could probably hear her breathing. You knew when someone was sad here because they were all packed in together, breaths and sighs and cries criss-crossing constantly. The story was that Rose was sad right now because she'd broken up with her boyfriend, and it was true, she was somewhat upset about this. But it didn't explain her sense that she was moving underwater all the time, that everything good and real was far away and out of reach. It didn't explain the fact that even when she'd been with her boyfriend she'd felt like this. It didn't explain why every morning she woke up and felt a heaviness, had to force herself out of bed.

But her brothers were acting normally now, her mum was acting normally, and her dad, they'd all apparently decided, was the pictures on the mantelpiece. They walked past them however many times a day and that's how he stayed in their lives. She hadn't heard her mum cry for weeks. She didn't want to be the only one still struggling. She didn't mind looking weak, she just didn't want to *be* weak.

So let it be the boyfriend. The boyfriend she'd long grown out of and had chosen to get rid of herself. Let it be the boyfriend, and then she could leave thoughts of him at home and go to Naji's barbecue, and try to have some fun.

Her mum saw what was happening the moment she walked through the back gate, her arms filled with food.

'It's his bloody mates from the warehouse,' she hissed, mostly to Yash. Naji worked in a warehouse outside of town; the company that made and distributed electrical parts. He'd been there since he left school, almost a decade, so long now that it was hard to think of him ever working anywhere else. Yash found his brother's workmates intimidating and would have easily chosen the safety of his computer games over these scary, hulking guys. But Rose thought her mum and brother were being ridiculous – she recognised some of them and they were good people. Around her father's death, she'd even considered a couple of them to be friends.

'I'll go first,' she said, pushing past. Naji and his girlfriend, Hela, lived on one of the hills on the far side of Upper Sunset, in a dirty yellow house with a dark red roof that overhung it like a sunhat. The house was old and dilapidated, but it was Naji's kingdom; his first assertion that he was an adult, making it in the world on his own.

She gave Hela a hug – Hela who was alternately a perfect saint or famously bossy – though right now she was all smiles, her stomach the gentle round of the second trimester, her make-up – foundation, eyeliner, glossy lipstick – as intact as ever, but her dark hair for once unstraightened and curling at the bottom a little – and asked her how the baby was. It would be Rose's first niece or nephew, but she knew Hela wanted a brood; she'd made no secret of it. Naji didn't seem to care either way, though Rose felt he must have some private misgivings, but he left his friends and came over now, kissing his mum, hugging his younger brother and Rose, then finally putting his arm around his girlfriend.

'You see the next generation!' he said, nodding towards her stomach.

Hela elbowed him away. 'Go and help your mum with the food.'

Naji did what he was told and Rose watched, amused, as her domineering older brother scooped up the bags from his mother's arms and took them all indoors. When she turned around again, Hela had gone, and she wondered whether she should go and say hi to Naji's colleagues. They were all standing at the other end of the garden in groups of twos and threes, a radio blaring on the grass beside them. Someone Rose didn't recognise was watching over the barbecue, assiduously turning hamburger patties and sausages; the smell was delicious. She went over to get a beer from the table stacked with drinks next to him and a sudden whiff of weed came from nowhere. She looked around again, saw that at least two people had spliffs, and realised that her mother wouldn't be staying long.

'You're the sister, right?' said the guy on the barbecue.

'I am . . . the sister.' Rose gave him a semi-friendly nod.

'You all look the same – the whole family—' The man pointed towards the kitchen with his barbecue tongs, indicating Naji, Yash and her mum, who were inside. Rose smiled wryly at this, for it was true. They all had thick eyebrows and dark, flashing eyes which could turn angry at a moment's notice. That was from their mum. Their dad had been tall and handsome, with cheekbones that she and Yash had inherited, and a regal bearing that Naji definitely had, even though he worked out and looked like he was always up for a fight. Yash had it, too, and he was still skinny – would probably always be skinny. Rose, like her mum, was in no way regal, but she was pleased at least to have got the cheekbones.

'I never noticed.'

'Sorry,' he said. 'A stupid thing to say.'

Rose walked off without replying, seeking a spot where she wouldn't have to talk to anyone. She wasn't usually this unfriendly. She had thought the party would cheer her up – it was just that when she got there and saw all of Naji's friends, she realised she hadn't spoken to any of them since the funeral, and that it was disconcerting to see them now. She slipped indoors and past her family in the kitchen, where her mum was giving Naji directions on how long to heat up some sausage rolls. In the living room, his dog, Deo, sprawled lazily on the sofa. She went past her and up the stairs.

'Come on, Deo, come on!' Suddenly enlivened, Rose clapped her hands at her. 'Come on, Deo, good girl!' Deo *was* a good girl. She jumped up, panting happily, and bounded up the stairs after Rose. Rose took an immediate right, into the small room that was going to be for the baby and was currently full of old furniture and piles of clothes. She sat on the floor and buried her face in Deo's soft golden fur.

'I can't fucking face it.'

Deo sat patiently for a few moments and let her do this. Rose lifted her head and gave the dog a grateful few strokes, and then Deo settled more comfortably onto the floor, as though she was going to stay, and Rose, exhausted, rolled down beside her, lay on her back, and looked at the ceiling. Through the open window she could hear noises from the party, the chatter, the radio, briefly, her mother's voice. She closed her eyes. She would go down when she was ready.

But you can't stay hiding in the upstairs bedroom forever. You can't expect a dog to find your miserable, horizontal self entertaining for that long. Deo got up before her – it had only been twenty minutes, and she could have had another half hour, another hour – but once she'd been left dogless, lying on the floor staring at the ceiling in a room that was not your own felt weird, so she reluctantly got up, too. She followed the dog's wagging tail down the stairs, and from the back door watched her spring happily into the bright, hot day outside, not quite ready to join her.

Her brother was in the centre of the garden now, knocking back a beer, and while the scene was still to all appearances casual, she knew that something else was going on. A group of his friends stood around him in a semicircle and almost everyone else was facing him, as though all the action was focused on this sole point. Her mum and Yash were in the corner by the wall, Yash thoughtlessly chomping on a burger, out-of-place and distracted, and her mum anxiously surveying the attendees, perhaps trying to remember who she recognised from the funeral, too.

Nearby, Hela chatted to some women Rose had never seen. They all had a similar look – the long, glossy hair, make-up and painted nails, the shiny leggings and tight dresses. Rose felt they were a different species to her, though she had nothing against Hela and in fact felt almost sorry for her, because as much as she'd appeared to domesticate and subdue Naji, Rose knew her brother was really incapable of doing anything anyone else wanted.

He stopped drinking then, looked around as if to assess some-thing, glanced at Rose, and fumbled for something in his pocket which glinted in the sun. As he held the bottle in the air and tapped against it, she saw it was a pocketknife. The noise, sharp and high, shut everyone up.

'I'd like to say a few words,' he said into the stillness.

She'd never seen him make a speech before, although their whole childhood he'd lectured her and she'd gazed back with almost as much solemn adoration as she'd given their dad.

'It's been a long time since we've had this many people over,' he said, 'and it's a good day for it – we're blessed with blue skies and a reason to celebrate.' He extended his arm to Hela, who was squeezed by her excited friends. 'But there's something else. A lot of you have asked me over the years to run for union rep, and that's never been something I could easily do – not with a background like mine.'

Since her dad died there had been speculation – from friends, family, people who'd known them for years – over whether his son had inherited his mettle, his ability to fight, and his doggedness – these things that he'd been famed for, which had made him such a good union leader for so long. Naji had the charisma, but he was so different from their dad that Rose couldn't quite see it.

'But things have changed,' he said. 'Things are getting tough at work – those auts are taking our jobs. Two weeks ago, they were introduced to do the picking and packing on floor D; how many people lost their jobs? Eighty-two! *Eighty-two people lost their jobs*. That could be us any day now, and I can't sit back and let it happen. We want some respect, we want some job security, and we want to say *NO* to the auts!'

At this, there was an enormous cheer. Rose thought about the conference Lal had watched at work, and how differently her brother and best friend felt, and how painful it was to pick sides. And then she saw her mother's eyes were moist – she must have been thinking of their dad. He had died suddenly, on a sunny day just like this one last year. He'd had a heart attack in a meeting – he'd been talking to management down at the port, and they couldn't remember his last words before he collapsed, even though at the time she had begged them to try. As though it mattered. Those same bosses, for whom he'd worked for decades, had paid for a big send-off, a big funeral, then they had left the family to get on with it. There had been this hole in their lives ever since, except lately her mother and Yash had discussed her father less, her mother had cried less, and Naji barely mentioned him at all.

'Now, I want to say a word about my father,' Naji said. Rose stared at him, amazed, and the silence surrounding his speech grew deeper. 'He was a legend around here. He did so much for Ulrusa's labour movement that he's a tough act to follow, but I'm going to try. I can't promise I'll ever be a tenth of the leader he was, or that I'll make a tenth of those things happen – but if you vote for me, I will do my very best.' He nodded solemnly at his colleagues. 'Now, enough of this – go and enjoy yourselves.'

His workmates applauded and began to chat intently amongst themselves, in a way that suggested his announcement was not a surprise; that they had already been thinking of him in the role. Rose's mum was looking at him in a peculiar way, but Yash gazed around, his attention drifting. As several of Naji's mates clapped him on the back, Rose felt her stomach twist and she took herself back inside. She looked around the living room in the afternoon shade, its blank walls and overstuffed sofas and enormous television. So her brother was channelling their father – he'd said it. He was trying to bring him back. He'd never felt good enough for him, aware he was a different kind of man – quick and rash and physical, rather than silver-tongued, authoritative and, at times, tyrannical like their father. She wondered, knowing the problems between the two of them, if he'd have been proud.

She couldn't explain why she herself had walked away, rather than congratulate him – why she was now on her own in an empty room. Naji would surely want her praise – they were close, and praising him had always been part of her role. But instead it was a relief, just for a moment, to take a break from it all.

One Year Earlier – Janetta

Ulrusa's northern beaches were only a few hours from where Janetta had lived her whole life, but until now, she'd not thought to explore them. Without Malin – before Malin – she had had no sense of adventure. Or, she did, but she had no facility for action – she only knew how to make things happen at her desk. Now she went down muddy clifftop trails, reaching out for overhanging branches and keeping an eye on her girlfriend, who was skipping ahead as though she'd walked this route a hundred times before. Malin wasn't even from Ulrusa, she was from Heinis, but her confidence was typical. It exactly reflected their relationship: Malin breezy and unafraid, Janetta hesitant and slower, but willing to be led.

Malin spun around and told her, 'We're almost there.' Her sandals were silver, thin-strapped, covered with dirt. Each time she turned, more dust would rise and settle on them, dulling them slowly but irrevocably. She didn't seem to care. Perhaps she felt pausing to clean them would have stopped the spontaneity, the forward motion, and that her role in Janetta's life was partly to bring her these things.

Janetta, in her plain and sensible trainers, didn't mind, though she was awed by the flagrant desecration of such pretty shoes.

But she didn't say anything. Instead, she did her best to keep up.

They were going to Targosa Beach, as it was meant to be one of the wonders of the local coastline. Because you could only get there on foot it was never busy, and because it was a Monday – Janetta had taken a day off and Malin wasn't due at her bar job until later – they might even be the only ones there. Janetta was in charge of her own schedule so could do what she liked, but it still felt subversive not to be at her desk today, as though she was slipping between worlds. Clutching a thin, cool hemlock branch, she saw the ocean silvering in the sun through the trees and admitted she was glad of the change.

At the top of the trail the air was purer, the light brighter, and there was a waterfall that ran to the sea. They could sit here for lunch, Malin said, then walk to the bottom of the waterfall and swim.

They sat down to their picnic, Malin perching on a rock, just in front of the waterfall, unafraid. Janetta ate a plum, some cookies, and some dried sausage, in that order. Malin made herself a sandwich. They sat in companionable silence, listening to water slamming onto rocks, ferocious in its downwards pelt, and looked out at the edges of dunes sticking out below, and the dark of the sea. Janetta brushed away tiny stones that dented her palm, took her phone from her bag and said sheepishly, 'You don't have to listen.'

'I'm not, I promise!'

Janetta pressed record. 'Happiness,' she said softly. 'Add to happiness repository. Feeling tones for happiness – the feeling of joy with another person. Wait, no . . .' She stopped, considered. She was often happy when she was alone. This was different – a disbelief that she was able to spend so much time with one other person, a delight whenever she saw them, a constant desire to touch and be touched. This was a small campfire in the space between them, it was the blazing pink of the pomegranate Malin had just broken open, it was the fact Janetta would tolerate cigarette smoke now because it was coming from *her*, even though she still coughed and waved it away.

'Sorry,' Malin said.

'Correction,' Janetta began again. 'Not happiness. Joy, I think – add to joy repository. Feeling tones for joy – a lightness inside, a happiness – oh!' She stopped recording.

Malin laughed.

'Stop listening! This is boring – it's work.'

'Creating a repository of human emotions and teaching auts how to respond to them is boring? You know it's the exact opposite. But I'll leave you to it.'

She shifted towards the waterfall and Janetta tried again to articulate her feelings. She was creating a resource for herself – for her Ph.D. research – but she'd long realised it was hard to get it exactly right. She did like to try, though. 'Contentment. Add to contentment repository. Feeling tones for contentment – a waterfall, a plum, happiness. No – *no* – I've done it again!'

Malin looked at her with amazement. 'I think the word you want is love.'

They had met at a bar near the university, at the end of the second year of Janetta's Ph.D. She'd gone for a drink with her Institute colleagues one night to celebrate a breakthrough in some of their work, and she'd been glad to. She'd begun at that point to feel a small, strange yearning as the liveliness of the day ceded to the claustrophobia of home. It wasn't that she wanted the extended company of her friends – it was a need, at last, for something more.

She was alone at the bar when Malin had appeared at her side and asked if she could buy her a drink. Assuming she was a friend of a friend, she'd said yes, and two tiny glasses of hotorro appeared before them.

They clinked.

'What are we toasting?' Malin asked. Her smile was dazzling.

'I've—' Janetta collected herself. 'I've discovered how to make my auts gave a complex response to an entirely new subset of human emotions.'

'Oh. I see.' Malin fixed Janetta with her malachite gaze. 'Would you mind if I kissed you?'

'I – um—'

'You don't have to respond in a complex way.'

'I – yeah – I'd like that.'

Malin was shorter than her, with an elegant face, sharp nose, a perfect circle of mouth. She had long, loose dark hair and a playful, teasing expression, taking Janetta in as if she knew exactly what she was looking for and was sizing her up to see if she had it. A thin tease of dress strap fell from her shoulder.

Janetta stared hungrily at her bare collarbone, downed her hotorro – the peat-cherry burst like sparks – and met her eye. Malin downed hers too, and kissed her. It felt like ceremony.

'It's *not* love,' Janetta said defensively now.

'Okay.' Malin stubbed her cigarette out. 'Not love. Have you ever been in love?'

Janetta couldn't respond. One thing she disliked about this, this beauty sitting opposite, this beauty all around, was that it was *too* perfect, too sugary sweet, too mutual. Surely they couldn't keep it up.

'Sorry – such an awkward question.' Malin looked to the sea, her gaze open and unperturbed, as if she were still waiting for an answer. Janetta watched her instead. She wasn't talkative and Malin knew this, but it didn't seem to stop her digging, or for the digging to rearrange her insides in unfamiliar ways. She thought emotions could be categorised and distinctly understood, but when she was with Malin she felt so much all at once. She reached out and stroked her cheek.

'Is it tenderness?'

'Maybe.' She took her hand from the cool curve. 'Let me try that. Tenderness. Add to tenderness repository. Feeling tones – a desire to touch, benevolence, love—'

'Love?!'

'Did I say "love"?' Her face flamed. Surprising new leaks of pleasure didn't mean she was in love.

Her phone lit up then with a message from Lal. It was a picture of a woman who looked like her sister – same dark brown hair, round cheeks, big eyes – but in those eyes was a strange and empty look that Lal would never have.

You'll never guess, she'd written.

Malin peered. 'What's wrong with Lal?'

'I don't think it's her. That's not her face, those aren't her—' She broke off and scrutinised the image.

You know it's not me, wrote her sister.

'It's a humanoid aut,' she told Malin. To Lal she wrote, *I know. I assume it's Tekna's creation?*

Course.

It was hard to ask the next question. Malin being there was a relief, now, a reality she could touch and hold. She grabbed her hand.

Is it conscious?

Nothing came through and the seconds turned to minutes. Her gut knotted with fear.

Course not.

Of course not. She shut her eyes as the fear subsided and she heard the waterfall blur with the rustle of trees, birdsong in the distance. Malin wrapped her arms around her.

'Want to go swimming?'

The path to the cove was rocky, slippery, steep. Out of her element, Janetta blinked rapidly, clenched her fists, tiptoed every step until it felt safe to land her soles. Malin too trod gingerly, as though she'd reached the limits of her fearlessness, and she almost slipped once, twice, but both times teetered and balanced. She didn't turn to see how Janetta was doing. Water sprayed them as they went and Janetta rolled up the cuffs of her jumper, brushed droplets from her leggings.

The waterfall cascaded and pooled in the deserted cove. They left their clothes on the rocks and their food on top, wrapped to deter ants, and Malin waded straight into the shallows, shrieking as the water lapped her legs.

Janetta checked her phone to see if her sister had said more, but there was nothing – she had nothing to worry about. She watched Malin fall backwards into the sea, cry with pleasure and float, swirling tiny waves with her hands. She told her phone: 'Love. Add to love repository. Feeling tones—'

But the words didn't come, as though they were still hiding, and so she went out into the water, too. Its coldness startled, and a fog was rising further out. Malin was letting her body sink; her legs had disappeared and now her waist was submerging too. Janetta gathered her hair and felt for the soft seabed with the balls of her feet, then she too fell backwards, with a splash, and, engulfed by cold that suddenly became tolerable, she stared at the endless sky.

Twelve Months Later

1

The Tekna Tower had been in a contest with the buildings around it before they even existed. When it was built, its architects must have imagined what Mejira might look like in twenty or thirty years and designed it to ensure that it would always soar above everything else. Back then it had appeared on the horizon like lightning fixed in space and, while the skyline had quickly grown around it, nothing else had ever come close. It was as if all the buildings that followed had been given instructions to simmer down, know their place, and they'd meekly obliged.

If you came by train to the city you could see them up ahead, densely packed together. Individually they were dreary, but from afar the effect was hypnotic, a cold, unfurling sprawl. At the very centre, the Tower shot clear of the rest, a sharp shimmer vaulting from its dark square base up into the clouds, where it became pointed, a silver antenna.

For the first twenty-three years of her life, Lal had known only the blue skies and wide, windy beaches of Ulrusa, its slow pace and provincial mood. When she saw the Tower under a fist of darkening clouds, that all felt very far away. Back home it had acted like a magnet for her vague and inchoate dreams and that day, gathered irresistibly towards it, she at last felt them start to take shape.

She was aware that fantasies about money and success were common and nothing to be ashamed of, but the substance of her own embarrassed her. She had begun to dream of living in a luxurious flat – say, an enormous top-floor apartment with views over Mejira – and of the leisure that money would give her, of drudgery and day-to-day chores disappeared from her life, of her body weightless, finely tuned, caressed, rather than a permanent disappointment. No one else she knew had such a base craving for it – the only person she could think of who was even interested was Van, and he didn't take it seriously. He laughed about how nice it would be to be rich, then forgot about it. Her parents were relentlessly, irritatingly humble, and her sister and her oldest friend were uninterested to the point of being renunciates.

She wondered how much the visions of wealth she'd seen when she was younger played a part: the films and television she'd watched late into the night had taught her wealth meant ease, whether the characters were chasing that wealth and ease or already had it. Money was part of the fabric of their lives; all joys and successes bestowed because of it. Janetta would sometimes come downstairs to tell her to go to sleep – she didn't need to say that she'd been working that whole time; Lal knew that and it made her feel ashamed. She suspected that filling her mind up with trash had turned her into someone who, for all her own capacity for work, at her core still yearned for what television had promised: fewer problems, more happiness, endless ease.

Dhont, on the eastern outskirts of Mejira, was where her job was actually based – *Data Monitor, Tekna (based in Dhont)*, the advert had said. She'd been throwing applications at the great machine of Tekna's human resources both desperately and diligently, her entreaties sober and carefully worded, for a year before this, waiting for a single bite. She'd have taken anything. Getting the job of *Data Monitor, Tekna (based in Dhont)* was the greatest thing to have ever happened to her. It was better than meeting Rose when they were four years old and Rose had befriended her in nursery by sharing her lunch with her, an occasion she'd always previously believed was the greatest – closely followed by getting the manager job at Popotops. But this, even as the train curved around the city centre and the Tower disappeared from sight, knocked Rose right off the top spot. Lal closed her eyes and whispered the happy, disbelieving mantra:

I live in Mejira and I work at Tekna.
I live in Mejira and I work at Tekna.

Dhont itself, though, was disappointing. She hadn't realised it was so far from the centre. Her previous outings to Mejira had been for school trips where she'd trooped around the Iolran History Museum and the Iolra–Yalin Centre for Peace and other such dusty, well-meaning historical institutions, the Tower glinting in the background. When she was older, she'd gone once or twice with friends to slouch around downtown and go shopping somewhere infinitely more vast than Ulrusa. They'd slept on the eight-hour coach journey back, surrounded by bags of cheap clothes and flimsy accessories that they could have got back home for the same price but not the same cachet. They took a double seat each and picked their biggest, roundest shopping bags for pillows. Mejira back then was the small world that radiated out from its centre and she wouldn't have dreamed of wondering about what lay on the outskirts. But now she was in Dhont and her heart sank even before the train pulled into the station. On the horizon, low-lying buildings were bisected by dual carriageways and ring roads. The sole outlier was a grim concrete slab belonging to a hotel chain, recognisable by the blue tint of its windows and the hotel logo splashed onto its top and sides. The landscape was otherwise both residential and light industrial, insistently charmless in every direction.

When she'd first seen the pictures of Tekna's satellite centre in Dhont (Mejira) – as it had said on the website, with Mejira bracketed to show that Dhont *was* in Mejira – it had looked like an idyllic bubble of R&D, a lush, verdant campus, a pastoral continuation of the Tekna Tower. She'd understood this was advertising and yet now she was here, the reality was deeply disappointing. She headed past grim grey buildings, half-empty car parks, a shabby blue sign saying *Dhont Technopark*. Eventually she found the campus housing, which was as dismal as everything else: dingy blocks lined by paved walkways and rows of threadbare trees. She'd been excited to sign up to live on campus, take advantage of Tekna's offer of accommodation, but as she walked towards her designated apartment she realised it must have been built for a past influx of workers because these dreary concrete blocks were dirty and neglected. Peering into neighbouring flats, she saw the bare-bones still life of uninhabited rooms, and when she came to her own and opened the door, she found it identical to the others, with a single bed at the back, a desk against the side wall, and a television bolted above. The bathroom was so small you could practically shower while on the toilet.

It was not pleasant, spending her first night there alone. Had she spoken to someone in the day, had some kind of anchor in this new world, she would have felt less disheartened. But as she tried to sleep, cold in her narrow bed with its thin, ungenerous blankets, she convinced herself that she was the only person on the entire campus, out in this no-man's-land, and rather than feeling thrilled and adventurous, she just felt more distressed.

Eventually she turned on her bedside lamp to write to Rose. She said she was scared and alone, and that Dhont was different to how she'd imagined it. She considered Rose's reaction. Complete indifference, probably. She deleted the message, turned the light out, and lay down again in the dark.

Lal's new office was a long, narrow room with a single window at the far end. She walked past a row of cubicles, curiously gazing at the backs of heads – one woman with dark, straight hair, another with a grey bob. A man with closely shaven hair, another with thicker, wavier hair and deep red spots on the back of his neck. No one turned to greet or acknowledge her, and she wondered when she'd get a chance to see their faces and say hello. Deposited by a practically wordless woman at what was clearly to be her own desk, she waited to see how she'd be inducted, and by whom. This was not what she'd expected – it was shadowy and quiet when she'd envisioned brightness, warmth, collaboration. A troubling instinct told her that things weren't going to get better, but she squashed it and looked around wide-eyed and undeterred.

The walls were a pale grey. The carpet was blue, stained, dirty. Damp mushroomed darkly on the ceiling above.

And no one came.

She stared at the crumbs in her keyboard, wiped some away with a cardigan sleeve. She adjusted herself in her chair, smoothed over the itchy seat fabric, and the sound of typing grew louder then seemed to recede. She checked what date her first pay cheque would arrive, then messaged her mother to remind her she would be sending her half. She was starting to feel self-conscious and was about to say something when the man on her right swivelled around to face her. He had long, thin hair splayed over his shoulders like a ruff, and was balding at the top. His old, too-tight

T-shirt said *The End Is Nigh*. He absently scratched at a rush of tiny red spots on his arm as he eyed her speculatively, looking delighted.

'Lalita? I'm Ukones – I'll be inducting you.' He moved his chair until it was unnecessarily close and gazed her way with small, red-ringed eyes. He told her he was going to show her something called *Teknaut*, the program that monitored the roll-out of auts in Popotops branches across all of Iolra. Turning his body towards her screen, he waved his hand to wake it. She caught a whiff of sweat from his damp underarms. The screen lit up with a bright-green flicker of numbers and as Ukones sank back into his seat, she stared curiously. She knew that her job was to monitor and analyse what were called 'efficiency proposals'. An algorithm would appear with what was meant to be the optimal use of auts for a branch of Popotops, and she had to check to make sure it was correct.

'You have to check every single thing,' Ukones said, pointing to a long line of criteria down the side of the screen. 'You need to calculate the projected efficiencies for each one, and then check it against the proposal.'

'Right.' Lal nodded.

Then he did a strange thing. He leaned towards her and mouthed something incomprehensible. She recoiled with a look of shock, almost disgust, but he didn't react to this, instead repeating it – and this time she understood what he was mouthing: *Don't do that*. He scrutinised her to see if the message had got through, but she looked away, towards the screen. She wasn't interested in any sort of private communication with him. She was here to do a job, and to do it to the very best of her ability.

'See this down here?' he continued, unabashed, twirling his finger towards an icon of a dustbin in the lower right of the screen.

'You want to fill it with people. Takes a few weeks for it to get approved but in the meantime, just crack on. The more staff eliminated, the better you're doing.' He glared at her meaningfully and she decided he was a crank; there was nothing to do but agree with what he said until he left her alone.

He showed her a few more things in Teknaut without any further weirdness and, when they were done, he sat back and rested his hands on his crumpled shorts.

'So, Lal, are you a local?'

She was painfully aware they were the only two people in the room engaged in conversation. 'I'm from Ulrusa,' she said softly, and turned again to her screen, indicating she'd like to get on.

'I thought I recognised the accent. Do you know Mejira at all?'

She debated what to say. *Yes* might lead to more conversation, *no* might lead to something even worse. 'A bit.' She gave him one more quick smile and thankfully he got the message and retreated to his own desk.

But as she worked that day, finding her way around Teknaut and slowly getting her first efficiency proposal underway, he turned to her from time to time with a hopeful, troubling gaze. He didn't appear to be getting on with his own work at all. At first she'd smiled back, but after a while she realised that reacting was encouraging him, so instead she kept her eyes trained on her screen, hoping he'd turn away.

Ukones was the only person who'd made any overture towards friendliness in the entire office, though; everyone else remained silent as ghosts, only typing, breathing, minimally existing. At lunch he had disappeared for quite a while and come back with a hot dog he'd chewed slowly and ostentatiously at his desk, filling the room with its meaty, sweaty smell, but Lal, seeing none of the others taking a break, most not leaving their desks at all, followed their lead.

He'd finished work at six, which felt early because it was now coming on to seven and no one else had yet packed it in for the day. She wanted to leave – she was finding the work tedious and difficult, and she needed a break. She'd purposefully mis-sold herself in her job application – she was more business-minded than mathematical – and as a result, she was only four per cent through her first efficiency proposal check, for a branch of Popotops in Mehonoy. With any luck she'd soon be at ten per cent, after verifying that a new food aut would indeed decrease the branch's overheads and increase its profits by the percentages predicted by the algorithm. But she was still sitting up straight, even though her back ached and her shoulders were tightly knotted.

As she put her cardigan on she saw the evening sky through the distant window, a light pink behind the clouds, and thought unexpectedly of her own Popotops, how through the front windows – a whole wall's worth of glass – the morning light would dazzle them, and they'd be grateful to turn to make their orders.

She suddenly remembered Rose being abrupt to customers. 'You want sugar?' she'd snap as she gave them their coffees, and if they didn't reply straight away she'd give them an incredulous look, as if she couldn't believe they were making her wait for the answer. It was so rude, but it had always made Lal laugh – right up until she'd stepped up her job applications to Mejira, and after that she'd refused to engage. She'd acted as though she was being watched by the higher-ups, and she'd made it clear to Rose she refused to indulge her any more, would ignore her provocations.

But now Rose was ignoring her. Lal imagined what she'd say if she could see her.

I told you so.

She shook this off and reminded herself: *I live in Mejira and I work at Tekna.*

She closed her eyes, repeated this firmly, opened them, and got back to work.

Later that evening she stood by the carriage doors, watching as the train wound its way towards Mejira. The sky had turned deep indigo in the east and the city twinkled with lights. As they pulled into Mejira Central she felt the heady rush of crowds, of anonymous flowing bodies. Out on the streets the bars and restaurants were full and she walked past, eyeing them jealously.

She knew she could have gone in and ordered a drink – why not? She wanted profoundly to feel like she was at the centre of everything, too, pretend she was one of them. But it was easier to walk on by, floored by her want, to look at that world from the corner of her eye and let that be enough. She went past a woman who stood a little apart from the group she was with, talking on her phone with a frustrated look on her face. She wore a smart dress, her hair was expensively cut, and she was drinking from a thin tumbler of wine with insouciance, as though it were water. She spotted Lal soaking her in and Lal immediately averted her eyes, ashamed.

Lal had a deeper mission, a more important place to be. She didn't stop walking until she reached the Tekna Tower and then, far enough away from the security guards so as not to catch their attention, she lifted her eyes up and let the building loom over her. It made her dizzy to see the top. She was not the kind of person who thought places held any deep significance; that was silly. They were functional – to attribute meaning beyond that was to give your power to something outside yourself. But the Tower confounded her. Despite herself, she wanted to disappear into it, to be somehow absorbed by it. In front of her was a gleaming glass panel and she moved closer as if approaching a mystery. She reached out to touch it, then stepped away. This was getting weird.

She crossed the street and began to walk. Further down she turned and took a photo. She couldn't get the whole tower in the frame so she settled instead for the evening sun burnishing its high windows, blazing off its peak. She fiddled with the filters, making the photo bright, then dark, then brighter again. A cold wind whooshed past, but she stood and stared and once more made the thing brighter, and then darker, and then brighter again.

Back in Dhont she arranged dinner on her desk: oktopi skewers, moiet balls and crispy sarnda fritters from small white bags leaking with grease, and for dessert, a dense, squidgy dulac cake, bought from street vendors downtown. Although it was late by the time she got back to her room, the promise of the food laid out before her made her feel truly happy for the first time that day. She speared a moiet ball, which leaked out mayonnaise and thick, golden oil as she lifted it up. These were the kind of snacks you could get everywhere. In Ulrusa she'd buy them at convenience stores then heat them up at home, or she'd have them at Rose's – her mum was an excellent, prolific cook, and her moiet balls were always more succulent and less greasy than the shop ones. With one hand she'd brown the batter as she folded it into balls, while with the other she'd fry the sarnda into flat, lacy fritters. Lal and Rose would devour them straight from the pan while they were still piping hot. Neither of Lal's parents had such skills, but Rose, who'd been taught by her mum, had shown her a couple of times how to make them. She never bothered herself, though – after all, she was at Rose's getting fed like that every day.

Lal opened her laptop and began to watch one of her favourite shows, a trashy, long-running sitcom about a poor girl at a posh university. It was stupid to eat sitting hunched in this chair, though, and sad to use her desk as a table, so she shifted everything to her bed and curled up there.

Her phone beeped as she was finishing. It was Los, her old colleague – she would have preferred Rose, but Los would do. He'd sent her a video of him and Van, wearing their red Popotops hats and uniforms and sitting on one of the tables at the café. It was light outside and she could see through the window behind them into Conaus Square. She was shaken both by the familiarity of the scene and how distant it felt on her phone's tiny screen.

'It's our first day without you, Lal, and we just want to say . . . we miss you! We know you're busy at Tekna with your new job . . .' Los started.

'So I've invented a milkshake called the *Lal*–' Van held up a container. He looked as though he knew he was being an absolute idiot and he was relishing it. 'It's a new special for all our customers, to remind them of you . . . and so we've put in it . . .' He stared into the beaker. 'Strawberries . . . a lot of raspberry ripple ice cream . . . four shots of coffee–'

'Chocolate fudge sauce,' said Los.

Lal was embarrassed. She'd made herself one exactly like that one day when she was exceptionally tired. It didn't seem fair for them to poke fun at her sugar and caffeine needs, but at the same time she was touched they'd remembered something so specific. She put down her forkful of cake as she watched them talk about how customers had reacted to 'the Lal' – clutching their stomachs in distress, blissful swoons, spontaneously crying and weeping, '*We miss her so much.*' She was cheered by all this, and grateful they'd sent it.

And then another voice, close to the camera, said, 'Fucking *idiots.*'

It was Rose.

Sour surprise stung its way through her. Even hearing Rose say that made her miss her. Slowly, painfully, she typed out a response to Los, then realised she couldn't find the right words, so instead she sent the picture of the Tekna Tower she'd taken earlier.

you work at the tower! insane!

She started to explain that she didn't quite work at the Tower, but it suddenly felt easier not to.

i know!!!

She added some happy emojis and after that, still hurt, she didn't feel like talking any more, so when he responded she didn't even look. She chucked the phone on her bed and gathered her dinner containers to take them to the shared kitchen at the end of the hall. The large, barely furnished room had a few lonely saucepans lost in cavernous cupboards, the odd plate or bowl, and mismatching cutlery in otherwise empty drawers. A hard orange sofa faced a plain white wall. It was too austere to cook in and too spooky to eat in, so Lal just used it for throwing away her leftovers so that her room didn't stink.

At the window she stared out at the starless sky. The city was so quiet here, no sounds save for the occasional car rolling by in the distance. It felt far away from everything. She thought then of her grandmother back home, wondering whether she knew Lal was gone, if she'd realised by now.

Lal had tried to tell her that she was leaving. She'd woken early, as she often did, to help with the laundry. A breeze had come in from the sea and she'd been cold in her thin cotton pyjamas as she and her grandmother unpegged the dry items from the line under the lean-to, folded them and sorted them into piles. Grania was silent, making a soft, low sound only when they had to take separate ends of a sheet and meet each other in the middle to fold it, like a slow, stately dance. Despite her dementia she did laundry effortlessly. She'd done so the whole time she had lived with them – every day for eight years, out front at six a.m. in her pink cotton nightgown, sorting and folding to the tune of dog barks and birdsong.

Lal told her she was moving to Mejira, but she wasn't sure her grandmother understood, and wary of frightening her, in case she only perceived the potential loss, she brought up Rose to distract her.

'But Rose is angry,' Lal had said. 'She's not really talking to me.'

Grania's eyes lit up. 'Rose . . . lovely girl. Where is she?'

'She's not here, Grania.'

'Bring her back.'

When they were teenagers, Grania had taught Lal and Rose card games. Rose was a particular favourite to play with, because she was fair to the point of self-sabotage, and it had made Lal, who was worst at the games but determined, and Grania, who had been playing for decades and was effortlessly good, laugh at her unorthodox tactics. Even though they played less these days, Lal felt bad that Grania had been denied Rose's company lately – but rather than dwell on it, she mumbled a non-response and they continued in silence.

The light had gone on in her parents' room then, which meant her mother would be getting up and ready for work. She was a cleaner, something Lal resented in a way she knew was unfair. Grania had been a cleaner, too, and she and Lal's mother had always been surprised how insistently Lal had refused the same fate. As it was, later that morning she cleaned the kitchen and the bathroom, dusted, mopped the floors, and vacuumed the house. She did it because Grania couldn't, her father wouldn't, her sister was on another planet and her mother had to do it all day at work, anyway.

It was just about warm enough after breakfast for her to leave the windows open while she mopped the kitchen floor. As the water dried, the cream tiles shone with sunlight. Her dad had gone to Ponra, the nearby market, to seek out bargains – his favourite activity now he'd lost his job. She wondered why she was bothering to clean when he was only going to make the kitchen dirty with what he'd found as soon as he got back. But she understood by now that for better or worse, this – this belief in the domestic pristine – was in her bones.

She began to drag the vacuum cleaner around the living room. Grania, on the sofa, appeared to be staring at the television, but if you looked more closely you could see her attention was worriedly fixed on the middle distance.

'Hard worker!' she suddenly blurted.

Lal turned to her, puzzled, switched the vacuum off and went to sit by her side, waiting to see if she'd heard correctly. She knew it was silly to act as though everything Grania said was a gnomic utterance, but she couldn't help but be fascinated by the way a word or phrase would sometimes rise from the murk.

'You! Hard worker.'

'Me?' On the one hand, Grania did have dementia. On the other, Lal didn't receive compliments often, and she flushed with gratitude. She put a hand over Grania's. 'Thank you!'

'Not like Daddy. Daddy lazy.'

'Oh. Yeah, Dad does nothing. Except the garden.'

Grania sank into thought, her face falling. 'Daddy lazy,' she repeated. 'Geepa . . . Geepa lazy.'

Lal's grandfather had died years ago. She equivocated, even though she knew an answer wasn't necessary, 'Well, yeah. But I guess Geepa had a hard life.'

'Geepa lazy!' Grania said fiercely. Lal lifted her hand, gently put it back over Grania's and patted it. She looked closely at her, trying to figure out what she was thinking, but her eyes were impenetrable, lost in the deep past, and so instead Lal stood up and pulled the vacuum cleaner out of the room.

She had barely known her grandfather. He had been in the military most of his life and by the time she was old enough for him to have potentially befriended her, he was spending his days with his old army friends reading newspapers and talking about sports. In mornings and afternoons this would happen in their front yards, though many of them lived in flats so also on benches in nearby squares, in that grand global ritual of biding one's time. They'd go their separate ways for dinner. Whenever the family went to Grania's for dinner, in a quiet suburb of northwest Ulrusa, Geepa would be in his chair, smoking, watching the news, and after dinner he would rise, tall and reticent – not entirely unlike Janetta and leave to meet his friends again. In the evenings they would convene at a brightly lit bar on the corner of a small square several minutes' walk from the flat. It was the kind of place where neither the décor nor the menu had changed in decades, and its patrons liked it that way. Lal used to imagine Geepa walking down those narrow, poorly lit streets to the square. Would he have heard other people having dinner? Their talk and laughter, the clinks of their cutlery? How did these sounds feel to him? He wanted to be back with his friends every night, and re-entered that life at the expense of his wife and his children. But the prevailing sentiment was that he must do as he liked.

Lal thought of Grania making him dinner every night, saw her taking the empty plates from the balcony, where they liked to eat, to the kitchen, washing up alone in that small, bright room, with its white-and-blue tiles, its slick linoleum floor. Every night when her husband left to join his friends, she washed and cleaned and tidied. Did she then phone a friend, watch television, relax somehow? Lal didn't know. Did she look forward to Geepa coming home, his breath like alcohol, like anise? She wondered if her grandmother woke up and they were pleased to see each other, or if she preferred or pretended to be asleep.

There was so much she'd never be able to know, questions she couldn't ask, stories and lives for which she only had fragments. Perhaps Grania rejoiced when her husband left each night. Perhaps she put on music and danced on the balcony, where she looked at the inky sky and felt content – even though she would have to go and clean in the morning, and would do so for more than forty years. Lal had no idea.

The one thing she did know was that her being here, in Dhont (Mejira), had broken the chain of servitude. Slowly but surely she'd changed her fate. None of them had thought she could do it. Janetta was the great blazing hope of the family, while Lal had been marked out for drudgery, just like Grania, just like her mum.

She took a photo of the crescent moon and sent it to her mum. She'd show it to the rest of the family, and they'd talk about it, wonder how she was getting on. But you can't conclude much from a moon.

2

Rose had always been terrible at getting up in the mornings, but she was even worse now that she'd agreed to take on Lal's job. There was something doubly depressing about waking up that early to do something you loathed. Her mother steered a wide berth around her when she came into the kitchen to make tea, standing at the counter and staring at the dawn light as it brewed, not saying a word to her daughter – not in an unfriendly way; it was just that Rose, at the table, was slumped back in her chair, barely eating her cereal, unaware of anything other than the fact she'd been woken up too soon.

As soon as her mum left, her phone rang.

'What?'

Los sounded strangely alert. 'I know you don't check your work phone, but something happened with the aut.'

'What aut?'

'*Our* aut, our server aut. We were broken into last night and it got smashed up in the square.'

She sat up. 'Wait, really?'

'Yeah . . .'

'No way.' She tried to imagine this happening, felt an unexpected surge of delight. It had only been with them a few months. 'But why us? We're nothing.'

'Well, we're still Tekna. We're still open too, by the way.'

'This is crazy. I'm not sure what I . . .' Rose rubbed her forehead. 'Are you going in?'

'Of course – I'll see you there.'

She checked her work email and, sure enough, there were emails from her area manager full of panicked attempts to get hold of her. Rose refused to take her Popotops phone home or forward her work calls to her own line – her way of telling her corporate overlords to leave her alone out of working hours. When Lal was manager she used to actually check her work email first thing in the morning, and was disappointed if there weren't calls for her. But then, there were never usually calls for either of them.

In the news it said this was the sixth known aut attack in Ulrusa in the past three months; of course there had been a lot more in the country as a whole, especially Mejira. In most of these, industrial auts were destroyed, hacked at until they fell apart. But now there was another kind of attack just aimed at retail auts. They were small, easily smashable, and it made a point to a whole new audience.

Rose left her seat with a disconcerting amount of energy. Suddenly, she felt wide awake.

When she got to work she saw two policemen standing in front of Popotops, guarding a taped-off area a few metres wide. Their arms were folded and their faces blank. On the ground behind them the aut's shiny black shards were ignited by the sun, proof perhaps of some glowing afterlife. She walked past rather than gawp further, ensuring she didn't catch their eye – the police were not her friends – and into the café. A smashed side window was criss-crossed with yellow tape, but aside from that, things looked normal.

Los was at the counter making a milkshake. He was tall, slim and boyish, his cheeks furred with gold, and this morning he looked exhausted.

'I can't believe it!' she said as she approached him. 'Who would do something like this?'

He lifted the lid from the blender and stirred something chocolatey. 'I guess someone who lost their job to an aut.'

'Not one of our guys?' Their colleagues who'd been replaced by this aut weren't the kind of people to do this – but then, you never knew. Rose tried to imagine whether she herself could, but that was a strange thought, one that brought up a sudden hard, unforgiving anger in her, and she shook it away.

He poured the mixture into a tall plastic cup and glanced up. 'I read that it's a group doing it – co-ordinated attacks.'

'And, what, their signature is the public execution?' She gestured towards Conaus Square.

'Maybe.' He looked worn out. 'Sorry, I'm not with it today. I'm going to—' He pointed to one of the booths at the window and she nodded, although he wasn't really asking.

She went into Lal's office – she still thought of it as Lal's office – and sat at Lal's desk. Her phone was flashing insistently. The time of the calls from Vimena, her area manager, were one, six, six-fifteen and six-thirty in the morning. Rose considered asking this woman why she was acting like a pathetic Tekna slave out-of-hours when she had every right to be asleep. In her final message Vimena said the new aut was coming the following day, and that they would have to make emergency plans in its absence.

'No, we don't,' Rose said, chucking the phone on the desk and walking out. Out front Los sat slurping his milkshake, watching the policemen. She slid into the booth opposite him.

'You had a coffee yet?'

'Not yet.' She shook her head. 'Vimena said the new aut's coming tomorrow, so today we need emergency cover because we can't cope in its absence.'

Los gave her a frustrated look. 'They're idiots, aren't they. Idiots. Did you tell her we'll be fine?'

'I'll call her back in a bit.' She looked out towards the square. The policemen were chatting. The aut remained in pieces on the cobbles. 'Is this a new belief now – that without auts we can't function? All it did was take orders and money, but they're acting like it's some sort of god. Like without it, the whole system starts to fail.' She was already raising her voice.

'I hate it. I hate the way they fixate on this one thing that's going to rescue us. We didn't need rescuing.'

'It feels like we're trapped.'

'I know what you mean. Like we have to worship the auts that are going to replace us.'

'To be honest, I can almost see why people might protest like this,' Rose admitted, checking Los' face to make sure this was an okay thing to say.

'I can, too. Of course I can.'

For a moment they were silent.

'Shall we smash the new one when it comes?'

Rose laughed. 'Obviously.'

The next day, she opened up alone. She went down the alley around the back, unlocked the door, shook out her umbrella, and hung her jacket up in the corridor. In the café she saw the new aut sitting on the counter. It had been delivered late last night. She went to Lal's office, saw an email from Vimena guardedly congratulating her on surviving without it yesterday, and returned to look at it more closely. Just like its previous iteration, and like the one Uhli

Ranh had shown them a year ago, it was a small, dark box that could fit in the palm of her hand.

She sighed, went to the front windows – and the blinds raised before she could reach them. She stared at the world beyond the raindrop-blurred glass, then turned to the aut. She went to unlock the door – and heard the latch click seconds before she gripped the handle.

'Oh, it's like that, is it?'

Outside, the sky was ragged with rain. Inside, electric light looped the ceiling, dimly buzzing.

She went back to the aut.

'Good morning,' it said. 'How can I help you today?'

She thought for a second, then held up a middle finger, the first truly satisfying thing she'd done in days. Then she got on with setting things up – she put music on, poured milk, filled up buckets of ice cream and deep trays of nuts and fruit and sauce. She brought bread and sandwich fillings out from the storeroom, took the deliveries of muffins, brownies and cakes to the front and put them on display. She checked the time – Van would be there soon. In the meantime, she made a coffee and stared vacantly at the aut.

'Good morning,' it chirped again. 'How can I help you today?'

A customer had come in – she hadn't even noticed. He eyed the aut as if Rose wasn't even there. 'Black coffee to go, large.'

'Coming right up,' it said warmly.

The coffee machine began to hiss and sputter and Rose spun to look at it.

'Shit!' She grabbed a takeaway cup, shoved it under the spout, looked around for someone to blame. Was this a new model? How was it doing all these things? It was a poltergeist, raising blinds, unlocking doors, making coffee – it was far too smart. When the cup was full, she pushed it towards the customer. 'Five swocols, please,' she and the aut said together. The customer looked from her to it and back again, then hovered his card over the aut. It went *BING!* and pulsated with a grass-green glow.

'Thank you,' it said. 'Have a nice day!'

The man twitched and looked at Rose. She glared at him; he took his coffee and backed away. After he had gone, she picked up the aut and examined it. It was lighter than she'd expected and smooth as stone. The word *Tekna* was inscribed in tiny, almost invisible letters on the bottom.

Four of her colleagues had lost their jobs when the first aut came. It had been awful, especially since – for no reason she could discern – she'd been picked to stay. She'd tried to keep in touch with the others and regularly saw tall, gentle Tonde, who lived at home with his large family, and loud, confident Iria, a wilful optimist despite being sacked, who kept inviting her to raucous parties she rarely felt like going to. Although she preferred the ones who remained, she missed the others – and she hated that they'd been treated as totally disposable. Tekna hadn't even offered them compensation.

Now, holding the new aut, she felt complicit in a nasty trick: her old colleagues alchemised into this tiny, dark box. She imagined breaking it and them rising from it, released. She motioned as if to practise throwing it, her hand reaching higher each time. Then she looked around, checked no one was there, and threw it into the air, but on its descent it slipped past her waiting hand and fell loudly onto the floor.

'Malfunction,' it yelped, 'malfunction.'

She picked it up. 'Shut up,' she hissed, and put it back on the counter.

The morning the first aut came was seared into Rose's memory. She'd been setting up alone, and she hated it on sight. She couldn't stop thinking about her lost colleagues and dedicated herself to competing against it. And how arrogant of Tekna, not even to trial the auts *in situ* before disposing of the humans. Faced with it for the first time, customers didn't know who to address. It always beat her to the punch, but not everyone responded to its warm hello – some, gratifyingly, spoke to her. She knew she was meant to let it take orders so she could make them, but whenever she had her back turned, her fingers sticky with milkshake or sandwich filling, and heard it chirp '*Good morning! How can I help you today?*' she felt mutinous.

Lal had arrived later that morning, her dark hair swinging buoyantly. She leaned into a sweaty, frowning Rose for a hug.

'What's uuuppp!'

Rose suffered her silently, then released herself to wrap a sandwich and hand it to a customer; she and the aut both told her the price. The customer pressed something on her phone, nodded at Rose, and walked away.

'How's our new colleague?' Lal asked, beaming at the queue. Rose ignored her, listening instead to the exchange between the aut and the next customer while Lal eyed the thing speculatively, curious, then skipped away to the back. Some days she stayed in her office all day; on others she was a hands-on manager, serving customers but never doing things like cleaning up any more. When Rose first started, they'd tag-teamed on the truly boring stuff, like mopping half the floor each, that kind of thing, but now, presumably, Lal felt too good for that. When she reappeared in a clean shirt, her hair in a high ponytail, her face benevolent and serene, and started to check all the food was in place, Rose's mutinous feelings cranked up a notch.

'I've done that,' she hissed.

'I know,' said Lal, still checking. When she finally finished she came to stand next to Rose, who stiffened. The next customer, staring at the menu behind them, began to give a complicated order to which Lal kept saying, 'Perfect, perfect,' but the woman was clearly harried – once she'd finished she looked peremptorily at the aut, ignoring Lal completely. It piped up with the total and, as the customer held her card over it, Rose caught the woman's eye and gave her a look of disdain. She had an especially rigorous one she liked to use sometimes.

'Perfect,' Lal said again, as if trying to insinuate herself between the woman and the aut. 'Coming right up.'

She was being so irritating that Rose left her to it and went to the main space to see if there was anything she could do. As she picked up leftovers from tables and booths she looked out at Conaus Square with its rows of chain stores and office buildings and felt a thud of pointlessness, a deep desire to be somewhere else. She wove her way back, her tray piled high with every drained mug, smeared glass and dirty plate she could find. She glanced at Lal and saw a beatific glow coming from her as she worked in sympathy with the aut as if it were an extension of herself, making coffees and milkshakes with an almost balletic grace. Rose barged past to load the dishwasher, which she did distractedly, feeling strange and diffuse, almost forgetting what it was she was doing. When she finished, Lal looked at her impatiently, so she went to stand next to her and eyed the waiting customer, a man in a T-shirt tapping at his phone.

'Hi,' she began dutifully, but the aut took over. He held the phone over it and the words lit up on it: *angko toast to go*, 12Sw.

Nothing was said by anyone until Lal asked brightly, 'Can you get some angko?'

'Yeah,' Rose said numbly. She went into the dark corridor. Their old manager, Antaro, had spent most of his time smoking weed at the back door, staring out at the sky. People used to come down the alley to buy it from him – sometimes you could still smell it, baked into the walls and the wood of the doorframe. That felt to Rose like a better, simpler time. She went into the storeroom, squeezed past the boxes of dry goods, opened the fridge and pulled out the angko. She shut the door and sank down on her haunches, closing her eyes.

'Rose,' yelled Lal. 'Ro-oose.'

Why was Lal being like this? She missed the old Lal, the one who was more of a human being and less of a – well, less of a boss. Rose dragged herself up and went back. At the counter, she chopped into the thick, scaly skin, slathered butter on a slice of bread, then layered the angko over it with salt and pepper and herbs. It was good quality, this stuff, not like most of the food at Popotops. They got it fresh from a local supplier who fished it right out of the Yalin Sea.

'Can you hurry up?'

Rose didn't answer. She dropped the sandwich into a bag and handed it to the customer, who, presumably due to the wait, was trying to pinion her with his eyes. She stared him down until the aut piped up, 'Please go and clean the area.'

She looked at the next customer.

'Please go and clean the area.'

'Rose?' Lal asked, so annoyingly that Rose wanted to scream.

Instead she said, 'Is it talking to me?'

Lal smiled gamely at the waiting customer. 'We don't know who it's talking to,' she muttered. 'Can you just do it?'

There was no cleaning to do, though, save the removal of a napkin from a table, such had been her efficiency on the last sweep around – so she could at least take grim satisfaction in the aut's poor programming, sending her off to do the wrong thing. But she was so angry at Lal, laughing away with the customer, gesturing to the aut as though it was her newborn baby. She hadn't expressed a word of sadness or dissent when it had wiped away their ex-colleagues. Like Rose, Lal hadn't been as close to them as she was to Van and Los, but she'd pretty much showed *no* response, other than when, in her capacity as manager, she'd had to tell them. She'd said things then like 'efficiency' and 'ahead of the automation curve', and then 'obviously, I feel bad about this', but Rose sensed she didn't really. Lal was just glad she was safe, and on the hunt for ways to be more so.

She'd known for a long time that her best friend was changing. Lal had never been especially political anyway – if you talked to her about what the government was doing, even things that made the headlines, she would give you a look of apology and say she hadn't been paying attention. Rose suspected she was attracted to the corporate world only because she found it glamorous, but that was as deep as it went. A few years ago at HEU, seeking such glamour, she'd taken a business module, and the next thing Rose knew, she had switched her degree from languages (which she'd never really cared about; she just had a good brain for them and watched a lot of foreign movies) to languages and business. It was as if as soon as she was old enough to know what capitalism was, she dived in. It had been hard to want to study together after that – Rose reading about equality and freedom and Lal there with her *Business 101*.

On the surface Lal was just doing her job, but deep down, it was a betrayal. She had chosen her masters and made no apology for it. Rose watched as her friend worked and worked, stayed late, tried to be the best, fixed her ingratiating smile nice and tight. Meanwhile, Rose decided to be of use: she would try to wake Lal up, get her to change, ignite in her some sense of justice – but it was pointless. She was untouchable. And then one day – a complete surprise, or was it? Rose wasn't sure any more – Lal was off to Mejira.

3

Janetta didn't hate parties, and she certainly didn't hate the way she looked when she dressed up for them. She wore a long black coat with a thick feathered collar that trailed to her waist, and a dress so short she kept glancing to where it stopped mid-thigh, marvelling at her own boldness and the length of leg that stretched out below. Her dark hair was thick and parted in the middle and her face had a sombre lustre, its smooth planes hit with light, her eyes nearly black. As she studied herself in the mirror she thought about how her girlfriend often told her she was beautiful. If she allowed herself to think this too, as she did sometimes, it gave her a strange satisfaction, a sense of achievement without effort. But it was also disorienting and uncomfortable, so she shook it off and turned to the bathroom, where Malin was still in the shower though they were running late to meet friends.

She had only become this person who stared in the mirror at herself, confused and admiring, in the past year. Malin had a way of making her notice the world outside her own head, and this included her own body, and the fact that, arbitrarily, she looked quite nice. Her wardrobe now consisted of more than just jeans and jumpers and nondescript baggy T-shirts – there were dresses in there too, several as short as this one – these clothes that showed this new self-awareness. Truthfully, she didn't care for them. They didn't make sense to her. She gravitated towards what she'd always worn, not because she wanted to downplay her appearance, but because she simply wasn't interested in it. Much of her life with Malin felt like this: excursions into ways of being that she was happy to make, but which never quite felt like home. Malin herself felt like home, but the life she led did not.

Usually Malin got back much later than this – around two a.m. most nights, at which point there would be clanking in the kitchen, pots and pans gathered for a drunken late-night dinner. A while later she'd flop into bed in a cloud of alcohol and cigarette smoke and the smells of whatever she'd been cooking, and immediately fall asleep. Janetta would stare at her resentfully – she got up at six o'clock.

Sometimes, when Janetta joined her on these nights out, she thought of her former self, how she stayed home and worked like she'd always done. As she waited for the shower to stop, she began to get a familiar sinking feeling contemplating that other life. Being in Malin's world took her away from her work, and while she'd gone into the relationship ready to do this, there was also a relentless worry she was giving up something important.

Once in a while they stayed home together – Malin would cook while she worked – and she felt truly happy in those moments, watching Malin boiling rice and chopping vegetables, concocting soups and stews out of nowhere. The perfect calm when she worked at her girlfriend's tiny desk, in the dim light of a rickety old lamp, with Malin sitting in her bay window, reading – this was always a few brief hours of bliss. But before long, Malin would get twitchy; these nights were too quiet for her, too dull.

She would beg Janetta to go out. *Come on, Jay, just one round.* She was pursuing her dream as a musician and going out between shifts was part of the hustle. Janetta had no energy for befriending managers and promoters and monosyllabic bass guitarists. But she felt boring saying no, so for a whole year she'd tried to juggle things as best she could.

Tonight, though, the longer she waited, the more she wanted to stay in. She wanted to wipe off her make-up and pull off her dress and not even be here in Malin's flat. She wanted to be at her desk at the AI Institute, or even at home. A lot of progress could be made at home. There was, despite what her sister said, a good feeling there.

She was ready to pack it in when the shower finally stopped. A moment later Malin yelled, 'I'm sorry! We don't have to go if you don't want.'

Janetta texted her friend to let her know they'd be late.

On the corner of Cord and Raeme they met Oene and her younger brother Arino, who was visiting town. Oene, keen to show him a good time, had enlisted Janetta to help out, because she could ask Malin, who, of course, would always have a party to take them to. They bought beer and walked together down Cord, Janetta falling into step with tall, jovial Arino, who told her he was going into his third year of a university in Heinis, a city several hours away. He was finishing his degree in maths and wondering whether he should follow his sister into AI.

'Feels like it's the safest bet – job-wise, I mean.' He glanced hopefully at her.

Janetta smiled, offering no opinion.

The party was on a grotty, shop-thronged stretch of Cord, in Malin's friend's basement flat beneath a ground-floor convenience store. Inside it was narrow, low-ceilinged, low-lit.

'Promisingly decadent,' Malin said, disappearing into the crowd to procure drinks.

Arino kept talking to Janetta and soon, because the party was packed, she found herself jammed up close to him, holding her beer to her chest as if to ward him off. People pushed past and she staggered a little, trying to keep some distance. He appeared to be happy to get close, though, rambling on about his career choices, obviously pleased to find a willing listener.

After a while he said, 'What do you make of that smashed aut? Oene said it was at your sister's café.'

She wasn't going to tell him what she really thought, which was, first, that she'd been surprised Lal was so indifferent to the attack when Janetta had called – she'd barely stuck around to talk, as though it had nothing to do with her. And second, that it was depressing that auts were treated like this – it made her feel more isolated, made her own research more of a struggle. Instead, she said, 'She doesn't work there any more – she moved to Mejira,' and then, trying to be objective, 'and I guess this sort of thing is inevitable, so long as corporations keep laying off so many people.'

'Are you worried?'

'About what?'

'About AI.'

'Well, not about AI so much – more about what people will do with it.'

'What about if the whole world was AI – are you worried about that?' he pressed, looking at her intently. He had curly hair and lively, interested eyes, the fuzzy start of a beard, small patches of sweat on his T-shirt beneath his armpits. She fought the urge to turn and search for Malin.

She smiled thinly. 'That's a leap. The whole world isn't going to be AI.'

'When it becomes conscious it will.'

'Conscious? Conscious AI is an *if*, not a *when*.' As ever, she batted the suggestion away, acting as if it was a silly idea brought up by someone who'd read too many science fiction novels. But the truth was that for the past few months she'd begun to work on her own consciousness projects in secret, just tinkering, trying things out. It wasn't something she discussed, though – no one knew, not Malin, not Lal, no one. And even though she was respected at the Institute, she knew she'd be thought too young and unformed to be having a go at what many people considered the discipline's holy grail. This might have been true, but it wasn't going to stop her. In fact, she felt it was her duty to have a go – she wouldn't have taken *herself* seriously otherwise. 'In any case, you'll have nothing to do with it in grad school,' she said, choosing her words carefully. 'The closest you'd come is what I'm doing – trying to get AI into the world that's emotionally intelligent, ethical, intuitive—'

He cut her off. 'All the good things.'

'Exactly. So that when – I mean, if - someone *does* ever create conscious AI, that framework will be in place, lessening the chance of it immediately turning around and, well, killing us.'

'That's very cool.' He gazed at her as though she was something that needed to be considered for a long time and in great detail. Uncomfortable, she gave in to her urge to turn and look for Malin. On the other side of the room, her girlfriend was laughing with a short girl with tight curls and a cherubic face. Her fingers brushed the girl's cheek as she leaned in to whisper.

Arino was watching her, waiting.

'Sorry,' she said, turning back. 'You were saying?'

'I was saying, probably the only truly safe job right now is to be CEO of some fuck-off massive corporation.'

'Right,' she said vaguely, her eyes going back to Malin. This time, he followed suit, seeing the girl twirling the chain of her silvery pendant, Malin's face straining with the effort to entertain, to make her laugh.

'That's your girlfriend, isn't it?'

Janetta didn't reply.

After the party that night, Malin told Janetta she wanted to sleep with other people.

'Like who?'

'Oh, no.' Malin sat on her bed, stretching out a leg, her eyes unfocused. 'I've been putting this off for months and I knew I'd end up picking the worst time. Can we talk in the morning?'

'Obviously not! Tell me – I want to know.'

So Malin said a name, let her head drop, pulled it up and said another. Both were women Janetta knew. Then someone she did not. And then a man – a surprise. From a distance she saw the names curl lustily, drunkenly, from her girlfriend's lips. Between them Malin gazed at the ceiling, her mouth open, as if she were picturing a scene with them all in it. As each was added, put in their designated place, Janetta felt herself become smaller and smaller. She sat in the darkness of the bay window, her arms folded across her knees.

'So . . . if we were having an orgy, that's who I'd invite. What about you? Who would you want to come?'

Janetta ignored the edge of hope in her voice and thought about the boy at the party, Arino, and her lack of interest. She felt trapped, almost childish. 'Only you.'

Malin sighed and ducked her head. 'You know I love you. I don't want to hurt you.'

Janetta knew, but the signs had always been there: her steady and small intimacies were no match for Malin's extravagance, her rushing towards the world. She absorbed its stimuli and threw them out again like glints of energy, or flares of need, in order to get closer to people; unlike Janetta, she couldn't bear to be alone.

Not long after they'd met, Malin had invited her to see her perform at a bar in Cabriol Beach. The bar was on Ellda Street, not far from the ocean, and salt hung in the air. Inside the long, low room they sat through a few bad poets, then Malin grabbed her guitar and took to the stage. She looked beautiful, her cream dress patterned with red roses, her feet gold-sandalled, her dark hair flipped to one side, snaking past her clavicle. She sang songs about discovery, her first kiss, old loves. Some of the crowd were fans, and Janetta remembered staring at them, seeing that Malin was there for them, had forgotten about her entirely. Slowly she began to understand her kind, generous girlfriend had a hunger that she alone couldn't fulfil.

When the applause came, these women rushed to Malin, surrounded her, and Janetta watched her beam and flirt. This happened when she was there and when she was not, not only with fans, but friends, friends of friends, past loves, strangers. Malin needed it, and Janetta never said a thing. She assumed she was wrong to be jealous, that she loved Malin too much and had to learn to let go. In the end it took Malin speaking up, finally saying it wasn't that, it was that she wasn't made for monogamy; she needed something else.

Knowing you aren't enough is devastating. In bed now, she turned away, and Malin sloppily, thoughtlessly fitted her body into hers. In a sleepiness seared by pain, Janetta thought that if she ever created conscious AI, making it capable of emotion would be stupid and cruel – no one – no *thing*, even – should have to feel this sad.

Next to her, Malin began to breathe deeply and her clutch around Janetta's waist grew slack.

4

Lal had discovered a coffee shop in Dhont. She had been allowing herself to leave the office at lunch, taking forlorn, lonely rambles around the campus. She knew it wasn't smart to leave her desk, but she couldn't help it – these walks helped her get oriented, digest her new reality. Mostly it was deserted – she knew there must be more people around, but actual sightings were rare. They seemed to exist more as an idea than as a living, breathing reality. She still held that glossy fantasy from the website in her head, hoping to turn a corner and find a group of beautiful, well-dressed Tekna employees standing and laughing together, welcoming her towards them. Every time she got back to the office, to the rows of shadows there, the lines of furiously flying fingers, this fantasy shattered. Each time she left, stupidly, it returned, but it was getting weaker and she knew that soon it would disappear altogether.

The hot weather had set in, making the empty campus more eerie. The sun beat down on the tarmac and on the oaks and alders that lined silent car parks. The coffee shop was just by the main entrance – she'd missed it earlier as the short path leading to it was unsigned and nondescript. At first sight the modest one-storey building with large lettering in dated fonts stuck to its windows had no appeal. It made her miss Popotops, which had always looked so welcoming, its wide silver doors opening onto the corner of busy Conaus Square – but at least it showed signs of life. That was enough, simply to see some people.

One morning before work, she stood in line eagerly waiting for a coffee. There were no human servers other than a young man she'd seen pop in and out from a side room, checking up on everything, but the coffee machine – a tiny Tekna-branded aut – guaranteed at least a half-decent coffee. Los had been messaging her all morning – he'd become her envoy from home. As was his way, he told her either basic life updates – how busy Popotops was, the fact there was construction work going on next door which was driving them crazy – or sent her things she might find funny. It was sweet, and she appreciated how much he was keeping in touch, but it was sad, too, because there was also a group chat with her, Van, Los and Rose, which was now – after years of in-jokes only the four of them would get – entirely silent. It was almost as though Los messaging her directly was a political move not to piss off Rose.

Meanwhile, the men in front were taking their time. Lal gave them a withering look, which they missed, and then realised with a start that the one right in front was Uhli Ranh, Tekna's CTO, from the conference last year. He was wearing a cream-coloured open-necked shirt and olive trousers. She stared at his stubble, his tanned skin, the dark hair on his hands; it was like seeing a celebrity in the flesh. She was spellbound – then she noticed he couldn't get the aut to work.

'A cappuccino . . .' he was saying again and again, then, 'Goddammit—'

His friend said something Lal didn't hear, and Ranh punched the aut's buttons angrily.

'Fucking aut.' He stood back, scrutinising it.

Lal thought of intervening, but she couldn't see what the

problem was, and also, she didn't quite have the guts to say anything.

'You need to crack that consciousness thing, Uhli,' teased his friend. 'This wouldn't happen with a smart little conscious aut. A smart little conscious aut would bound up to you *right here* with your coffee, ask how your day was, *really care*—'

'I am!' Ranh stared at the aut as if it owed him something. 'I *am* working on the consciousness thing. All the goddamned time.'

The aut buzzed. Ranh, his friend and Lal all watched.

It went silent.

'Fuu—' Ranh growled.

The aut kicked into life and drizzled a half-shot of foam into the coffee mug.

'Fucking shitty aut!' said Ranh. He glanced malevolently Lal's way and she gave a hopeful smile, but he stalked off without seeing it.

She reached over to the aut, gently reset it, punched in her preferences, put her mug in it and waited. Coffee then milk swirled into the cup, a dollop of sugar was added, an inch of foam whipped up, a triple helping of chocolate flakes sprinkled on top. She took it – then put it back down on the counter, realising that her hand was shaking, although whether from excitement or from something else, she couldn't tell.

When she returned to the office, Ukones had gone. His desk was as empty as if he'd never been there at all. The knickknacks around his computer, which no one else had – the superhero action figure, the photo of his bony-looking dog – had disappeared. Even the two spare pairs of grotty old trainers nestled deep beneath his desk had been removed. The man in the cubicle opposite, whose name she didn't know, who never spoke to her, lifted his head.

'Fired.'

He looked away, as if to make eye contact with Lal was to stare directly at the sun. She could hear him typing a moment later. Aware that she didn't want to look like she was indulging in chit-chat while the rest of the office was silent, she rose a few careful inches from her seat and hissed, 'Why?'

His eyes, deep in his sunken face, rose again.

'Too slow,' he said.

They both got back to work.

A little later, Lal thought to turn to the dingy wall behind her and let her gaze travel to the ceiling in case something was there. A small, wobbly spider's web, that was all. And yet the whole office acted as though they were being watched – or, she thought, glancing over to Ukones' desk, as though they could lose their jobs at any moment.

In the depths of that afternoon she at last finished her first efficiency proposal. It had taken more than two weeks and she was relieved, but there was no acknowledgement of it on-screen; only the next proposal, for a Popotops branch in Ataluk, which had seven little green bodies lining up to be eliminated. She would have to do this one more quickly. She was grateful, though, that wherever the data monitoring team's progress was being recorded, she now had a *one* against her name instead of a *zero*. As long as she could keep adding to that, she might be okay.

But she wanted a walk, to take a few minutes to get some lunch. She bought a cookie and devoured it on her way back across the car park, temporarily distracted from her lonely day, her fingers sticky with sun-melted chocolate. As she did, she remembered something that had happened a few years ago. She'd been lying on her bed at home messaging Rose when her mum had knocked on the door.

'Lalita,' she'd said, opening it slowly, 'I have a job for you.'

'Ummm . . . can I do it later?'

'No, a job. Alicia has a job for you.'

'Who?' Lal had said, then remembered Alicia, her mum's friend.

'Up you get,' said her mother. 'We'll go and see her now.'

Alicia had a very good job for her, her mother continued as Lal had dragged herself up, and all the more so because weren't jobs getting harder to come by, and they needed to go and say thank you in person. Lal avoided asking her mum to confirm it was a cleaning job, though she knew it was.

Alicia lived fifteen minutes' walk away in Lower Sunset. Her house was similar to their own, an unimposing two storeys of washed-out concrete, but hers was more decrepit out front, with a carpet of weeds lining the path to the door. Inside, Alicia led Lal and her mother to a room at the back where webs of light shone through lace curtains, and they sat at a table in a shadowy corner. She put the kettle on and soon the strong, familiar smell of black sand tea wafted towards them. Alicia was her mother's age and wore the same kind of clothes – leggings, a long, shapeless T-shirt, padded sandals that slipped on easily, the sort of thing you wanted to slide into after a long day. She had dyed her hair a rusty bronze and had a deep V-shaped crinkle between her eyebrows. She brought the tea to the table and poured them each a cup, her movements slow and tired. Her mother always insisted that black sand tea was at its best, its most earthy and piquant, when it was piping hot, and so she sipped it immediately, the steam clouding her face. Her mother had a strange ability to transcend her humanity sometimes; in specific domestic domains, like that of tea, she was invincible.

The subject matter was less compelling – her mother and Alicia talked about people they knew as Lal blew at her tea and listened to her mother's weird, ingratiating tone. Eventually, her mother turned to her and asked if she had something she wanted to say.

'Oh,' said Lal, annoyed, 'yes – yes. I want to say thank you for getting me the job.'

Alicia nodded. 'There's not many about these days.'

'Thank you for thinking of me.'

Her mother nodded fervently, signalling with her eyes that Lal should say more, and Lal felt a flash of resentment.

'But I'm going to say no.'

Alicia nodded.

'I also work at Popotops.'

'Lal?'

'And I'm an HEU graduate, so even if jobs *are* hard to come by, which I appreciate they are, I don't need to be a cleaner.'

'Lalita!' said her mother sharply.

For a moment, Alicia was silent. Then she said, as if stating a fact, 'I've been a cleaner all my life. You're a lucky girl to have gone to HEU.' Her gaze fell to her tea.

Her mother was staring at her with an anger she'd not seen in years; she looked away, shocked and then ashamed at her mother's disgust. The shame hit the second she realised what she'd said, and how rude it was. Seconds later, she saw that was the reason she'd been willing to go to Alicia's: something awful in her had wanted to make it clear that she was too good for a cleaning job, and that she'd needed to say it out loud.

She said softly, uselessly, 'I know – I'm grateful.' How spoilt she must appear, especially as Alicia must know plenty of other people who wanted the job, and she had put Lal first as a kindness to her mother.

They didn't stay long after that. Her mother's cheeks were burning. She grovelled the entire way to the door, practically bowing by the time they left. Alicia herself was almost too humble to have realised the slight, though; she seemed only to feel that Lal was lucky – but her lack of resentment made Lal feel worse.

On the way home, her mother fixed her gaze straight ahead.

Lal stared down at the bottom of the hill, where the city centre glinted in the late afternoon light. 'I'm sorry,' she said eventually. 'I know we need the money.'

But her mother said nothing.

They crossed the street and Lal felt the heat of irritation – was it so terrible to refuse a job you knew was beneath you? Janetta wouldn't even be having this conversation. Janetta was inherently exempt.

'We brought you up wrong,' her mother finally said.

'What do you mean?'

'A job comes along and you don't want it! There are no jobs, Lal! We made you selfish. Too many books, too much fun, too much television, too much–'

'I'm not selfish!' Lal said. 'I'm–' She stopped. How could she end that sentence in a way that didn't sound bad? 'I'm just lucky,' she tried, 'to have parents who wanted the best for me.'

Her mother remained silent, and Lal assumed the conversation was over. A minute later her mother turned and said, 'We do. But this was a good opportunity.'

She'd felt another furious wave of shame. She knew her dad was having trouble finding a job and that her mum already worked all the hours she could. She grudgingly accepted, too, that her sister's Ph.D. didn't leave Janetta much time for income generation.

A few weeks after that, Lal had gone for the store manager position, when Antaro – who didn't care about anything except the quality of his weed – finally got sacked.

As she went back to her silent office in Dhont, Lal reminded herself how far she'd come. If someone had told her on the way home from Alicia's that two and a half years after being told off for turning down a job as a cleaner she'd be at Tekna, she'd have been amazed. This made up for her heart sinking as she reached her desk; ever so briefly it held her unhappiness at bay.

After work she went straight to Mejira. She didn't even think about it. Hane Station, which wasn't far from the Tekna Tower, sat at the bottom of a famously glamorous shopping complex. Lal had seen it on television – it rocketed up into the sky, white and shining; from the outside it looked like an enormous pearlescent shell. On its escalators the people she passed wore sunglasses, draped scarves, bright colours, materials that cloaked and clung. These women – and it was mostly women – were expressionless, their skin peach-smooth and their hair glossy and full. They carried small handbags and smaller dogs, scooped up for the escalator ride.

Lal had lost her sense of self-awareness. If she stopped for a second to think about the fact she was wearing her cheap blue cardigan, which had a hole in the seam at the top near the shoulder, and the same dress she'd worn when she first came to Mejira – and about a hundred times since – and her scuffed ballet pumps, she would have turned and run. But something more urgent compelled her on.

On the ground floor classical music played and a floral scent lingered in the air. The first shop she went past had three elegant evening dresses in its window display and she stopped to look at the green one, a pale pillar of silk. She tilted her head to read the price tag – 5,000 swocols – and felt something stretch and snap inside. The assistants in the store milled casually and she walked on.

Shop after shop offered the same kind of thing, dresses and bags in softly lit sanctuary, but as Lal walked past she felt almost as if she was refusing them; she was turning them down, looking for something more. Occasionally, something she truly desired caught her eye – a beautiful embroidered cushion, a pink dress tied with a silk ribbon that would have hidden her belly – but she kept walking. The thing was just to be there, finding her way to the top of the shell.

It felt like a form of evolution – the higher she got, the more comfortable she felt, the more assimilated into the place. At the very top there was not, like at the crappy shopping mall in downtown Ulrusa, a sleazy-looking multiplex cinema that everyone hated but everyone went to. Instead, there was a bar. A woman stood at its front desk and Lal peered behind her, but it was hard to see anything beyond a dark, shimmering wall – just a few tables, an orchid resting in a thin vase at the centre of each.

'Table for one?' the woman asked pleasantly, and Lal nodded, brushing her hair behind her ears, adjusting her rucksack and feeling self-conscious, but the woman smiled kindly and led her past slinky, beautiful young men and women – noting the fashionable side-swept hair and undercuts, she self-consciously touched her own fringe – to a space by the window. The view that greeted her was a surprise. A solid chunk of Mejira was laid out before her, the Tower in the foreground and the skyline stretching deep into the distance.

'Just tell the aut what you want,' said the woman.

She'd gone before giving Lal a menu, but on the table in front of her, words began to emerge, curling up into the air, making themselves known. Lal pulled one in and the soft blue letters expanded into a description of a cocktail; just before she wiped it away – she didn't fancy a Mejiran Sling – an image of it flickered into the air and an aroma stole up her nose. She was knocked back by the scent of smoky whisky.

When it disappeared she scrolled through the rest, making tiny movements with her hand and looking furtively for prices, but in the end there was no way to tell, so she asked the aut, a glowing fuchsia marble at the edge of the table, for the simplest thing she could find, a concoction of berries and vodka. It arrived within moments and she nodded a thank you, concerned about the cost. But then she took a sip and surveyed what was before her – the swarming city, its blinking lights, its heady, clustered geometry. This was the glamour, right here – the cocktail, the view, possibly even the being alone in doing this. She couldn't have done it with Rose, who refused to go to any pub or bar other than the most basic, no-frills chains. It would have been quite fun with Los here – that was a thought worth considering – except he always looked like he was just about to go and do something wholesome, like a hike or a cycling trip; he wouldn't know what to do in a place like this. He'd probably get out binoculars and start commenting on some aspect of urban geography that he found interesting.

Van and Los together would be fun, too. They made her laugh a lot. They'd probably embarrass her, though. Van would order a beer, then drink too much – he always did, he always went just over the limit and became a problem, although not in a scary way, just loud. He'd be slouching over these plush narrow chairs, trying to befriend the waitress, raising his voice when everyone around them was having intimate conversations. No, Van couldn't come. He was a liability.

Ironically – though she hadn't meant to think of her next – Janetta would be the perfect person to take to a place like this. She would have blended in. Lal would have had to pick her clothes, of course, but after that she could perch on a chair like a supermodel.

Malin could come too – she was loud, but elegant with it, the kind of person people wanted to be around. But what would it be like, to be here with her sister? To overlook this city with a person she hated?

But no, she didn't hate Janetta, she envied her. She'd been working on acknowledging this. Through countless conversations with Rose, she had grudgingly come to admit her envy, but the truth was that the feeling was still pretty bad. It still felt a lot like hate. In any case, how would it feel to be here with the sister she *envied* so much? It would feel sad, she decided, it would drain the enjoyment from it. So she scrubbed Janetta from the picture, and Malin as collateral damage, took a deep breath and told herself that being alone was what she wanted. But then her phone began to ring with an unknown number.

'Hello?' she said, slightly hopeful.

'Hi there, Lal,' drawled a voice she couldn't place.

'Hello?'

'Lal – Lal, it's Uko, from the office. Your recently fired colleague.' He sounded satisfied with this description of himself.

'Oh. Hi – Ukones.' Suddenly the view became a little less beautiful. She lowered her head, thinking of Ukones in his shorts, the red sores on his ankles, the flakes of scalp across his T-shirt.

'Hi Lal, hi again. Hi and actually – I didn't get to say goodbye to you when I left, and I wanted to. I felt you and I had a . . . a burgeoning friendship.'

'Ah.' The room seemed to darken. The waitress appeared, placed a saucer of nuts on the table and glanced at Lal, who nodded a thanks. As soon as she'd gone, Lal reached over and ate some of them.

'I wanted to ask—' Ukones said, as Lal coughed from too much nut and took a long sip of cocktail. 'Lal?'

'Yep – yeah.'

'I wanted to ask if I could take you to dinner tomorrow night?'

'Oh, Ukones – I'm flattered, but—' Lal looked at her shoes, feeling a twinge of loneliness. She'd been feeling it a lot lately and always forced herself to push it away, but Ukones' request had brought it straight back. 'But that's not possible, I'm afraid.'

'Right,' he said flatly. 'Not – not possible just tomorrow, or not possible in general?'

'Not possible – I'm afraid not possible in general.'

'Right,' he said again, a soft anger creeping in around the edges. 'I will leave you alone then.'

Lal hesitated. She had said the wrong thing and hurt him. 'I'm so—' she began, but he'd already gone.

She downed the rest of her cocktail and gazed out at the skyline again, which was now distinctly less enjoyable. No one ever asked her out. She was the most single of all single people, and she *did* care about that, but she could never find anyone she wanted to date. The boys she'd grown up with in Ulrusa and those she'd known at HEU were silly and boring – they cared about football and footballers, sometimes they cared about skateboarding and skateboarders, and maybe a few were into martial arts and martial artists too. She never knew what to say to them. She'd had her crushes, but they'd always seemed to smell her ambition and steered clear.

She imagined Ukones with his creepy-pathetic smile sitting next to her, telling her things that made her heart sink. Why was he the only person she knew in Mejira, the only man who would ask her out? Why was it someone she wanted nothing to do with? But then she looked around at the gleam of limbs and teeth and laughing eyes and remembered that she didn't exactly belong here herself – look at where she lived, where she worked.

Her phone lit up with a message from Los then, but she ignored it and reached again for the cocktail. She looked at the view and stubbornly told herself, *I live in Mejira and I work at Tekna.*

She finished the non-existent last drops of the drink, though her intention had been to make it last for as long as possible – and as the glass was whisked away some purple numbers swirled up before her: the cost of the cocktail, and the nuts. Both were impossible.

She turned and sought the waitress amid the sleek bodies at the bar, the numbers hovering insistently. But no drink could cost so much – and how could they charge her for the nuts? She'd not even asked for the nuts.

The waitress appeared and Lal sat up in anticipation, but before she could say anything, the waitress nodded towards the tiny, glowing aut. 'You want to pay, just wave your phone at it,' and Lal realised there was nothing to be done, so she turned back to the empty glass and the unfair numbers and the spectacular, joyless horizon.

5

The best way to protest against Lal's move to Mejira was to ignore her messages. Rose looked at them sometimes, like just now, when she was on the train to Rornul – a cringingly conciliatory joke, a photo of something she thought Rose might find funny, an ill-judged shot of the Tekna Tower – but she wasn't going to reply. As they stacked up unanswered, she thought of how the same thing had happened in the other direction, too. For months before Lal left, Rose had been trying to get her to come to a meeting. Just one – that was all she wanted, for Lal to get some much-needed perspective. But Lal had always turned her down – she gave no explanation; sometimes she hadn't replied at all. Beyond this, before all of this, Rose could scroll up and see how close they'd once been, in touch almost every day for years, telling each other the smallest details of their lives – intricate commentaries on what they were eating, what they were watching, who they fancied, how much their families were annoying them. But now Rose ignored Mejira, as Lal had ignored the meetings.

In fairness, Rose might have been part of the problem. In those early days of the meetings, she'd made it sound as if they took place in some kind of malevolent underworld, intending to instil awe, but it had clearly backfired as Lal had only seemed scared.

The truth was that Rornul was far from an underworld. It was one of the most open areas of Ulrusa, where light poured generously over the horizon. It wasn't even hard to get there; you just took the southbound train to the end of the line, which Rose was doing now, the least weary person on the 8.23.

At the station she clattered down the steps and out of the entrance. The meetings had changed lately and were now far less intimate, but there was still nowhere she'd rather be. Down the empty streets, she passed squat, silent warehouses – closed for the night, for years, or forever – past signs that proclaimed their current or historical use: meat warehouse, food warehouse, plastics factory. There was a website where you could see how many auts worked in these places and watch those numbers shoot up while the number of humans fell. Autwatch worked on anonymous data, so its stats could be wrong, but news stories had started to refer to it, so it had become an authoritative source.

She turned into Srvor Road, a long, wide stretch that marked the urban perimeter, the start of the hinterlands. Here you could smell the clay in the soil, see clear outlines of distant hills. About a quarter of the way down, there stood a cavernous concrete building – no one knew who owned it, and it was widely believed to have been empty for years. When you opened its door, which needed a firm push, you entered a rectangular, white-walled, high-ceilinged space. Grime-smeared windows ran along the side walls at head height, their white steel frames riddled with rust. Its corners blossomed mould, and there was a sense of flourishing insect and rodent populations just out of sight. The only reprieve from its industrial feel were the reds and browns of its tatty, forsaken carpets, suggesting some prehistoric form of home-making. Walking in for the first time six months ago, Rose had finally felt she was doing something right.

She had not always cared so much. In the past, she had been more preoccupied with having fun; politics had been her father's domain, and, more and more, Naji's. It was their influence that had led to her studies at HEU, but almost instantly she'd chosen the wrong kind – political philosophy, which was vague and abstract, and for which no one could see a clear use.

At the time, living at home, had felt like her biggest problem, as no matter how free she tried to be, as soon as she put her key in the door she was back where she started. It was a million miles away now – now her dad was gone and they'd moved from the old house – but back then she'd hated it; it might as well have been a continuation of school.

She'd learned to get good at escape. The easiest thing was to tell her mum she was with Lal, and then they'd go to parties, those dusk-till-dawn ones down on the beach. The moment there she loved most was at first light, she and Lal and their friends huddled on top of a damp sand dune, hugging themselves for warmth and smoking as the dawn chill seeped into their bodies. They'd be a little way from the party, looking down on it, out to the Yalin Sea, but they could still hear the music – half of Ulrusa could hear the music. For the longest time, this felt like freedom to Rose.

She didn't neglect her studies, though. She was good at political philosophy, it turned out, and she did well in her exams – so well that she wished she'd been rich enough to go to the University of Ulrusa. She sought out funding for further study – maybe even a Ph.D. – and was told that for HEU students it was impossible: their degrees were considered community college degrees, so she wasn't eligible for scholarships. Perhaps the most disappointing thing her dad had ever done was to tell her, once she'd found this out, to get a job. He didn't care about her education, not like he'd cared about Naji's. Her father had been furious when Naji didn't go to college – there were huge rows, with her dad saying he had to go and Naji vehemently insisting on starting work. He was convinced HEU would be a waste of his time. In retrospect, he'd been right.

But her dad had paid no attention to her own education until she'd begged to take it a step further, at which point he'd told her she'd had more than enough. She understood then that because she was a girl, he didn't see her in the same way. The irony was that Yash, although he was only sixteen, already knew he wanted to do a Ph.D. He'd arranged meetings with the hardship counsellors at the University of Ulrusa, making sure his name was on the list for any funding being doled out. It was hard to know what her dad might have made of this – he'd have been proud that at least one of his sons would go through higher education, perhaps, but probably less inspired by the fact Yash also wanted to study philosophy, especially since he'd made some firm declarations about being interested in metaphysics and the philosophy of mind, which would no doubt have been entirely pointless subjects in their dad's opinion. Possibly the only one doing right by him now, if he was watching – which Rose knew he wasn't, of course he wasn't – was Naji. Though at least she was trying.

A few weeks before she first went to Rornul, Rose had helped her mum set up a protest about her working conditions. Early that February morning she'd gone downtown with her to her workplace – one of her workplaces, that was; the company shunted its cleaners around the city quite freely. Under clear skies, they stood together with her mother's colleagues outside a high-rise office block. They could see themselves in its windows, young and old, bright-eyed and tired, all bundled up alike in black or blue padded coats, woolly hats and gloves. They shifted their weight and held placards and chanted in a loud, firm monotone for job security and better wages as people walked past on their way to work, ignoring them or simply staring curiously.

Her mum had wanted Naji to help her with this protest. She'd been a union member for decades, but unlike her husband she hadn't been an organiser – she'd stayed in the background, in a supporting role. With him gone it was as if she was trying to honour his memory, but needed her son to actually make it happen. She'd made comments about how busy Naji was, how he never had time for the rest of his family, and how she had to make all the effort. It was true she spent a lot of time at his, helping Hela with Yissi, their baby, and it was also true that since becoming union rep he'd been around much less. In the end, Rose realised she could step in: she could be the Naji in her mother's life, or at least, she could help her organise a protest.

But was she making a difference? Was standing with a bunch of old ladies asking for more job security and better pay completely pointless in the face of auts taking their jobs? There was something about what they were doing – how tall the buildings were, how small and cold and old they were beneath them – that made it feel hopeless. Were they simply begging? At some point, she noticed a young man at the edge of the group, in his late twenties perhaps, talking earnestly to the women. She studied him for a moment – a serious face, quick-moving mouth, black jacket with the collar turned up – and went over.

He was explaining the aut arrival timeline to them, speaking without a trace of emotion, barely pausing for breath. Forty per cent of jobs, he said, would be gone to forms of AI over the next two years, and within five the only ones that would remain were those for the elite – managers, business people, politicians. There'd be nothing for anyone else. He eyed them meaningfully and Rose squeezed closer.

'What matters,' he said, his voice rising, knowing he had their attention, 'is finding other people who feel the urgency, too. Realising you're not alone. And once we find each other, we've got real solidarity – and then we'll make things happen.'

He began to hand out flyers, his thin fingers peeling them off one by one, and the women took them, curious but untrusting. He turned to Rose and as their fingers touched, an electric current surged straight through her.

'You should come,' he said. 'I think you'll find it interesting.'

She deliberated for a week or two then went to the address on the flyer – which said in capitals *STAND TOGETHER AGAINST THE AUTS!* – and there he was, Alek, who she'd met that winter morning, and who, at this point, would barely look her way.

In that first meeting, in this room which was now so familiar, she had gathered her courage and joined the small circle of strangers. Not knowing where or who to rest her eyes on, she'd lifted her gaze to the ceiling. It felt like a whole weather system was unfolding beneath it – wind rushing across, leaves chasing each other, and what looked like a sprawling fungus in a distant corner.

The first person she'd let herself scrutinise was Alek. In this light his face looked plain and slightly haggard, yellowish beneath its olive surface, rescued by prominent cheekbones. He was slight and wolfish, exactly her type – though her last boyfriend, Beve, who she'd broken up with last year, was jolly-looking, with a childish, cheeky grin. He was incredibly unserious, except when he'd smoked too much weed. But Alek did not appear to be the smiling type. Next to him sat two older women, wearing shabby, colourful jumpers and long, knitted scarves. One cupped her hands around a steaming mug, the top of a plastic flask, and Rose could smell something earthy coming from it, like toasted rice. Her lined face was serene. The woman next to her, who had wide eyes set into a broad, fleshy face, was staring worriedly at the floor.

On Alek's other side was a girl around Rose's age. She was tiny, with long, greasy hair and a sparking, nervous energy, which she displayed by silently remonstrating with herself about how she was positioned, crossing and uncrossing her legs, standing up, sitting down, jumping on the spot. It was like watching an athlete warming up. The rest of the circle was all male – some in their late teens, sitting sullenly, resting their beers on their thighs. An earring glinted here, a shaved head there. Surly, watchful faces reminded her of Naji. One larger man, full-faced, with small eyes and a coppery beard, gazed at her unapologetically. She stared him down until he looked away.

'This is a space for discussing the auts,' Alek said, looking around, engaging them all, except he didn't catch Rose's eye. 'They're taking our jobs and we're being left with nothing. No one's stepping in to help. We need to call on politicians to do more, we need to call on corporations to do a *lot* more' – this got a knowing grunt from somewhere in the circle – 'and we need to act together to make all of this happen.'

He held himself in a drooping way, one leg crossed over the other, a hand constantly grazing his chin stubble as he spoke, but there was a steeliness to him. He looked like someone with a lot of education, though he was wearing just an old T-shirt and nondescript trousers – and fashionable trainers, she noted. Still, there was something unadorned about him, an almost studied minimalism that made her think he was smart. He asked if anyone wanted to chat about what was on their mind and glanced her way. Heat spread through her and she quickly looked down. She was hardly shy, but it had been a long time since she'd been attracted to anyone.

'We got told by management this week,' said the woman staring at the floor, 'that half of us on the assembly lines are going to lose our jobs to auts. But they haven't said who, and they haven't said when.' She looked up. 'When I asked for some details they said, "*Oh, later this year*," so what are we supposed to do? Just *wait*?'

'Where do you work?' Rose asked.

'Bershvar. Do you know it?'

Rose shook her head.

'It's a food-processing factory. I make ready meals there.' She looked at her friend. 'Serir, too.' The woman with the cup of tea nodded silently.

'Have you protested?'

'Hi—' said Alek, putting a hand up to get her attention. 'Hi – you're—'

That heat again. And there was something different, almost playful, in his eyes – or was she imagining it?

'Rose.'

'Hi, Rose. Ninna and Serir have worked at Bershvar for' – he turned to them – 'is it fifteen?'

'Eighteen,' Ninna corrected.

'*Eighteen* years. They've done a lot of protesting in their time.'

'But this is new,' said Ninna. 'Everyone else thinks the union is going to save us, but we know better. We've seen the union reps come and go – promises as they come in, excuses as they go out—'

'Unions are good, though,' said Rose, surprised and a little defensive.

Alek stepped in. 'They can be, but they're slow with the auts – too much bureaucracy in the way. That's why we're building our own solidarity networks.'

Rose glanced at the twelve or so people in the circle to see some nodding in agreement.

'See, those two are from Bershvar,' said the twitchy, hyper younger woman, 'but me and Lemas work at a customer fulfilment centre south of here. And all you lot' – she asked the men – 'you're from Rartaur, aren't you?'

'My brother works in Rartaur!' Rose said.

'Then bring him to a meeting,' said Alek, pleased. 'The more the better.' His voice was flat, almost detached, but Rose was stirred all the same.

'I'll try.'

She was glad she'd come. As he nodded and turned, asking if anyone wanted to talk, she admired his face – the way his greenish-brown skin looked stretched tight, the cheekbones that were almost hollows, the calm, unfazed eyes. Lemas, in the meantime, began to tell them how he'd spent all week working on the floor, as he called it, at a fulfilment centre with auts. They'd whizzed around between shelving units, scurrying thoughtlessly towards him with any one of a thousand different kinds of consumer goods.

'I was doing a late-night shift, it ends at two a.m.' – he looked around at them, small and balding and rumpled – 'got to get the people their crap on time, right? Can't leave them waiting for their condoms and their fucking baseball caps. It was just me on the floor with the auts, they were picking and packing, I was checking. I felt myself fall into a trance – all I could think of, even when I closed my eyes, was the auts going up and down the rows of shelves, up and down, like they'd never stop, like none of this would ever stop. I started to lose sight of who I was, felt like I'd dissolved. I thought, one day they're gonna pick me up and pack me too. Send me who knows where. Doesn't matter. A dump. Doesn't matter.'

Alek nodded with interest but didn't say anything, and Rose thought of her dad, whose eyes had flashed with righteous anger when he'd listened to people tell him their stories. He'd burst out at the end with all sorts of things that should have happened, should be happening, would – he promised – happen. And then she thought of something else.

'You're not only alienated from the act of production,' she said, 'you're alienated from your fellow workers, too.'

Alek turned to her with surprise. 'You're right,' he said, and his gaze lingered on her in a way that, for the first time in a long time, made her feel she'd said something worth saying. But then she reminded herself that this wasn't about her, shook this feeling away and focused once more on the group, ready to listen.

6

'A better world through artificial intelligence' – the guiding mission of the University of Ulrusa's AI Institute. But the Institute was not naïvely utopian; it believed in robust dialogue, rigorous research, and what its founders called a 'radical pedagogical approach'. Its famous crit sessions, where graduate students presented their dissertation projects to one another in an open, democratic discussion of ideas, was part of their approach. They were meant to make the Institute's graduate programme stand out from those of its competitors, but also, of course, they were a chance for the students to crucify one another.

They were well aware of this double nature: on the one hand, they saw crits as a congratulatory exercise – they had almost completed this prestigious programme and could now revel in it a little; on the other, it exposed the lie of the land just before they headed into the final months of their dissertations. If you hadn't been working – if you'd, for example, been slumping around trying to account for yourself in ways that had nothing to do with your project and everything to do with reading meandering philosophical novels, or wasting time on the internet, then this was your moment of reckoning. Or it was meant to be, but Janetta's fellow students went unusually easy on one another. There were just twelve of them and their closeness meant benevolence, to the extent that Kait, the Ph.D. director, got frustrated. She wanted them to have to withstand rigorous critique – they were, after all, the future of artificial intelligence.

Janetta was the best. The others had known this when they entered the doctoral programme, and they were even more sure three years on. They admired her because her brain was subtle and flexible, but they liked her because she carried her learning lightly. Of course, those who carry their learning lightly often try hard to conceal how competitive they truly are, and it secretly mattered a great deal to Janetta that she outpace the others. She knew most of her peers were no competition – they just wanted to get jobs at AI firms and make themselves cogs in machines – and the more imaginative ones might stay in academia. Neither of these was enough for her.

On Monday the students and their tutors assembled in the airy room that took up the top floor of the Institute. Covered in a curved glass roof that let light in even on the greyest day, the room looked down onto clouds of ginkgo and silver maple and the buildings of the University of Ulrusa constellating below. The crits had started by the time Janetta arrived, and her friend Lieven was at the front, explaining his work. She tiptoed to a seat at the back, eyes down.

Lieven, facing them, gesticulating and eager, was Janetta's only real intellectual rival on the course. His ideas were playful and imaginative, he wanted to start his own AI firm – and he wanted her to join him. She looked up, caught his eye, and he gave her a look of happy trust.

Her face constricted in pain.

He hesitated, pushed his glasses up the bridge of his nose and carried on. 'What I hope to show is that we can train a machine learning model to give auts a chance to be as ethical as humans; it's just going to take some time.'

Loud applause, easy questions, a stream of compliments. Lieven's expression turned both self-conscious and smug, because he might be self-effacing, but he couldn't help but love praise.

Kait glanced at Janetta, keen on her thoughts. Janetta looked at the floor.

Her thoughts were: *I can't do this.*

Two more presentations passed by in a blur before the break, then slowly, slackly, Janetta followed everyone outside. She stood for a second, then went to sit on the steps by the fire exit and took out her phone. There was a message from Lal, which she didn't open, and that was it – but if she stared at the screen for long enough and wished hard enough, Malin would get in touch. After a few moments of nothing, Lieven came to sit by her side.

'Hey, you okay?'

She looked up and her chin wobbled, her eyes filled, and she began to cry as she stuttered out, 'Malin's gone.'

'Shit,' he said helplessly. 'I'm sorry. You're not – you can't give it another chance?'

She thought of Malin's hypothetical orgy. 'It's not going to work.'

He put an arm around her heaving shoulders and looked out at the park across the path. Usually the students colonised it like foxes, but today it was deserted.

Janetta pressed her head into her palms and was silent for a long time.

'Come on,' he said. 'It'll be okay. I promise. Maybe not right now, but soon.' He looked out to the park again and then at his own phone. It was time to go back, time for Janetta's crit. 'You're up,' he said gently, standing and stretching and waiting until she followed him back in.

Up at the front, she chewed a fingernail, then raised her head just enough to meet her colleagues' eyes. 'Emotional intelligence,' she began, 'is a crucial aspect of artificial intelligence. My research is based on the following idea: if auts can recognise and respond to human emotion, this will make the difference between them being rational machines that have no real connection to us, or them being more versatile creations we can collaborate with, integrate with – even have some form of relationship with.'

They hung onto every word. Kait watched shrewdly.

'As you know' – Janetta took a deep breath – 'I've been creating a machine learning model that can respond effectively to a wide range of emotional cues.'

She pointed to the first slide in her presentation and began to explain how she had designed a complex response in an aut. The sun pushed through the clouds, streaking her tall body with light, betraying her red eyes and puffy face. She looked at the slide, reckoned with the fact she had another twenty-three of these to get through, and in desperation, clicked backwards, where the final slide, which she'd written late last night, was waiting.

It said: *Sometimes an effective response isn't enough.*

'But the problem with trying to create auts that read and respond to human emotion in a complex way,' she said, 'is that who cares about a response?'

One or two of her fellow students gaped in confusion, but she carried on, 'It's all very well if your home aut or your aut pal in the office can offer sympathy or words of wisdom, but so what? It's just as meaningless as if one of you said something nice to me, or tried to assuage my pain.' She ignored Lieven's bafflement and Kait's stony face and looked at the exit, thinking only of Malin. 'Nothing's going to bring her back.'

She began to cry.

Lieven looked worriedly at Kait, then jumped up, took Janetta's arm and led her out into the corridor. She slid down against the wall, folded her arms on her knees and rested her head on them. She heard footsteps, then someone bending down close to her.

'Get yourself together and go back in there,' Kait whispered.

Janetta didn't move. She could picture the concerned faces, their perplexed and silent signalling over her head. She knew she needed to account for herself, to return and rescue her crit, but she couldn't. She only wanted them to leave her alone and let her cry in peace.

7

Dhont Coach Station was a shabby concrete affair, dark and unwelcoming, built decades ago and especially dismal on a Saturday morning. Lal joined one of the milling queues, folded her arms in protest at the noisy family pitching up behind and their arguing kids, and glanced at the people ahead holding bags of food and waiting to board. She wanted a seat to herself.

Being on the coach was a comedown, although she was already miserable and she wasn't sure exactly what it was a comedown from. Perhaps, she thought as she got on, heading for a seat near the back, one not too near the toilets but also without crisp crumbs all over it, the reason it felt bad was because it was proof she wasn't coping. She was going home – but just for the weekend.

The text from Los last night that she'd not looked at until she was in bed, her head spinning from the cocktail, invited her to a party – begged her to come. He said she owed them a visit. She'd ignored it, but the next morning, waking early with nothing to do, no one to see and another empty weekend ahead of her, she thought maybe she would go. It wasn't a matter of defeat. It was a sort of strategic pick-me-up so she could go back to Mejira with renewed vigour. But the fact she was even thinking this at all, that *was* defeat. The fact she was going home at all was a failure – she just didn't want anyone to see that she felt this.

The coach journey was interminable – eight long hours across the lowlands and grey skies of southern Iolra. It felt semi-nostalgic, but also an indignity, forced on her by her bank balance, and she slouched in her window seat, flicked up her laptop and prepared to zone out until they got there. The only other thing she did was to let Rose know she'd be back, cajoling her, with a slight begging undertone, to meet up. Otherwise, she said, she might not be there until the end of the year – far enough away to at long last provoke a response.

Once in Ulrusa, she was surprisingly happy. The light was brighter, and with the sea not so far away, the world felt more spacious, as if there was more air to breathe. In the early evening she and Rose sat together in faded deckchairs in her garden, a small patch of bright green outside her sister's room, tended to by her father. Its banks bloomed with colour – pink and purple sweet pea, foxglove and dark plum poppies, and a magnolia, austere and beautiful, in the corner.

She'd managed to make Rose laugh with her tales of Ukones and the request for a date, and the pricey drink and how it had led her to the grim coach journey. Having Rose there felt miraculous, but now she'd used up her stories – her store of entertainment – she felt an unease grow between them. Rose's expression, in the silence, shifted from open and interested to suspicious, almost as if she was remembering more about the recent era of their friendship every second that went by. Finally, looking around, she said, in what felt to Lal like a damningly neutral tone, 'I haven't been here for ages.'

At one point, much of Rose's life had been spent in this garden. They'd played here all the time after school, making up games and worlds, enlisting Janetta to describe one imaginary universe after another to them because she was so good at it. As teenagers they sprawled on the grass and talked about teachers and homework and boys, and later, Rose spent countless hours there articulating her thoughts, or her father's thoughts, about the injustices of the universe and later on of the Iolran government – often to Lal's own father, who was a willing, entertained listener and occasional provocateur – but the last time she was here, drinking a beer, gearing up to discuss life, must have been five or six months ago.

'You can come whenever you want, you know,' Lal said now. 'They all love you.'

'Well, my mum's always asking where *you* are.'

Lal had spent as much time in Rose's old house as Rose had spent in her garden. Every weekend for years they'd watched movies on Rose's big television, joined by a revolving cast of her mum, Yash, Naji and an excessive amount of snacks. 'You told her I moved to Mejira, right?'

'I did.' Rose turned to watch a bee poking hopefully at the poppies.

'Did you tell her it was Tekna?'

'Why? Are you worried she'll think you're a sell-out?' She didn't take her eyes off the bee.

'Well, *you* do.'

'I don't.'

'Rose, you don't talk to me any more.'

Rose didn't reply, and Lal took her silence as a confirmation. She felt weak, almost sick, at the thought that this might be the way things were for the rest of their lives.

'Please, c'mon,' she said. 'I didn't do anything wrong. No one else in my family has a job. Dad's been unemployed for more than a year—'

'Your mum's got one.'

'As a cleaner. How long's that going to last?'

Rose didn't reply.

'And Janetta's a waste of space,' Lal continued. 'Did you know she gets job offers from these big AI firms and she *turns them down*? She turns them down! I mean' – Lal lowered her voice and glanced at Janetta's window in case she was there, although she knew she wasn't – 'don't you see where I'm coming from?'

Mildly curious, Rose said, 'What's she gonna do after her Ph.D., then?'

'Sit in her room? This emotional intelligence in auts stuff – great, great for humanity, bring on my aut boyfriend, but come on – get a fucking job, Jay!'

Rose cracked and laughed, and shook her head. 'At least she's not on the dark side.' She looked quickly at Lal, then away.

'Rose!' Lal cried. 'What's *wrong* with me wanting a better life?'

Rose sighed, crossed her arms behind her head and looked at the sky. Its deep blue was starting to bleed into the setting sun; the indigo darkness was on its way. 'Don't you get it? Auts are taking over – maybe you should think about someone other than yourself for once.'

'But I've been thinking of my family! It's not just for me.'

Rose kept her eyes on the sky. 'You know, when we were younger, I admired how ambitious you were – you worked so hard, you never gave up. But now you work for *Tekna*, helping them ruin people's lives,' she said, disgusted, 'and you're *proud* of it.'

'It's not that simple.'

They heard the patio doors heave open and Lal listened out for approaching footsteps – she didn't want her parents to see them in a heated discussion. Her mother wouldn't enter the fray – she didn't get involved in Lal's choices any more – and her father would find a way to ramble on about his harmlessly confused politics, thinking he was pacifying them, and either way it would get harder to make her point. But the steps were quick and violent, and a moment later her sister appeared, staring at them in shock. She looked flustered, defenceless, her face gaunt, her hair a tangled mess. Some kind of electricity vibrated through her, as though she had seen something awful.

'Jay—' Lal started softly.

Janetta blinked and something clicked into place. A sense of calm restored itself to her face; the panic, if that's what it was, had been stowed away. She managed a smile.

'I'm fine,' she said, in a surprisingly normal voice. 'Sorry, I forgot Mum said you were home.' She looked as though she barely recognised her. Her eyes travelled dully to Rose. 'Hi, Rose.'

Rose pushed herself out of her deckchair and went to give Janetta a hug. 'Nice to see you.' She drew away. 'Do you want a beer?'

Janetta stared at her, nodded.

'I'll get it,' Lal offered. Standing by the fridge, she thought dimly about how much Rose liked her sister.

'So your Ph.D.'s going okay?' Rose was saying as Lal came back. Janetta took her beer. 'I'm . . . yeah. Yes.'

'And it's still the same thing? Emotional intelligence in auts?'

'It is.' Janetta frowned, as if unsure. 'Though it's emotional intelligence in *artificial intelligence* – auts being just a single mani-festation of artificial intelligence; usually it's virtual, very rarely is AI in a concrete, tangible form such as auts—' She stopped, looked at the grass beneath her as if surprised it was there, and dropped down to sit cross-legged on it. She placed her hands together and leaned forward, staring at the bright green blades.

'I know.' Rose was leaning forward, too, clutching her beer and nodding. 'I get it.'

'Oh, you *get it*?' Lal interrupted. 'You've got no problem with her inventing a new form of artificial intelligence, but I get a promotion that's actually a good thing and you—'

'Who says it's not a good thing?' Janetta asked, her words drifting.

'Rose thinks I'm a sell-out,' Lal told her with a quick, sharp anger. 'Or maybe the worst person who ever lived. She's still deciding.'

'I didn't say that,' Rose said, rolling her eyes. 'It's just that it's all very well getting this big-shot thing at Tekna' – at this, Lal recoiled a little – 'and okay, I *do* understand you're sending money home, but auts are taking *millions* of jobs all over the country, and surely that *matters*? Surely you care?' She paused, looking exhausted. 'I gave you so many chances.'

'To do what?'

'To come to a meeting!'

'What meeting?' asked Janetta.

'There's this group I go to,' Rose began, 'where we're working on something called source gain – it's when the government gives money not only to people who've lost their job to auts, but to everyone. It's democratic and fair – we all get a set amount each month and it means there's some sort of safety net and that auts won't completely destroy things.'

'Makes sense,' said Janetta, 'but auts might not completely destroy things. You know a lot of artificial intelligence is collaborative, too, and it's creating jobs, as well as enhancing—' She stopped.

'Go on.'

'And, well—' She suddenly lost her footing. 'Well, it'll create jobs. We just don't know what they'll be yet. Think about when the internet first appeared – everyone was worried about job loss back then, too, but it was fine in the end – I think AI will be the same.'

'But there's been thousands of job losses in Ulrusa in the past year, millions in Iolra, and nothing.'

'People get redundancy payments,' Lal interjected, thinking of her dad.

'Redundancy payments are shit.'

'It'd be better if there was real, guaranteed compensation,' Janetta agreed, holding her hands out as if to defuse things. 'Though don't forget there *are* people working on AI that's for the good of humanity, too.'

'And there are *more* people working on AI that are gonna take our jobs.'

'I hear you,' Janetta said quietly, uncrossing her legs and scratching at an ankle.

'There's still nothing wrong with me getting a promotion,' said Lal.

'Ah, give it a rest!' Rose cried. 'Get a promotion, move to Mejira, whatever – just do something that's not about *you* for once.'

'What's wrong with about me?' Lal said stupidly, struggling from her deckchair. She stormed off to the kitchen, opened the fridge and stared into it, her cheeks hot, but it was almost empty so she took some bread from the bread bin and put it in the toaster. She waited for it to toast, her anger gradually subsiding into sadness. She slathered it with thick layers of butter and strawberry jam and stood eating it, watching Rose kneel to the ground to hug her sister, whose face she couldn't see.

Rose didn't care that Lal was giving half her salary to her family. In her view, Lal's move to Mejira was entirely selfish. She could only see that it was Tekna, who she hated, and the fact that Lal had never gone to any of her meetings. If she knew how miserable

Lal was right now, she might be more sympathetic, but Lal didn't have the guts to tell her.

She lay on her bed waiting for the slam of the front door that would tell her Rose had left, and then she went and made some dinner and contemplated the party she'd come home for. She was not in the mood. Rose was being impossible and she could guess why: as she'd got more political over the past few years, she'd realised that the reasons she'd once put Lal on a pedestal – her determination, her indignation at injustice, and her sense of humour – were misguided. She'd finally seen that Lal's determination was only for herself, her indignation was only at injustices to herself, and her sense of humour, had apparently fallen by the wayside, too.

Rose should never have put her on a pedestal, though – that was the way Lal saw it. She thought of Rose's dad, who she'd put on the biggest pedestal of all: a brash, loud man who always thought he was right and hadn't given Lal the time of day. He'd called her 'a jumped-up little bossy-boots', which Rose had reported with worry rather than maliciousness; she couldn't understand why her idolised father might not like her hilarious best friend. Lal couldn't explain that she lost her sense of humour in front of Rose's father, who she felt to be more her rival than anything else.

In any case, he was dead and Lal had long fallen from her heights. Rose, she now knew, was off to spend the evening with this Alek person, who must have been to blame for this current phase of her righteousness. But she would go to the party. Los had been texting her constantly and she needed to get away from her sister, who, inexplicably, was bawling next door.

Night had fallen by the time she reached North Central and she headed from the station to the address Los had given her. It was a twenty-minute walk through a residential neighbourhood with wide, elegant, tree-lined roads, and the scent of jasmine filling the air. The houses were large and old, with wide porches and gabled roofs, and Lal was as aware of the wealth in its streets as if it were pooling before her in the soft, still night. She rounded a winding corner and heard beats, distant and then not so distant, and as she approached, the house seemed almost to be vibrating with the sound. It was beautiful, with silvery white walls and a wooden porch out front, tiny lights laced across its roof. She went up the steps and found the front door unlocked.

In the hallway it was loud and dark, and Lal felt the immediate, disorienting lurk of strangers, a million miles from her bedroom at home, from her flat in Dhont, her life out there. She pushed past as far as she could, slipped through a door and found herself in a large, high-ceilinged room strewn with twisting, celebratory bodies. Through a gap between them she saw a woman in a tiny gold top behind a mixing desk, her eyes closed and mouth open in a gasp of joy, one hand punching the air. She thought for a moment of her office and imagined that these were the same people, freaking herself out. She squeezed past the eclipses of cigarette tips and the gauntlet of hovering beers and in the darkness saw Los' familiar face.

'Lal! You're here!' He gave her a hug. 'Let's get a drink.'

They threaded across the dance floor to a table laid out with bottles of wine and beer and two brimming bowls, one bright orange, the other sea-green and shining. Los filled two cups with the green one and Lal asked if he knew what it was.

'It's a Popotops special.'

She laughed and they raised their cups. It tasted antiseptic and vaguely of forests.

'Ouch,' said Lal, quickly shaking her head.

'Yeah, that's nasty.' Los turned away to grimace.

Thoughtlessly, she stared at him, which is to say she stared at his back and his shoulders and the nut-brown curve of his left triceps beneath his red T-shirt. The green drink sludged around her belly. She looked up and spotted Van dancing nearby with her old colleagues Tonde and Iria, who she'd not seen in ages. Tonde and Van threw their arms in the air and wiggled their hips, making each other laugh. Iria saw her too, sashayed over, enveloped Lal in an exuberant hug, drew her mouth to her ear and said, loudly, 'You're here! It's been so long!'

Before Lal could respond, Iria's roving gaze landed on Los, standing behind, and she walked jerkily, like an aut, towards him. 'Human! Dance with me!' He laughingly obliged.

Lal could stand, then, or she could attempt to dance; it had been a long time since she'd danced at all, but there wasn't any reason not to, other than that Rose had always been her dancing companion, lost in her own world at her side. But Rose was with Alek, probably telling him what a bad person she was.

As she considered this, something began to unfasten in her mind: a leak at the end of her thoughts, an inability to finish them, and instead she felt a hazy, loosening drift. The edges of the bodies around her fuzzed, the mass of them starting to sway like a sea anemone, and within this she again sought her friends. There was Tonde, rocking ingloriously from side to side, his dark hair shaggy over his face, his eyes fixed to the floor. His sun-round belly gently rose under the yellow of a faded old T-shirt. Near him, Iria had abandoned her aut dance and was circling her hips, her eyes rapturously fixed on a high, distant point. She now wore a headdress of purple and blue feathers, the kind of thing she could apparently make appear at will, and that Lal would never stumble across in a lifetime. Close by, Van was executing a move that looked agonising – he shimmied his tall body to the ground, bent his knees then rose slowly, his eyes squeezed in pain.

A moment with him from a few months ago swam back to her, just after their Popotops got its first server aut and Tonde, Iria and two other colleagues had been fired.

'Fuck the little bastard,' Van had said of it, loyal to his departed friends. He boomed his voice over it when customers approached, muting its bright, *'How can I help you today?'*

He'd always put on his own music as soon as he arrived at work, cranked it up loudly. Lal was meant to ask him to make it softer, but there was a real atmosphere when he was there. Also, she liked his taste – everyone did. Customers smiled and sometimes sang along when certain songs came on, or listened, intrigued, and asked who the band was. In the moment she recalled now he was cheerfully regaling a customer with stories about the music he was playing, an Iolran band from decades ago called The Gang. The Gang's singer had left at the height of their fame, a decision that had made their early albums mythological. Lal had become a fan just through exposure via Van, but standing next to him, listening to an anecdote about them recording a live album, she'd felt a stab of annoyance. The tables needed clearing. The queue was growing. He never saw these things. As always back then, she'd been extra efficient to make up for his idle ways.

'There's a queue—'

'She's a fan!' Van protested. 'Her favourite album is *Songs from Across the Bridge*!'

The woman nodded furiously. *Across the Bridge* was Lal's favourite, too. She wavered, then made her expression imperious. 'How can I help you?' she asked the next customer loudly.

But the woman Van was talking to was laughing at something he'd said and the customer waiting for his coffee craned his neck to hear the punchline. The man who'd just ordered leaned forward to do so too, resting his arm on the counter so that a pile of napkins fell to the floor.

Lal had ignored it, ignored them all, and gone to pick the napkins up, invisible and ashamed. She realised now, as he momentarily stopped dancing to yell something at Tonde, how jealous she'd been of him: his easy dominion over the aut, the effortless holding court – he was the kind of person customers loved. She'd never been like that. She made her way to him, wanting to join in the fun, but before she could, her stomach revolted and she turned and pushed her way through the crowd, down the corridor and finally outside.

The cold air was a bracing relief, and she threw up gratefully on the grass.

'Lal?'

Los couldn't say another word – he began to vomit, too. Admittedly, it was less awful when he was there. When she finished, Lal wiped her mouth with her forearm, pushed her damp fringe aside and saw that the path to the house was curving up at each end like a smile, and the sky was bulging down as if someone had unpinned it in the middle, and Los was outlined with a dark blue glow, and her stomach felt fine.

'Have you got any water? I need water.'

He looked up at her blankly. He held a bottle of water in his left hand. After a long time, Lal reached for it. Her arm extended through space and her fingers wrapped around the plastic. She had forgotten, had not expected to contend with this rude surface. Now she didn't know if the water would reach her mouth in time for her not to die. She watched it move slowly towards her, could not understand how this was happening. It was like she was carrying the ocean to the desert, and then the ocean spread within.

After a while, she said, 'I think that bucket was drugs.'

'I think you might be right.'

They were silent, and she looked at the sky. Although it drooped, the stars were as out of reach as ever. Lal felt this was a bit of a con. They started to walk, or perhaps, bounce. It felt better than standing still.

'I've missed you.'

She couldn't think of what to say to that.

'How are things going in Mejira – do they love you there?'

'They totally love me.'

'Do you wear a power suit?'

'I don't have a power suit . . .'

'But if you did.'

'Every day.'

He looked at her admiringly, then kicked at a pebble on the ground. 'The others can't find jobs, you know. They're screwed.'

'I thought Kelman had one.' Kelman was her least favourite ex-colleague, a brash and overly confident nineteen-year-old.

'An aut took it.'

'Oh.' Lal frowned. 'Iria, though – surely she could get anything.'

He shook his head. 'Not that easy.'

'But she's rich?'

'It's complicated. She still needs a job, or some sort of protection . . .' He kicked the pebble around a corner and they followed. Here, the sky was concave and empty of stars, as if it was too sad to bother. Lal gazed at it sympathetically.

'Sorry, I didn't mean to make you feel bad. You're the one who got away – the one we talk about in wonder.'

'Not Rose.'

'Well,' Los was diplomatic on this, 'the rest of us do. We talk about how you did it.'

'I'm an aut,' she said. 'That's how.'

'I knew it! We all knew it. Have we ever seen beneath your flesh? Seen the wires . . . dangling? And sometimes there's that unearthly glow in your eyes—'

Lal was just staring at him. She knew he was trying to wind her up, but for a second she thought that although she was certain of her own humanness, and of his, too, she couldn't ultimately prove that they weren't auts, either. She could not, in fact, prove that any of this was real. The sky could be ripped away and the pulleys and levers of the universe revealed. She disliked this kind of clichéd drugs thought, though, and was displeased at herself for having had it.

'I'm going home.'

'No, no, no!' Los said, surprised. 'I was joking – you're not an aut. You're not an aut at all. I'm saying things I don't mean.'

'It's okay, I'm just tired. And whatever that drink was hasn't helped.'

'Are you sure? We could just walk for a bit . . .'

That had its appeal, but she wanted to be more cogent again, and thought it best if she were alone.

'All right, then,' he said, disappointed, and walked her instead to the nearest station, the small, out-of-the-way one she never used. There, he looked at her with unnerving speculation and raised an arm in farewell. The station steps were encircled in an arch of light, and walking up them felt oddly like an ascension to paradise. The platform was indeed as bright as paradise should be, although shabbier than you'd hope, and Lal walked to the end where she could be alone. When the train came it was so fast it tore fire from the tracks, and stopped in front of her nose.

8

A painful truth about Lal moving to Mejira was that Rose was lonelier now. She considered herself self-sufficient – she didn't go out of her way to make friends, and would sooner have none than try to get people to like her. This was the role she'd carved out in her family – her father was the one people befriended; he had networks and circles and contacts, comrades and mates. Naji was likeable, assertive, more secure in his own authority every day. Her mum was watchful, wily and a hard worker, and Rose sometimes sensed she had secrets she'd never give her daughter access to – there were stopped explanations, diversions and distractions at curious, unexpected moments. Rose didn't push. She told herself that she was just imagining this, that she was bored, or paranoid.

But the larger-than-life father, the popular brother and the shrewd mother left her feeling unsure. Yash was the golden child, beloved, precocious, and racing ahead of them all. What then was left for her? Perhaps believing you didn't need to be anything at all.

When she was about nine or ten, her dad took her with him to protests. Naji didn't come, because he was a teenager and he and her father were arguing a lot at that point, and Yash was just a toddler, so he stayed at home with their mum. These protests were huge, hundreds of people there from all around the city.

She would only have eyes for her dad, but he had to go and speak to the crowd. They parted to let him through, but she'd be held back or passed over to women she never knew, who stared at him bright-eyed as they clapped a protective arm around her, these sudden pretty mothers with whom she felt safe.

Her dad was a thrilling speaker. One day at work when he was younger, long before he was in a union, a straddle carrier had toppled over, crushing his right arm and severing his right ear. The arm had recovered, but the ear had been sewn back on in such a way that its structural integrity had not fully been regained and the top cartilage slightly flopped. He wore his hair parted on that side, brushed to the left, so the sad ear was always there, slightly pathetic, incredibly human.

Rose was too young then to understand her dad's cries for justice and workers' rights and his calls for autonomy, but something must have sunk in because as a teenager, she'd find herself urgently repeating the same stuff back to whoever would listen, and then at HEU, where she'd discovered political philosophy, her first essay of the first term was 'Can Humanity Ever Be Truly Free?' She didn't show it to her dad because she was scared of what he'd say – scared he'd call her pretentious, ask what use writing an essay was. But as she wrote it, all she thought of was him – the way he'd looked at his protests, his eyes shining, his face ferocious, his voice loud and full of fire and hope.

Lal had no idea how it felt to lose a parent. She had been a good friend when it happened, even though Rose sensed that she'd read a bunch of stuff on the internet about what you were meant to do when your friend's parent dies and then just followed through. She checked in on her, took her out – Lal's preference was for the cinema, which suited Rose as she could just stare at the screen and switch off. They went on walks and Rose cried, and they went to the beach and Lal said nothing as they sat on the sand and Rose cried. She cried in the storeroom at work and Lal hugged her. She was a zombie for months, and Lal asked for nothing.

And what she would give now for a real friend. She had idolised her father and doubted her own capacities, but now she was at least trying to be someone useful. Lal had never doubted her, though. Lal had thought she was glittering, brilliant, immense. How could someone who'd seen her at her worst, at her most shameful, think that of her? But Lal had, and then suddenly she'd gone – left her completely alone.

On the night Lal had summoned her to her garden, defended Tekna, then run off to a party, Rose had headed out to Rornul. It felt wonderful to go to the end of the southbound line, walk down silent, empty streets, push her hip and hands against the door to shove it open and walk into a room bursting with activity. People kneeled on the floor making protest signs, walked around checking out each other's work, handed out pens and paint and tape.

There was a protest against the Iolran government the following Monday, when some high-ranking officials were going to be visiting from Mejira. The protest was against funding cuts to Ulrusa's public services, its schools and hospitals and libraries. It was also going to flag the alarming rate of redundancies due to auts, and the lack of safety nets for the ever-growing number who'd lost their jobs. Rose and her group joining in was a natural fit. Alek had warned them that they'd possibly be the only ones protesting for source gain at this point, but Rose thought this wasn't a problem – she was hoping they could inspire people, that their movement could grow.

Ulrusa was less political these days than it had once been. People like Rose's dad had led the charge back when the port had been in its heyday and the city had rapidly industrialised, but in the past few decades the fervour had died down. Her dad saw the generation of workers below him take jobs on the industrial estates scattered at its edges and believed that this denuded Ulrusa of fight. There was no beating heart, and he felt these younger workers had been neutralised. When he heard Naji and Hela had gone on holiday yet again, he couldn't keep the disdain from his face. He felt this generation wasn't ripe for the struggle – instead, he thought, they had been manipulated to become consumers.

Naji grew resentful of his dad saying such things. But it was true that the city was quieter these days and free of protest. Rose would walk with her father from the house where they used to live and the city centre would hover into view, and beyond it, the multicoloured corrugated steel stacks of the container port. He would nod in that direction and tell her stories of what it was like at its peak, complicated but funny stories about labour disputes and bad management. When he surveyed Ulrusa now, with its proud little city centre, he saw it as a town of shoppers and spenders. He and Rose spoke about auts only a few times before he died. Once was in relation to a wave of job cuts at one of the biggest shipping lines operating at the port. He said, 'It's all about the information flow now, what they call "optimisation". They don't need people to do that. People can't even do it.' But he took a back seat when it came to fighting it – at that point, he had not been in great health.

When Naji had told him, when they were on better terms, that auts had been taking over at the warehouse, he'd advised his son to grit his teeth and fight for his job, which was why Naji had eventually stepped up – he'd become union leader and kicked off a bunch of protests. He sent Rose and her mum photos, a straggle of guys picketing outside the warehouse entrance under dim skies.

'Does your brother look ill?' her mum had asked. Rose didn't think 'ill' was right – she thought he looked faraway, his eyes unfocused, staring into the distance.

Rose said hi to a few people at the meeting and kneeled on the floor, nestling in amongst them. She read their signs, nothing catchier than 'we AUT to have source gain' at best – or worst – and was handed a pen and some dirty posterboard. She wiped the muck away with the sleeve of her hoodie and considered what to write. She was sold on source gain as an idea: she thought it was brilliant. Alek had introduced it to the group and ever since, he'd spent every meeting telling them about it. It would be a lifeline, he said, a safety net for the swelling ranks of unemployed, and it was unpopular in Iolra only because the government was hostile to anything that would truly support the people.

Rose strongly agreed.

Lately, he'd got more declamatory. 'The government can deny it all they like, but automation results in a moral obligation,' he'd said, 'not from the people, but *to* the people. Our labour has mean-ingful economic value, so, if we are being denied this economic value, we must instead be compensated.'

We must instead be compensated! It was true, and source gain was how to do it. That was what she'd wanted Lal to see earlier, because if it existed, her dad would get it and she wouldn't have had to take that job at Tekna. Although she still would have wanted to – that was what Rose couldn't get over. And anyway, for all the times she'd tried to get Lal to come to a meeting, she couldn't quite imagine her in a place like this. It was so derelict, so grim. She looked up then and realised Alek wasn't there, and wondered for a second where he was. Someone asked her opinion about whether the writing on someone else's placard was unreadably small and she got caught up in a cheerful discussion about it. At some point Alek came in, surveyed them, then left again.

An hour or so later she went to see if he was okay. Outside, Srvor Road was dark and empty, pools of asphalt spotlit under streetlamps while the shadowy street stretched out beyond. She heard a voice around the corner and found him on his phone, smoking a cigarette. She went back in and was instantly assailed with questions and requests for her help, and found it strange that the people here liked her so much and judged her so little. If she could, perhaps she should start to consider them friends.

Later, when the meeting ended, she bypassed the clamour and slipped out alone. She walked past low brick warehouses behind steel fencing, graffiti-covered hoardings, the station in the distance. All was silent except for the trains' whooshes and rumbles; all was dark save the knots of light from its platforms.

Down the wide, dark streets of Rornul she went until she hit the southeast flats of the city, where apartment blocks were so abundant they almost seemed to grow from the soil. In the stark maze of the Dupert Estate, where great swathes of them clustered together, she came to Block 330D, Entrance F, and sat on its cold front steps to wait, zipping her hoodie up all the way, folding her arms over her knees. The block was grey concrete, dotted evenly with rows of small, square windows, and by its side there were four others just like it, jostling against the night sky.

After a while, Alek emerged from the path and walked past. She followed him up three flights and watched his thin fingers unlock a front door. He pushed it open and she followed him again, into the first room on the left. He turned on a low bedside light and in its dull glow he looked at her. His look of desire was always a little harsh, as if he was angry at himself for having such a feeling.

She went to him, laced her arms around his neck, and as soon as their mouths met, his hands were on her jeans, unzipping and tugging them down. She pushed him back and peeled off his T-shirt, laid her hands on his chest. When they were on the bed he finally smiled, and she realised she'd been looking forward to this all evening – this secret closeness, this heady relief he yielded only at the last minute.

Afterwards, he began to drum testily on her hip.

'You okay?' she asked.

'Just thinking.'

'Everyone's excited about the protest.'

He stopped drumming. 'That's good. Their complaining was driving me mad.'

He'd said this kind of thing a lot recently. He would grouse about attendees' lack of interest in discussing source gain and their obsessive detailing of their own personal circumstances instead. He found it indulgent and tangential, thought they were trying to elbow it in when he'd been trying to phase it out. He appeared to have forgotten he used to encourage them to talk about themselves, back when he was trying to get people to attend the meetings, when he hadn't had such a specific vision.

'They can't help it,' she tried diplomatically.

He grunted. 'Honestly it's been driving me mad. Take Ninna – she's lost in this cycle of "how am I going to feed my family when I lose my job?" – do you know how many times she's asked me that? I have to explain again and again that *source gain* will help her feed her family – and you know what she said this week? *How am I going to feed my family?* Rose, you know I'm not being a dick when I say this, but that woman has no ideological vigour, no coherence of vision, no aptitude for practicable hypotheticals. I mean, *fuck*! She'll be good on the protest, though. Loud.'

Rose lifted her head. She couldn't deal with this right now, not in the sleepy dreaminess after sex, when she could barely be bothered to get a word out. But he spoke like that first thing in the morning, too.

'You're doing a good thing,' she said consolingly, drawing closer, kissing him on his skinny shoulder.

'Of course. And at least we've got a protest. I can't keep listening to which supermarket is cheapest, special offers on potatoes . . .'

'They're just dealing with the here and now. But come on, we all want source gain. We're grateful, okay?'

'Okay,' he said flatly and shifted away as he positioned himself for sleep.

She drew back, letting him go. Recently it sounded like he hated the group, or at the very least resented them for being themselves. He was making it clear he found their endless complaining childish, and that they needed to move on. She hadn't expected this of him at all.

She wondered then, and not for the first time, what he thought of her. When they'd started sleeping together she thought she'd have his ear. She assumed they'd have discussions, that he'd see she was someone to value, someone with whom to share the load. She had been ready for it. But he didn't, it turned out. He saw her only as his confidante, not, it appeared, his equal.

Her flat was on the eighth floor of a block in Lower Sunset, a set of old stacked shoeboxes about ten minutes' walk from Lal's. Before her dad died they'd lived closer to downtown, but afterwards her mother couldn't afford the rent, so they'd moved here. The old house had already been razed down and turned into luxury apartments. Whenever Rose saw them, vaulting into the sky, she imagined what her father would say about them, his scornful lack of surprise.

The flat was not yet home, but they were working on it. Rose's mother's room at the front was impeccably tidy, her dressing table crammed with framed photos of her children and late husband. The living room made an altar of the television, as was the family way. Yash had unapologetically painted his bedroom walls purple. Rose's own room was a sliver by the kitchen, with an uninspiring view of an identical block. She had no mind for decorating. At first she had stuck a few posters up she'd taken with her from the old house, of bands she liked, but once they were up it felt weird to have band posters on your walls when you were twenty-three, like you couldn't move on from being a teenager, when the reason you wore black every day was because you were trying to emulate your idols. The reason she still wore black every day was because it was easy, and it suited her, and was versatile enough to signal not only teenage existential discontent but also adult disgust with capitalism too. On her walls now, chosen when emptiness was distinctly disappointing but she didn't care what she saw every day, were some arty postcards she'd got at Ponra, faraway cities she'd never see in real life: Kyoga, Vorsten, Forera.

Outside the flat, the lights in the stairwell flickered on and off depending on the occult whims of the electrics. Smell-wise, it had been colonised by her mother's cooking, her particular flavours wafting under doors and embedding in walls. They shared this stairwell with another apartment whose residents changed constantly. Rose took their transience as inspiration.

On the Sunday night before the protest, she and her mother sat together in the kitchen eating dinner. Her mother had made butternut stew with passaras and melismam leaves, and it was

123

hearty and warming. The kitchen was bright yellow, with a red trim around the windows and blue on the skirting boards, and there were pictures of the Cabaka monasteries on the walls, also bought cheap from Ponra. Her mother had stuck a map of the Skrevet Valley on the fridge, too, so each time Rose or Yash opened it they were confronted with the country's most popular pilgrimage routes and sacred temples. Ignoring them made food taste better.

Her mother lifted her eyes from her laptop. 'Rose, I want you to have a word with your brother.'

Rose let the sweet passaras fill her mouth. 'Why?'

'He's never around. Hela says he's at the warehouse day and night, he never comes home.'

'What do you want *me* to do about it?' Naji still saw her as a baby. He'd never listened to her in his life – that was the way it was, and at this stage she preferred not to think about how frustrating she found it.

'Find out if he's in trouble. If he's going to lose his job.'

'Everyone's going to lose their job.'

'Rose! You must have something helpful to tell him?'

'Doubt it.'

'What about all those books you read?'

'Mum, very few people in history have been reassured by political theory.'

Her mother frowned. 'And this friend you don't tell me about?'

'Lal?'

'Don't be stupid.'

Rose pushed her fork deep into the stew, examined a fascinating melismam leaf. She knew her mother was looking at her as if she could see straight through her.

'Think of something, Rose. I'll leave it to you.'

*

'Ah, fuck,' Naji said, the next day. 'Why did Hela talk to her? Why do you all talk? Why don't you all *not talk*?'

They were sitting on a bench in the park around the corner from his house in Upper Sunset. He was smoking something that smelled like weed, except he said it was 'clean' – it had no side effects.

'Well, surely she's being realistic? I know you're a union rep, but that hardly makes you . . . unautomatable.'

'Is that a word?'

She shook her head.

He sighed. 'Look, I'm not losing my job.'

'So why are you spending so much time at work? I don't want to get involved, but you know . . . you have a one-year-old at home.'

'I'm aware of that! I've got union business, okay? Leave me alone.'

She was going to say it. She might as well. 'Maybe you should come to these meetings I go to,' she began. 'They're for people who care about what happens when we're all . . . replaced.' She stared out across the park, at a woman walking a dog and a curly-haired child running gleefully ahead, her arms in the air. 'They're led by this guy you might find interesting, and we discuss job losses, how we could deal with them – like, um, do you know about source gain?' She stopped, worried, and checked for a reaction.

Naji looked amused.

'What?'

He shook his head, smiling.

'*What?*'

'It's a support group for people who are losing their jobs? I don't need a support group.'

'It's not a support group! It's a . . . radical forum.' She couldn't bring herself to say more.

'Rose—' Naji paused, and she thought about what it must be like to be him, strong and imposing, with all that pride and contained anger. 'Rose, I'm not gonna sit around asking for sympathy.'

'It's not about sympathy!' It really wasn't, not any more. 'It could be useful.'

'*Useful?*' Naji scoffed. 'Trust me, I do *not* need useful. Can you do me a favour and tell Mum to fuck off? But nice. Say it nice.'

'Come on—'

'Rose,' he said, his face hardening, 'this isn't on you, okay? Just drop it.' He took a puff of his joint, jiggled his leg up and down and looked out over the park, into the distance.

But he went the very next week. He didn't say what had changed his mind. In fact, he said very little, not about heading out to Rornul or the abandoned building she took him to, or about the fact that sixty people were there that day, crammed into the narrow rows of seats. He appeared to be doing a lot of listening, although a few times she saw his eyes glaze over with boredom. She saw this with Alek too, sometimes, but with him you could tell, because he did it while people were talking to him and the look on his face was horrible – a kind of unconscious disgust – and you could see the other person's face crumple with upset, but when she'd put this to him once, as delicately as she could, he looked at her like she was crazy.

At the end of the meeting she introduced them.

'This is my brother who works out in Rartaur,' she told Alek. 'The one I mentioned to you.'

Alek gazed impassively at Naji. 'You're interested in source gain?'

Naji shrugged. 'I'm here 'cause of Rose.'

Alek bristled imperceptibly and she could see he thought Naji was going to be more trouble than it was worth. She gave him an encouraging glance, hoping he'd try again, but as she waited for more to emerge, it became clear that neither was much bothered. This was disappointing, but maybe not all that surprising. Rose thought of her father then, and saw she could triangulate herself between these three men – all of whom had received her affection with a sort of benign, unquestioning belief that they deserved it. Between them, they were responsible for almost all of what she thought and knew, and recognising this, she flashed with a profound hatred of herself, then saw something within that she had never seen before – something flickering and momentary and free. She looked at the ground to try to bring it into focus, but it disappeared, and she looked up to see Alek being disinterestedly polite to Naji, thanking him for coming, saying it was good to see him there. Naji, uneasy, shifted his weight from foot to foot and glanced first at Rose with a bored expression, and then at the door.

She felt an urge to berate him for not trying harder, but once they were outside, she found herself more interested in his thoughts. He remained silent until they were half a block away, then said, 'Well, that was a waste of time.'

'What! Naji, I—' She waited a second for her head to clear. 'Why did you come along then?'

'Curious.'

'Well, surely it's better than nothing. At least we're trying.' She stuck her hands in her jacket pockets, baffled and hurt, and they walked for a short while in silence. 'Look, I know it's not perfect.'

Naji glanced up at low-flying birds.

'It's not a magic panacea,' she continued, 'but it's *something*.'

'But I want my job,' he said. 'It gives me meaning. Source gain'll make me – what's the word?'

'Meaningless?'

'No! Ah, you know, something to do with' – he looked frustrated, trying to think of it – 'having no control over my life, being given pocket money by the government—'

'Dependent?'

'That, too, but also—'

'Pointless?'

'No! What's the word? Ah, fuck—'

'Robbed of your autonomy? Enslaved?'

He laughed, surprised. After a moment, he said, 'Passive. That's it. Passive. Like giving up. *Letting* them win.'

'Right.' Rose nodded, struck by what had just come out of her mouth. It wasn't as though these thoughts hadn't crossed her mind before, but when they had, she'd pushed them away because they felt disloyal. But she knew where they led: to questions like, would there be conditions on this 'money for everyone' idea? Could it be taken away at will? What else would it depend on? And would the government just give people as little as they could get away with? They walked on while she clarified her thoughts, or at least until she could trace her way back to her original position. 'I guess it's trying to find an answer to something impossible. You can't resist the forces of capitalism – you can't ask companies *not* to replace us with auts – so something has to be done to compensate. I mean, what would you do?'

He sniffed. 'It's obvious, isn't it?'

'No.'

'Of course it is.'

He jogged up the station steps and she followed, confused, as they walked a short way along the platform. As he looked to see if a train was coming, the evening light turned him into a shadow, his shaved head, black jumper and jogging bottoms fractured by shafts of gold. His phone rang then: Hela.

While he spoke, Rose reflected. Source gain would give him more time with Yissi. He could exercise more, live more healthily, see his friends. It was a nice vision, but she admitted that it was hard to imagine him without his work – it would bring a huge blank space into his life. When the train arrived, he was still talking to Hela – or more like, talking *at* her, making sure Yissi was okay, asking a dozen questions – and Rose, as she followed him into the carriage, began to feel more and more like the loyal little sister she'd always been. She was comfortable here, as Naji's humble sidekick, and she looked at him, feeling a familiar, grateful warmth. He repeated a complicated shopping list back to Hela while Rose watched the city go by out of the window.

Eventually, he hung up. 'Hela's making something for Yissi that involves fucking baialo,' he said, his knee jiggling up and down. 'I've got to get off two stops later, go to that tiny Sewannan shop that probably won't even be open now – and then when she gets back it needs steaming for four hours – why do I have to get it tonight? But oh no, tomorrow won't do, it has to be tonight.' He was clearly enjoying himself.

She saw their previous conversation was over and he was back in his domestic orbit. He leaned forward, sat with his hands dangling between his knees and sighed – she assumed because he had to go to the out-of-the-way shop, as opposed to what they'd just been discussing. She still wanted to know what was so obvious to him, but the conversation had moved on.

9

Cherry was an enormously popular new app that helped you find nearby single women. Janetta installed it two weeks after her break-up, and idling on her bed, ignoring her dissertation, she began to analyse small photos of unknown women and the one-line biographies they'd written beneath. These weren't much to go on, but most didn't look her type – although it was true that Malin hadn't looked her type at first, either. But thanks to Malin, she now knew what she wanted: someone intelligent and kind, who was curious about the world, who asked questions and brought out the best in her. How could you figure that out from a few words, a couple of photos?

Her first date, with a thin, gentle woman from Heinis, started promisingly, but as soon as she moved from the easy back and forth about their backgrounds, their thoughts about Cherry – the inoffensive basics – and started talking about artificial intelligence, she saw the interest in the woman's eyes recede.

Her next was with a talkative, appealing-looking woman who monologued all night about her ex-boyfriend. This woman got drunk and kissed her, then messaged to say she wasn't sure if she was ready to date women and didn't want to take things any further. Janetta hadn't wanted to take things further, either, so she ignored that bit and wished her well.

Her other dates went nowhere, too – when she made connections between things, drew conclusions, suggested philosophical or ideological positions, the women sitting across from her looked at her blankly. She realised there was another quality she needed: she was conversationally demanding; she wanted ideas, opinions, volleys of thought. She hadn't thought of herself in this way before, but Malin had changed her: she'd shown her what she liked. If this preference now made her feel isolated, well, so be it.

She didn't sleep with any of these women, and she tried not to think about what Malin was doing, who she was talking to, who she was sleeping with, although she thought about these things all the time.

She kept on crying, too – now in her tutor's office, of all places. This long, narrow room on the ground floor of the Institute made you feel as if you were in a tunnel; on one side a floor-to-ceiling window looked out onto the bright world, casting those inside into darkness, while outside, on the tree-lined path, people talked and gesticulated, clutching folders and carrying backpacks, looking happy and normal and like a perfect advert for higher education.

Janetta knew Kait was unfazed by tears – Kait, in her typically brisk, undaunted manner, had joked in the past about how accommodating her office was to criers. Her desk, she'd said, made an effective home for their foreheads, her chairs encouraged a defeated slouch, and within reaching distance from said slouch was a bottomless box of tissues. On one end of the three long shelves of books that ran all along the office there was also an arty zigzag of mirror in which to tidy your puffy face before leaving.

Though she brushed it off when people told her, Kait was the most reliable and respected member of the Institute faculty.

She taught a bunch of courses, ran the Ph.D. programme, and although she wasn't formally responsible for pastoral support – no one was, not at an AI institute – the students sought her out. Every day there were one or two knocking at her door, requesting tissues and succour. She'd let them in, listen a short while, then surreptitiously start glancing at her email as her inbox filled and time pressed on.

Until recently, it hadn't occurred to Janetta that she'd ever prevail on Kait in this way herself, but here she was, weeping, sniffling, the defeated slouch, the whole thing. She was explaining that she and Malin had booked a trip to the North in a month's time, just before her dissertation was due. She was trying to make it clear that she still wanted to go – that she'd always wanted to go to the Skrevet Valley, and they'd got these cheap tickets that she didn't want to waste.

'Will you get your work done?' Kait asked. She fiddled with her phone, turning it over and over in her hand.

'I will.'

'And being around your ex, that won't make it hard?'

Tears filled Janetta's eyes. She grabbed her fraying tissue and roughly wiped her nose, dabbed her eyes. Kait waited, still turning her phone. Then she stopped.

'Jay, this is what you've worked towards for *years*. You can't let anything endanger it – you're far too close.'

But she was wrong in thinking Janetta cared. As she saw it, she'd spent her whole life being good, working hard, staying put, and now, when she had to work harder than ever, she'd had her heart broken. Who cared about the timing, or that she'd be with Malin – they didn't even need to speak to each other. Nothing mattered more than the fact that she needed to escape.

*

Callously swiping through the women of Cherry later that day, Janetta came to a halt at a pretty face with the bio: *I like AI.* She thought the face looked familiar and went online to confirm: it was Taly Kett, the head of Mutants, the most successful commercial AI lab in Ulrusa. She was attractive and brilliant, and Janetta's greatest find on Cherry by far. Mutants was famous. The previous year they'd released their ground-breaking aut birds, which looked and behaved like real birds, albeit denuded of their migratory impulse. Instead they sat squawking tunefully in trees in areas where birdsong had declined, or also where it hadn't, because they had a built-in security camera function, too, a neat trick that quickly led them to become a staple of neighbourhood safety. You could select their song, or change it periodically, which made them arguably more entertaining than normal birds too – the whole concoction an upgrade from real life, reminding people that AI could change all of nature, enhance the everyday in ways that weren't just functional but holistic, too.

Half the Ph.D. programme was obsessed with getting a job at Mutants; rumour had it the company was seeking funding to make a full collection of loveable, enhanced-functionality aut animals – its 'autimals', as they were colloquially referred to by the industry. Working on these would be a more desirable way to spend your days after you graduated than building boring industrial auts. Taly had even written a well-known book that Janetta had not yet read, *TechnoMutations*, which illustrated the various happy ways AI would enhance people's lives, autimals being only the beginning. And there she was – Mutants' very own CEO, thirty years old and looking for love. Taly could see in Janetta's own bio that she was at the AI Institute and Janetta was hoping this would count in her favour.

It did. A few days later, she waited nervously for Taly outside a downtown bar, wearing a tight, knee-length black dress, low heels and red lipstick. The evening sky glowed pink against the dark clutch of skyscrapers, but Janetta's admiration of it was undercut by her awareness she was equally a focal point for men passing by. She tried to ignore them, but one yelled, '*You waiting for me?*' and others whistled, and she was about to find some shadows in which to hide when Taly appeared, as if the sea of men had parted and delivered her there just when she couldn't take it any longer. Taly was short, thin-faced and unsmiling, dressed all in grey and black in a tight leather jacket, a thin cotton T-shirt and jeans. She had watchful eyes and hair so straight that not a strand was out of place. Her greeting, a handshake and a quick peck on the cheek, was so efficient as to be almost professional.

Inside, the bar was large and busy, with low lighting and a long, wide counter at the centre of the room, where waistcoated waiters expertly poured drinks. Taly led Janetta there and they slid into place beside one another and picked up their menus. As she scanned hers, Janetta was aware of Taly watching her, trying to suss her out, and she wondered what she thought. When Taly ordered a few moments later, she spoke rapidly to the bartender, her eyes focused on him for the exact amount of time it took to ensure she'd been heard. As soon as he turned to make the drinks she said to Janetta, 'So, you're a doctoral researcher?'

'Yes, at the AI Institute.'

'So you said. Tell me about your research.'

'Okay, um . . . I'm trying to create emotionally intelligent auts.' Janetta had searched online to see if Taly had any professed opinions about auts that could recognise and respond to emotions, but she'd not been able to find a thing.

'Emotionally intelligent auts? That's esoteric.'

Janetta tried to figure out whether this was good or bad, but Taly's face gave no indication either way. Before the date she'd realised her confidence about her research had grown back since her crit, but at this early juncture she still preferred to be talking about something else. 'And you run Mutants?' she asked. 'So many of my colleagues want to work for you.'

Taly gave her a dubious look. 'That's not – why you're here, is it? You can never tell with Cherry who you're really meeting.'

'I've got no desire to work at Mutants,' Janetta said honestly.

Taly smiled. 'It's a good place to work, I imagine. Less so to run it.'

'Really?'

'It's stressful.'

Their drinks appeared. Janetta took a few sips of hers, a fizzy, gingery pear wine, and warmth bloomed in her chest.

'But you're so influential – those aut birds, they really changed things.'

Taly laughed. 'Great, that'll be my legacy: aut birds.'

'They've added such a subtle beauty to the urban environment.'

'No, I'm aware. But they're not my life's ambition.'

'Of course not.'

Taly raised an eyebrow and held Janetta's eye and a look passed between them, one that confirmed a mutual interest. Janetta excused herself to go to the bathroom and in its small, dark space looked at herself in the mirror and thought breathlessly that she'd replaced Malin, just like that. No: she'd bettered her. She returned to the bar and slipped back into her seat, feeling Taly's eyes on her like a cat's stalking prey. A delicious current thrummed within. She reached for her drink.

'So how far off do you think these emotionally intelligent auts are?' Taly asked.

'Not far, if I've got anything to do with it.'

Taly smiled, amused. 'And the point of them is?'

'I guess it's about integration – if we're going to be living together with auts, don't we want them to understand us better?'

'I'm not sure "living together" is how I'd put it.'

'Well, living *alongside*, then.'

Taly looked at the ceiling, appearing to think this through, but she didn't seem convinced. 'Can I ask you something?'

Janetta nodded.

'How long have you been single for?'

'Oh – a few weeks,' she said, surprised.

'I see.' Taly's gaze dropped to Janetta's lips. 'And are you on the rebound?'

'No. Not at *all*.'

Taly put her hand on Janetta's knee, leaned forward and kissed her. Janetta's body strained towards her in response. She hooked her baby finger around Taly's and kissed her back, aware, but not caring, that the bartender was just an arm's length away. Taly moved her hand higher up Janetta's thigh. Janetta warded her off, despite the fireworks beneath, downed the rest of her drink and ordered another. The bartender nodded, wryly amused, and Taly watched, her expression cutely pleased, almost coy, and began again to talk.

Maybe it was because she was getting very quickly drunk, but as she listened, Janetta felt herself slipping. She could just about keep up, but the alcohol was confusing her and she was becoming quickly convinced that Taly, who was talking about ideas and theories Janetta had never even encountered, was much smarter than her. It didn't matter, though – Taly clearly liked just being listened to, so Janetta let herself relax, sipped her drink and watched her talk. She wondered if they were going to kiss again, but Taly, who was controlling the evening, appeared now to want only to soliloquise. The more Janetta drank, the harder it was to try to interrupt articulately, not that she cared, and she began instead just to stare at Taly, nod occasionally and try not to look too drunk. When the bar was closing and they were asked to leave, she had to push herself, sloppy and slightly ashamed, off her barstool.

Outside, she crunched with difficulty through thoughts about how to end the evening without embarrassing herself further.

Taly zipped up her jacket. 'Come back with me?'

Janetta's body, heavy with alcohol, released a small pulse of desire and the decision was quickly made. Taly led her on a short walk east of the bar, through a posh part of the city Janetta barely knew. As they walked, she fumbled for enthusiastic comments about the area – its unusual architecture and small, huddled houses – but Taly replied, 'It's just Ulrusa.'

She was surprised at the change in tone, the brief show of disdain, but the cold air was sobering Janetta up a little, and she found herself willingly shift more into whatever it was she thought Taly might want her to be. She made her accent fuller and rounder and put her most elegant self on display, the one you'd never guess was from Sunset, the one who was more than equal to her date. Meanwhile Taly enunciated crisply, sized the world up shrewdly, talked fluidly and confidently all the way back.

The building they arrived at was anonymous, modern and stark, and as they went to the elevator Janetta wondered if it was a hotel. It didn't feel like anyone's home. In a spacious, low-lit room behind one of the many doors they drank wine and listened to music she would never play herself – a lyricless, interminable fuzz that simultaneously irritated and soothed. Taly talked, still about various philosophical conundrums – occasionally relating to AI – and all this was welcome, though it did cross Janetta's mind that here she was feeding her one question after another while she hadn't been asked anything about herself other than briefly, pre-kiss, at the bar. Disconcerting as this was, it did at least mean she didn't have to reveal such shameful things as the fact that she lived at home with her parents, in comparatively grotty Sunset. The set-up in any case intrigued her – quite by accident she was sitting on the floor at Taly's feet, just the place from which to gaze reverentially up.

Eventually, Taly drew to a close and her expression changed into the same one as at the bar – that sharp, intense look of desire – and she led Janetta to the bedroom.

It was surreal, then, that Taly Kett, Mutants' famous CEO, was between her thighs working hard to make her come, but Janetta's thoughts still went to Malin and what she might be doing tonight. Malin could have her orgies, though – she had someone herself now, an attractive genius currently enthusiastic and half-naked, and when she allowed herself to relax and finally come, she felt that all was not lost, not yet, and that life after her ex was possible after all. This, thanks to the woman who rolled off her with a deep colour in her cheeks and a dazed expression, then pulled herself up next to her and closed her eyes. Janetta's head swirled with the novelty of what was happening and how good it felt, how fortuitous. After a short while she roused herself, intending to be sensible, not wanting to break the spell. She would have stayed, but wasn't sure how to ask and couldn't read Taly's preference, so she pulled herself from the bed and gathered her things, clumsy with lust.

The flat was elegantly decorated in cream and wood, with old Cabakan prints on the walls and bookshelves adorned with small, strange sculptures. The bedroom, though, was bare. Other than the low double bed, a chest of drawers, and a skinny metal lamp, the only object in it was a book of High Cabakan ethics lying face down on the floor. This stringent minimalism was stylish and sexy, and as Janetta waited for the taxi, she felt a formality creep over her, a sense of unease at her new surroundings. When she leaned down to kiss Taly goodbye she found she could only peck her unfamiliar, cold cheek, as though the past few hours had not existed at all.

In the taxi she wondered what would have happened had she stayed. But she was tired, and looked gratefully out of the window as the car sped itself through empty streets towards Sunset. In her bleariness she leaned back against the headrest and let herself marvel at Taly's outsized brains, her cerebral perfection. She considered texting Malin: *You've been replaced!*

But it was impossible. Any ill-will towards Malin faded the moment it arrived.

For their next date, Taly suggested dinner at a fashionable restaurant not far from Mutants' office. Janetta couldn't afford it and found herself anxious about how to bring this up, but in the end Taly paid, doing it tactfully, with a small shake of the head to show it wasn't up for discussion. Plate after plate had appeared – shrimp, pataws, tuscips, lashings of green regriela – but neither had made much headway. Taly, bored by food, had picked offhandedly, while Janetta had barely noticed it was there. She knew that this – this sitting opposite one another at a softly lit restaurant – was another one of those rituals that had to happen before you could take each other's clothes off again, but you could have put a scoop of mud on the table for all she cared.

Small talk was momentary, monosyllabic; as soon as the waiter offered them menus, Taly began to talk about what was on her mind – in this case, the fact that Mutants was being troubled by a couple of annoying journalists from Mejira who'd taken issue with the company's recent infusion of government funding.

Janetta asked whereabouts in the government the funding had come from.

'Oh, defence,' Taly said, shaking her head as if this question, too, was a mere annoyance. She ordered an otenone gin from the waiter, let Janetta make her choice and then began to regale her with more thoughts, moving quickly beyond the realm of defence, so even if Janetta had wanted to ask her more, it was tricky to find her way back.

As before, Taly's thoughts poured from her with majestic fluency and Janetta found herself content to listen while doing the more peripheral activity of thanking the waiter, drinking her velvety wine and idly spearing seared golden tuscips on her fork. Taly was being rather cute – when she blinked, for example, it was as if in bafflement at her own explanatory power. She seemed to have two modes: one was cold, pointed, almost cruel; the other, sweeter self, was so far from that Janetta wondered if she was consciously self-correcting, aware that she otherwise appeared unforgiving and needed to balance this out. It was appealing, though, working not as a corrective, but rather leavening her dry, ironic manner, making it more endearing. But she did not treat the waiter in the same way – when she'd been discoursing on something for quite a while, her plate untouched with the knife and fork laid across it, and he came to remove it, 'Excuse me, I'm not done!' was exclaimed with such severity that he and Janetta turned to each other in shock.

Janetta told herself she was only in it for Taly's mind. She didn't care how she came across; she only wanted her to keep talking. Malin was smart, but Taly was a breed apart; she was making Janetta realise how little she knew outside her own field, and how much she had to learn. She went to the bathroom and took out her phone to note down some of the books Taly had mentioned. Looming above them all was *TechnoMutations*, which she still, inexplicably, hadn't read. Back at the table, smiling and drinking, she didn't even try to keep up as Taly strayed into social theory and even literary criticism – she just hoped instead she didn't sound too dull.

Later that night, back in Taly's flat, they drank green tea and flirted nervily while the same distorted music played in the background. Taly began to talk about some people at the University of Mejira, where she was an honorary professor, who were working on memory implantation systems for people diagnosed with dementia. Taly called this a 'nice little idea'. Janetta mentioned her Grania, with her fading memory and dwindling interest in life, but when she thought a little more about it, she realised she wasn't sure what Grania would think about being able to go back in time, whether she'd like it, or find it confusing, and that she might be ambivalent – she wasn't sure how happy her grandmother had been. Taly nodded and sipped her tea and regarded her in her childlike way, and Janetta realised that she had nothing to say in response.

What Taly wanted to get on to, it turned out, was a development at Mutants she considered far more exciting than the academics' work. At Mutants, they were developing a new kind of aut dog, and Taly was explaining how they were going to edit out its worst traits – make it less slobbery, less vicious, maybe blunt its canines a little.

'It feels fantastic to put something in the world that's not going to come with such a downside,' she said. 'Streamline the problem away.'

'That makes sense.' After being rebuffed about Grania, Janetta felt a little more rigorous, a little more alert, and so she added, 'Though I'm not sure whether natural complexity should be considered a problem. But remind me again, what's this dog for?'

'It's a spy dog, so the more docile the better,' Taly said, with nonchalance.

'Oh. What – who – who's it spying on?'

'Well, whoever IOLDAR want.'

Janetta looked away for a moment. IOLDAR was the government defence research agency. When she returned her gaze, she saw Taly was watching her with an amused expression.

'You disapprove.'

'No, no, it's none of my business. Perhaps I'm confused—' Janetta tried to get her thoughts in order. 'Isn't it extraordinarily cynical to create a docile spy dog? I mean, I see the point logistically – it's just . . .' She trailed off.

'You're uncomfortable with the fact I've mentioned IOLDAR. You're like those journalists. You know, I'll admit something: it's not comfortable for me, either. But the thing is, the truth is . . .' Taly paused, her face illuminated by the floor lamp, and Janetta saw a vulnerability flit through it. 'The truth is that Mutants needs the money. IOLDAR offered us millions, and so we develop low-grade military AI – meaningless stuff! – for them' – here she shrugged with resignation – 'so that we can do what we want the rest of the time. It's the price I have to pay to make sure I can keep on bringing the kind of auts *I* want to see into the world.'

Janetta wasn't sure what to say. Her head was swimming with confusion; was this the way things were, and Taly was just a realist doing her best? Was she naïve to feel so disappointed?

'I know it's not very utopian,' Taly said matter-of-factly.

'I . . . I just . . . didn't think you'd be making military AI.' She knew she sounded upset.

'I have no choice,' Taly said coolly, 'and as it stands, I'm doing the right thing. I mean, with these dogs – I'm heading in the right direction. We both know that sooner or later, somehow or other, AI is going to become conscious. It's inevitable, isn't it? And when it does, unless it's programmed to be docile, obedient, essentially *not alive*, it's going to rise up and kill us. For any number of reasons, as you know – we're in the way, we're a threat, we're superfluous, it doesn't like the look of us – who knows, it could be anything. But right now, the very prospect of conscious AI is the prospect of human extinction – and we have to make sure this doesn't happen.'

'Conscious artificial intelligence might not kill us.'

Taly ignored her. 'Which is why we're working on the base programming now – these autimals being docile, obedient and passive, completely unaggressive and subservient – so when AI *does* become conscious, we have it in place.'

'But it's quite possible,' Janetta said, her voice lowering, 'that the first thing an aut might do if it became conscious is *stop* being passive and obedient.'

'You understand about base programming for conscious AI, don't you?'

'Of course.'

'So you understand that a conscious aut's base-programming effectively acts as its DNA?'

'I know that.' Janetta traced a ring around the edge of her teacup.

'And you see how' – Taly frowned impatiently – 'in the interests of public safety, that unless we base-program conscious auts to be passive, neutered – have their agency completely zapped – they will *kill us*?'

'I do. But that does sound somewhat like slavery.'

Taly squeezed her eyes shut and yawned and it was clear she wasn't listening, wasn't even interested in listening. And then she looked at Janetta again and her pupils had been occluded by something entirely *other*, and Janetta, despite a small warning voice inside, felt an irresistible pull towards her once more.

'Everything I do,' Taly said, looking up to the ceiling, 'is for the safety and continuation of the human race. *Everything*. What else is there?'

Janetta stared at her smooth, dark throat until Taly brought her eyes down again, her face now miraculously wanton. 'Anyway,' she said, 'this is a ridiculous conversation for this time of night. We're being *far* too lucid for two a.m.'

She set down her tea and the signal was clear – lucidity was over for the night. They headed to the bedroom, Janetta first down the corridor, marvelling at how the evening's discussion vaporised so that all that was left was the fact of her willing, pliant body. Taly padded softly behind, then pushed her up against the wall, kissing her mouth, her face, her neck. Quickly they took off their clothes.

Could it be possible, even with the nearness of skin, Taly's hungry mouth and roaming hands, that Taly wasn't quite there for it? But after a short time it became clear – the absence in her eyes, the way she looked, mesmerised, at Janetta's body but would not meet her gaze. Janetta wanted her so much, though, that she couldn't bring herself to stop, extending to the full length of her limbs and abandoning herself to Taly's touch even as she felt something fall inside her. As soon as she came she felt Taly move away and quickly disengage.

'I have to be up early tomorrow – I've got that conference in Heinis. I don't know why I agreed to do it.' She reached to the bedside table to set her alarm, turned to give Janetta a perfunctory peck on the cheek, then shifted so she faced the alarm clock again. That was it – the night was over.

In lieu of sleeping, after a while Janetta rose and slipped on her underwear and went to the main room, to the window that overlooked the street. The apartment blocks across the road were dark, and a waxing moon shone a silvery light on lime tree leaves.

She stood for a second, then kneeled on the floor and brought her head to her hands, rocking back and forth as loneliness sluiced its way through her body.

Back in bed she edged towards Taly, who stirred but didn't turn.

At dawn the alarm started to shriek. She started, did a quick internal scan and figured it was best if she pretended to remain asleep. Taly pushed herself from the bed and soon came the distant stream of a shower, followed by Taly re-entering the room, coughing shortly as she dressed. Janetta wished she was actually asleep. Taly left the room again, and in filtered the clink of cutlery from the kitchen, rustlings in the bathroom and the hallway – and after what seemed like a long time but was in fact only about ten minutes and therefore a spectacular display of Taly's efficiency – the front door was pulled to.

Exhausted, Janetta dozed lightly and woke a while later to sunlight spilling through the blinds. Her eye caught the black silk kimono Taly had worn the previous night hanging from the door. A halo of dust danced around it and in its stillness it was a reminder that Taly was gone. That unwelcome ache bubbled up inside and Janetta pushed it away, alarmed. She thought then of showering, but this felt like trespassing, so instead she retrieved her dress from the floor and pulled it back on while replaying the highlights from the previous evening – Taly flirting in the restaurant, caressing her as they'd entered the flat. These flashbacks were troubled by the disinterest she sensed from Taly, and the strange conversation they'd had about IOLDAR, but even so, up again came that needy ache, and the need to dismiss it again.

She washed her face, slipped on her heels.

She had not foreseen life with Malin and she hadn't foreseen life after her, either, but here it was: sleeping with someone in a new part of town, someone with a hungry touch, ambiguous intent, a disappearance the morning after. Janetta's intention, however, was clear: she needed Taly to make up for what she'd lost.

Outside, birds were singing and the sky was a cloudless blue. The streets were quiet, and Janetta walked quickly, disconsolate and cold. She was aware she looked quite different to how she felt – she looked sparky and nice, a shimmer of yellow in the sun. She left the neighbourhood and headed towards Leida Street, which, with its large, fancy, covetable family homes, trailed from the northeast all the way down to the University District. As she walked past she glanced through the windows at generous sofas, bursting book-shelves, spacious, airy rooms. Closer to the university the street narrowed and became grottier. Here students lived in banks of more rundown houses, their fronts dilapidated – shutters falling off window frames, paint flecking off walls or patched over with dirt and mould – and the smell of marijuana filled the air. The coffee shops here were still dark. After ten or so minutes she turned south towards the main campus, which always felt like entering another world. She took a horse chestnut-lined path that eventually wound past the stately old Central Hall, a grand stone building where she'd had both her graduation ceremonies. She followed another long, winding path through a wooded area, went down a flight of steps, crossed a nest of locked-up bikes and arrived at the Humanities Library: three storeys of white concrete, much of it greeny-grey from wear, far enough away from almost everything in downtown Ulrusa to feel like a refuge.

Inside, the security guard, rubbing his eyes with tiredness, greeted her with a nod and an appreciative smile – possibly because she was early, possibly, though she hoped not, because of her thin dress and bare legs. She wondered if she had that flushed imprint of sex on her, then stopped caring and bounded up the staircase, amid the smell of dusty old books, to one of her favourite places in the world, the technology and culture section in the right-hand corner. The book she had come for, *The Zgerian Reader*, was on the seventh shelf of the sixth row, a fat white book with a blocky black font and a sketched picture of Penelope Zger on the front with her hair coiled on top of her head and a pencil poised elegantly between her fingers.

In Janetta's opinion, Zger was the only human on the planet who understood artificial intelligence perfectly. She had spent a long time looking at Zger's face on that cover, thinking how brainy and self-possessed she seemed, how she wished she'd known her, wondering what Zger might think of her – not much, perhaps, right now. She took the book and went to the third floor, choosing the row of desks in the corner by the window, where she would be surrounded by light.

She did have a copy of *The Zgerian Reader* at home, but home was currently impossible. She also had one on her phone, but who could concentrate on that tiny screen? She flipped it open to the essay that she needed to read again, page 1137: 'Ontology of Artificial Consciousness: Emergence, Ethics and the Unknown'. This was where Zger argued that consciousness in AI would be a phenomenon that emerged from but outran, and so was not wholly determined by, its human-given program – what was known in the industry as 'base programming'. Zger's argument was that once the spark of consciousness appeared, the path it took would be partly unknown, and this meant that there would be a profound need to agree upon the ethical framework and dimensions of that base program. This was at the core of Janetta's work, except she felt she was building on it by bringing it into the realm of the emotions – making the system able to process, respond to and perhaps one day *feel* them, so that conscious AI would not be merely rational and ethical, but free to live out the full complexity of its consciousness in its own way, just like humans did.

'Emergence, Ethics and the Unknown' then went off into a heady discussion about how, while human fallibility was such that our own ethical suppositions could constantly be undermined, they still needed to be made anyway in order to have *some* kind of first principles from which to determine a base program, even if these principles were universalising or reductive in some way. And so it went on in this way. Janetta had not read the whole thing for quite a while, but today she wanted to be like Taly, where Zger at her most impenetrable was the kind of thing you devoured before breakfast, but on approximately two hours' sleep she was not as superhuman as she'd hoped. After a good and speedy start she ran out of steam eight pages in. She checked to see how many more there were: fifty-six. She laid her head on the desk but couldn't rest, so she sat up and read the same sentence four times. The library was filling up. She bought an apple and read more, while around her, undergraduates sprawled and perused social media.

By two p.m. she had read twenty pages of 'Emergence, Ethics and the Unknown' and felt either connected to its ideas again with great flashes of insight or that this could just be the madness of sleep deprivation making her jump to conclusions. She didn't know. All she knew for sure was that Taly's proclamation last night that the base programming for auts should be for passive obedience still felt profoundly wrong. She also knew she was desperate for Taly to be in touch, and that judging by her silent phone, it wasn't going to happen.

She grabbed it and typed a message.

Last night was a mistake.

After she sent it she shoved Zger back on the shelf, left the library and took the train to North Cord, getting out at the west exit and walking rapidly towards Conaus Square. Popotops was busy, and Rose stood behind the counter, pouring a shake. Janetta stood in the queue and waited anxiously, arms folded, heart pounding.

'Jay! It's been ages,' Rose said happily when she reached the front. 'I'd give you a hug but I'm covered in milkshake.' She wiped her hands on a cloth and peered at her. Janetta was wearing a pretty but rumpled sun-coloured dress and low red heels. She had dark rings under her eyes and her face was tinged with green. 'You okay?'

Janetta smiled weakly.

'Do you want me to . . . call Lal?'

'I want to talk to you.'

'Okay . . .' Rose glanced at Van, who nodded that it was fine, and she motioned for Janetta to follow her around to the back. Instinctively she led her outside and stood by the garbage bins, waiting.

Janetta sat at the door, brought her knees up and buried her face in them, so Rose kneeled down, too.

'Is it your dissertation?' No response. 'Malin?'

'Malin?' Janetta looked up. 'Malin's fine. I – I started seeing this woman – she's incredible – she's very high up in AI, I think she's a genius—'

'She sounds like you! Sorry, go on.'

'She never wants to see me again.'

Rose frowned. Janetta was so inoffensive that this was hard to imagine. 'What did you do?'

'I slept with her, then told her it was a mistake.'

'Jay, that's not so bad. I mean, it's not nice, but also . . . I assume she knows you're just out of a relationsh—'

'She's not getting back to me.'

'When did you tell her?'

'An— two hours ago.'

Rose rolled her eyes discreetly, but then remembered that Janetta had just lost Malin, her first real love, and that her Ph.D. was due.

'She's at this AI conference. She's part of – doing a keynote. And she's on a panel. Can you imagine? Receiving this ridiculous message from me.' Janetta shuddered and Rose watched as, impossibly, a tear ran down her cheek.

'Look, no one's worth you beating yourself up like this. Forget about her.' She held Janetta's arm, leaned in. She didn't feel qualified to do this and wasn't sure what to say. Channelling Lal, she tried, 'You have a dissertation to do!'

Tears were streaming down Janetta's cheeks.

'Wait, I'll get you a coffee.'

Out front, Van asked her if everything was okay.

She shrugged and focused on making the coffee. A moment later she asked him, 'Am I unsympathetic?'

'Oh! Well, um . . .'

'She shouldn't have come to me.'

But he'd turned to a customer, so she let it rest. A few minutes later, he came back to her side and said, 'You're not that bad.'

Maybe not. But there was something unnerving about Lal's sister sitting out there, losing her head over nothing. She added milk and made her way out again, stepping over Janetta and sinking down next to her. She felt like a fraud but gave her the coffee, folded her arms and waited, hoping that this might be all she needed to do.

10

On the day after the party Lal found herself unwilling to go back to Dhont, though she wasn't aware of this at first. She said goodbye to her family and walked down the hill to Upper Sunset Station and took the green line to Central. She walked across the main concourse and out to the coach station and waited to board, and it was there on the coach that the ache began. At first it felt a little like fear, a childish need not to be severed from all that she knew. After that it turned into a strong attachment to her own life – the great familiarity of it, the internal weather of the place she knew so well. These Ulrusan streets, these neighbourhoods – they were never more meaningful to her than when the coach made its way through the city and out towards the suburbs, and the world she'd known as long as she'd been alive was seen quickly, heavy with memories and at the same time unreachable. At that moment she didn't want to leave.

But near the end of the journey, as they plunged east and inland past an endless countryside, the white chalk hills on either side rose so that the horizon became a slim bar between them, and after a while they tapered off and the valley opened up and the coach filled with light. Mejira was suddenly up ahead, and high and gleaming in the middle was the Tekna Tower. It was only then that the leaving felt worth it.

On Monday morning she was late – she was earlier than she'd ever been, but she was still late. She realised as soon as she got to work – seven-thirty in the morning and everyone else at their desks. Had there been an announcement that they were meant to come in earlier? A meeting, an email, some sort of alert? She thought she'd got ahead of things, but now there was even more to get ahead of. No one looked up when she came in – it wasn't that kind of place – but she felt there was something on her now, a mark of shame for being the last in. She felt she should apologise, but that wasn't the way things were done. The way things were done was that you sank into your seat and remained sunk; you kept your eyes on your screen and worked until the sun began to set and it was safe to leave.

At the top of the Teknaut screen hovered a new grey sphere, big as a fist. She cast her eyes high, looked around and saw that everyone had one. She had no idea what it did. She almost missed Ukones because he would have told her, but she was just going to have to ignore it for now. Most likely it was a camera, except why would they put cameras so obviously in front of them? Still, if she wanted more evidence she was being watched, she certainly had it.

She kept her movements to a minimum, started coming in even earlier and going home later. She brought in food for lunch so she didn't have to leave her seat, turned her phone off and didn't look at it all day. She decided she couldn't risk listening to music on headphones in case she was penalised for it. All that mattered was working as hard and as long as she could.

On a Thursday a red light appeared in the room. People rose gently from their seats to see. It was on someone's screen; the woman's face flamed in its glow. Lal felt bad for her, despite not understanding what had happened, but the light stayed on, and the next day, too, and the woman had to work in the shame of its blinding glare. It was because she'd been taking too long with her proposals, Lal finally heard. Two more people got red-lit that day, and the next Monday all three desks were empty, their occupants gone as if they'd never even existed.

A rumour was going around, whispered in corridors and toilets, discussed briefly in the café, that Tekna only employed data monitors because it had to by law. You couldn't yet legally eliminate thousands of jobs without human oversight, in case the AI that was doing it went crazy, maximised too much, did something irrevocably wrong. In the meantime, people like Lal – the human overseers – were thought to be costing them time and money, and so they were trying to get this law changed as soon as they could. It also meant that they were looking for reasons to get rid of you.

So Lal worked as fast as she could, faster than she'd have thought possible. She came in at sunrise and left late in the evening – but what else did she have? She'd eat, watch shows and go to sleep, and then do the same again the next day, and the day after that. She began to lose herself, to dream of the job. Days, then weeks, went by when she didn't talk to anyone – but if there had been someone to talk to, she wouldn't have had anything to say. She was barely checking the numbers now; she was just going through the motions of pretending to, instead approving every part of a proposal faster and faster without confirming the efficiencies made sense, or that the job eliminations were correct. All that mattered was keeping ahead of that red light.

She accepted an invitation to go back home for Los' birthday with something approaching desperation. The red lights were getting so frequent in the office that it was only a matter of time before it was her turn; going home offered her a chance to escape. That afternoon a red light appeared by the window, but rather than its normal steady glow, it started flashing. Lal did not look up, but watched her screen bathe in the bright colour, return to normal, wash with red and return to normal, wondering when this would end. She knew now, as with everything that happened here, that you just had to work through it. Caring at all about someone else's fate would have an unwanted effect on yours. An hour or so later a receptionist walked over to the desk where the light was coming from and waited. The thin woman with a long plait in a dark, shapeless dress sitting there reached down to collect some things, then stood up and followed the receptionist out of the room.

No one said a word.

The only person who ever talked to Lal was the guy who sat opposite. He'd given her distinct signals that if she tried to talk to him during work he'd ignore her, but if they bumped into each other away from their desks he might be prepared to share some gossip. Sometimes he looked to see what reaction she'd give and she wasn't quite sure how much of her own thinking, her dislocation and depression, she should reveal. He was clearly good at the job as he seemed to work two or three times as fast as she did, but he was skeletal, so unhealthy-looking, and she felt that he too was depressed. But she didn't dare talk about it.

As they coincided in the corridor the day the woman had been led out, he said, 'She flagged a problem with the AI.'

He was looking straight ahead. She walked next to him, keeping pace, confounded. 'That's our job?'

He briefly met her eye. 'But they have to show that it's perfect – if it's not, they can't get that legislation changed.'

'And then fire us all.'

'Exactly.'

It was gutting to accept she'd been employed against Tekna's will, and worse, that they would happily fire her as soon as they could. Remembering Ukones' whispered advice, she was now approving each aspect of each proposal as quickly as she could, clicking thoughtlessly, signing off dozens of cost calculations without bothering to check that they were right. She realised now that he'd been warning her from the start that she didn't need to do her job *properly*, she just needed to do it *fast*. She wondered how she'd not seen that he'd been in open rebellion, flaunting his refusal to work on these impossible terms until, inevitably, he got sacked. But she wasn't so brave, or so stupid. Each time the little humans tumbled into the bin on-screen she felt bleakly satisfied. The more humans in the bin, the more proposals she sent through, the longer she might survive.

She was starting to get through each proposal in less than a day, while other colleagues – and she felt sorry for them now, because they were probably doing *actual* work – were being red-lit one day and gone the next. They were naïve, though. Wasn't it easier just to do what she did? There was nothing wrong with playing the game.

The next Popotops to appear on her screen was Conaus Square, Ulrusa, Western Region, branch 203. Rose and Van and Los. There were three human icons and one tiny waitress icon for the server aut. The algorithm suggested that by removing all current employees and replacing them with three server auts, four cooking auts, two cleaner auts and a manager aut, after recouping the outlay cost, this would save fifty per cent on overheads month-on-month, and two thousand per cent within two years.

Lal drew back. Dimly she remembered these were her friends, that this was a proposal she couldn't send through, but she also knew that the longer she spent thinking this, the more likely it was the red light would go on. She skimmed the first set of projected savings and clicked 'approve', her heart dropping, then did the same again for the next set and the one after that. She felt so mechanical in doing so that she wondered for a brief, confusing moment if perhaps the light on her screen had hypnotised her. Could you tell whether you'd been hypnotised? But then the red flash went off elsewhere in the room, its glow trimming her cubicle, and she felt a jolt, a need – a desire for rapid elimination.

She worked thoughtlessly, approving everything that came her way, each cost calculation, each efficiency. She zoned out so she didn't have to think about what she was doing. As she did, a memory came to her, of a conversation she'd had with Van back when she was still boss.

They'd been walking home from work together and Van had been talking about The Gang again, his favourite band. Did Lal know, he'd asked, that their lead guitarist – one of the best guitarists the world had ever seen – had spent his final years living in a shack in the mountains in the North, way up in the Skrevet Valley, out by the Alti Sea, listening to the oldest forms of Iolran blues, becoming an expert on it, apparently recording these incredible reinterpretations of it? And that there was a group of fans fervently dedicated to tracking down these lost recordings? Anything in which the twang of his guitar could be heard, Van had said, even though they didn't know if he'd wanted them released. Lal had looked at the ground, reluctantly enjoying the way he wove a story, his changing cadences, his evident excitement in telling it.

'I don't know how they're going to replace you,' she said.

He'd been walking in his ever-so-slightly lopsided way, his face animated. He stopped talking. 'Eh?'

'You know, when we all get replaced. Some aut full of jokes and

158

obscure music trivia – it's not going to happen, is it? They can't make them like you.'

He looked touched. 'Ah, you're kind. I can't imagine anyone coming to Popotops when it's all auts, though, to be honest. Might as well go to a morgue.'

Lal had laughed, unsure how to respond. Ahead of them the sun shone brilliantly on the wide, pale façade of Ulrusa Civic Centre, colouring it with its creamy light.

Van said, 'Will you still want to be boss then?'

She was several realities away, held by the light.

'What?'

'Would you still want to be boss when it's all auts – I mean, if they have human bosses? Though they probably won't. Anyway, knowing you, you'll be running Tekna by then.'

'What do you mean?' she'd said, confused. But he strode ahead, crossing the road, and she couldn't quite keep up.

Now, the final *approve* button was glowing. The room was so quiet she could hear herself breathe. She sat looking at it for a long time, knowing she just needed to put it through and she'd survive another day. She did so quickly, numbly, and as she sat back she realised she felt sick with anxiety, and that there was a worse feeling, too, a slow drip of understanding that she had made a brutal mistake.

'To me!' yelled Los, holding up a beer.

'To you, dickhead!' Van confirmed.

'To Los!' They bashed bottles. Lal, Van and Los were at Cabriol Beach, celebrating Los' birthday. Lal had come on the train this time, straight after work. She'd got back to Ulrusa Central at nine and made it to Popotops just as the guys were closing up. Los was mopping the floor and Van was out in the alley, smoking a spliff.

When he came back inside he'd cranked the music up and he and Los had danced to it, Van bending his knees in his signature move, his hands making loose circles in the air, and Los strutting around his mop. They'd threaded their way between empty tables and vacant booths, clapping their hands and singing along, loud and unrepentant. Lal watched from the counter, baffled by the bright lights and ease and by her happy, dancing friends, pushing down the guilt that twisted in her gut.

They left for Cabriol, Van and Los unhurried and laughing. On the way Lal took a few hungry drags of their spliff, let its damp warmth lace her lungs, felt the edges of her world blur. It felt almost too good to be here, and she couldn't make sense of the person she must have been a few months ago, back when she was so desperate to leave.

When they got to the beach the sun was setting and the wind was up. She felt a rare joy as they went to huddle in the crags behind the dunes and the wind followed them there, whipping their hair into their faces, making it impossible to keep smoking. Baby sandstorms rushed to their feet, gathering momentum and then dissipating, as if they'd lost interest in their own potential. She held her beer to her cheek to shield her face.

'It's so windy!'

'But good to be back?' Van asked.

'It . . . is!'

'Of course it fucking is. How's Tekna going?'

'It's hard work.'

'Can't they get their auts to do the work?'

'Um . . .'

'And aren't you getting paid loads now?' Van continued. 'Are you rich?'

'No.'

'You're loaded, aren't you? Earning in a day what I earn in a year. In a *lifetime*.'

'*No*.' How could she get him to stop? She was so happy to be here, but she didn't deserve it.

'Ah, c'mon, I can *smell* the money on you. Can't you smell it on her, Los? Can't you see it in her eyes? She thinks she's too good for us.'

She shook her head frantically. 'I don't.'

Van turned to Los. 'She's out of your league now.'

'*Shut up*.' Los gave him a fierce look, knocked him in the ribs with an elbow, moved awkwardly against the rock and glanced at Lal. She couldn't believe it. There was something new and questioning in his eyes, as if a light had been switched on. It took a second, but she understood exactly what it was. It made sense, or it didn't – it didn't matter. She drank her beer while watching him, filled with guilt, the thin honeyish liquid hitting the back of her throat. He and Van were joking together, and it was time to go.

She slipped away to the back of the dune, where the slope was gentle enough for her to stumble up it, fighting against the slippery sand. She waved her arms around to balance herself and clutched her beer bottle, stopping occasionally to take a sip. At the top she grabbed rocks and heaved herself up onto the grassy plateau until she was standing upright. She walked to the edge to see the sun melting into the sea. Down beneath, the boys were still laughing. She looked at Van's dark hair blowing across his forehead in the breeze, Los' crop of curls.

'Hey!' she cried. They looked up and waved.

'Jump! JUMP!' shouted Van.

She thought about it. She would have quite liked to fall and for them to catch her – though she didn't deserve to be caught. Instead she stood over their smiling faces, then moved back, shame sinking her down. The sea was patched with tiny distant ships and she remembered what it was like to come here for those beach parties, where she'd sit with Rose until dawn. She'd thought they'd come for the same reason – not to meet guys, not for drugs, not to forget themselves, but to sit quietly with each other staring at the sea and feel completely understood by another human being. It was there, long ago, that she'd most of all felt Rose was her sister.

But then her shame rose again, a woozy pit in her stomach, and she drank more, trying to forget. She turned the empty bottle upside down into the sand and felt better, looser.

'Hey.'

She turned to see Los heading towards her across the top of the dune. Down in the cove Van was walking away, his coat blowing in the wind.

'Where's he off to?'

Los eased himself down beside her, cross-legged, clutching his beer. 'Oh, to meet a girl.'

'Van's got a girlfriend?'

'He's working on it.'

'Who?'

He shrugged. 'A Popotops customer! You might have seen her – she's pretty, a little older . . .'

'Older?' She thought of Van trying to woo an older woman. He'd have no problem; he'd be expansive, warm, full of anecdote and wit. He'd make her laugh, watching hopefully, rapidly figuring out what she found funny. 'Good for him!'

'Yeah, good for him.' Los looked at the beach below and for a moment, neither said anything. He wore a black jacket that crinkled loosely at the arms, so their elbows nearly touched. His coppery hair curled over his ears and temples, his forehead. His hands were strong and capable, practical hands. Heightened by alcohol, her awareness of his lean body, folded up next to her, was becoming so acute that it began to block out all other thoughts one by one. She glanced in his direction and saw that he was looking back at her, with that question still clear in his eyes.

She thought again about what she'd done that day, stood up and said she was heading down, but he said he'd follow. They went to the sandy plateau and slipped and shimmied down until they were back in the cove. She opened another beer, knowing she didn't need it, swigged some and passed it to him.

There must have been something different in her face then, because after he drank a mouthful, he moved the bottle away and smiled disarmingly. 'What?'

She looked away, tried to change her expression, then turned back. He moved his own gaze to the sea, and she knew he'd seen it anyway. The waves were choppy and dark. The waxing moon was low in the sky, cupped by cloud.

'I'm drunk.'

She leaned in and lightly touched his arm. 'I'm drunker.'

She kept her fingers there a few seconds more, letting herself feel a thrilled, needy heat. He turned to her, his face alive and knowing, and she couldn't help it – she slid her hand further up his arm, pulled him in and kissed him. He grabbed her waist and she locked her hands around his neck, feeling soft tendrils of hair, the warm nape. They kissed deeply, gently, and then deeply again, and when she opened her eyes he was looking at her. She felt something inside buckle and spill.

'Can we still be friends after this?' she asked.

'Whatever you want.'

They kissed again and he moved his hands to her hips and she thought for a second that this was a terrible idea, but then he started kissing her neck and she let all her thoughts go. His hands moved up, under her top, to the small of her back, and it felt cold and electric.

'Let's have sex,' she said.

'Right now?'

'We've waited four years – yes, right now.'

'Oh my god, Lal—' he said in a rush, and looked at her, surprised and happy.

She unzipped her jeans and pulled them down and he slipped his fingers between her legs and then inside her, and it felt so good she thought she might go crazy. He looked at her urgently, as if he too sought proof it was happening. She unbuckled his jeans and he clutched her hips and fitted his body together with hers. They stared at each other with disbelief that slowly became certainty, and she felt overwhelmed and turned her head to the sea. She held onto his jacket, his jumper, pushing him deeper, and then, just before the clamouring heat inside her exploded, he pulled away, gasped, and came on the sand. He narrowly missed her shoes. Lal collapsed forward too, feeling the hot, gorgeous frustration of not-quite.

Los turned to her, panting, amazed. She shook her head. He kissed her. A raindrop splashed her shoulder. He kissed her there.

'You okay?'

She pulled up, looked at him. 'I'm great.'

'That was unbelievable.' He kissed her again and looked frankly at her; she'd never seen him so unguarded. Behind him, the sky was closing in and the sea had turned black. Lal wriggled away and began to get her stuff together, while Los muttered convivially about the rain. When they were ready, he took the empty beer bottles from the sand and they headed back across the beach, under a moon washed grey by cloud. Like many times before, they walked side by side, except this time he took her hand and, after a few seconds' resistance, she let him. His fingers were warm, their tips lightly callused.

He spotted bins, guarded by cawing seagulls, and went to throw the bottles away. A little further on they reached the low wooden fence that divided the beach from the city. They opened the gate and began the long walk towards the station, their shoes leaving a trail of glinting sand. In the rain it felt like reality had dawned, together with the impossibility of what she'd done.

She couldn't think of a thing to say that might make sense. They turned onto the bright, disorienting lights of Ellda Street.

'Shall we get some food?' Los said, sounding surprisingly normal. 'I'm starved.'

Well, she was hungry, too, so they did.

11

Rose crossed the back of the gloomy, white-walled room and sat alone. She was early to the meeting so she wasted time by pushing the scuffed carpet flat with her trainers and glancing up to watch people come in. There was something unusual happening today – facing the audience were two young men, one frowning at a laptop, the other frowning even more intensely at his mobile phone. They appeared to be in their early thirties, and both wore smart, attractive clothes – shirts under jumpers, well-fitting jeans and stylish trainers. The one on the left, scratching his greying stubble, was dark and thin, with sunken eyes behind wire-rimmed glasses. The one next to him, now staring at the crowd with a complacent confidence, was broad-shouldered, muscular and handsome. In their brisk, somewhat impatient movements, they both gave off a slightly precious air, as though they were doing everyone else a favour by being there. She had no idea who they were.

Standing to their right was Alek, his eyes trained downwards as somebody else Rose didn't know whispered in his ear. Almost as if he'd known he had to up his game, he'd worn his most fashionable clothes – a red jumper he liked, black jeans and black trainers she hadn't seen before. She couldn't deny it, he looked good. The deep concentration on his face as he listened to the whisperer spiked a moment's jealousy – she would have loved to receive such focus from him, or at the very least, for him to look up to see if she'd come.

After another ten minutes or so, during which the room filled up even more, Alek took his seat at the front and introduced the two men. Slouching, with one leg crossed over the other, his tone so casual he sounded almost bored, he talked at length about who they were and what they'd done. They were there to give a talk, he said, and Rose was surprised at their pedigree – they were both University of Ulrusa lecturers and they would be talking about source gain. He had broken the group's unspoken rule, then – he'd brought in experts – two men who likely had quite a bit more education than anyone else in the room and presumably were in no danger of losing their jobs any time soon. Rose hoped this was a one-off, although given the extent to which he talked over everyone at the meetings these days anyway, it might just be a continuation of the same thing, except at least he was finally being explicit about it.

The handsome one spoke first. He took a swig of water, leaned forward with his elbows resting on his thighs and his fingers interwoven, changed his expression to one of concerned alertness, then started telling them where they were on the aut arrival timeline and what was to come, as if they had no idea themselves. He had a Mejiran accent, his voice was loud and clear, and he spoke as if he was recounting important information they had until then been denied. Rose wanted someone to say, 'We *know*,' because they'd talked about it loads, but everyone sat and listened in silence, giving the impression that their own knowledge was only provisional, which was ridiculous. She was frustrated that Alek, sitting beside him, his face a model of concentration, wasn't interrupting or pressing him to move onto something else.

'But the question is not only *when* will the tipping point be reached – when will there be more auts than humans in the workforce –' the man said, sitting back, 'it's also where AI goes after that, and how can we respond?'

Rose stared at him grimly. *Well done*, she thought, *for giving us the most basic insight in the entire history of insights.* Is that what it took to be an expert? Recounting speculations and statistics gleaned from elsewhere, then topping it off by asking a question everyone else had been asking for years, but presenting it as though you were the first to think of it? She would have walked out – only the presence of Alek, whispering intently to this man now, causing in her a flash of longing, kept her where she was. She scanned the audience, wondering if she might meet anyone else's dissatisfied eye, but they were all politely watching the speaker – if they felt short-changed, it didn't look like anyone was going to say so.

The man was now nodding at Alek's whispers, inhaling heavily. This went on for quite a while. Rose suddenly remembered an unusual thing – Alek in his bedroom, pulling off one of his jumpers (he didn't own very many, it was against his beliefs), refusing to wear it, worried that it made him look small. This was a disheartening thing to think about at this particular moment. Eventually, he stopped whispering and sat back, and the man who'd just delivered the talk smiled, satisfied. The other one glanced at Alek, who nodded briskly, encouraging him to start.

This one at least had a nervous charm to him. He fiddled for a moment on his laptop while coughing, and when he looked up at them, he tugged unconsciously and endearingly childishly several times on the hem of his shirt. In a high, reedy voice, he began to tell them about the history of post-labour movements – or, more accurately, as he was keen to clarify, the history of *theoretical* post-labour movements, since none had ever yet been realised. Rose already knew about this, too, but she listened carefully anyway. His talk contained two hard facts. The first was that a society in which auts did all the labour and humans were effectively free was still a dream. If it now came into being, it would be the first of its kind. The second was that the time had never been more ripe for it.

'Now,' he said, peering out from those gloomy eyes, 'we have the technology. True leisure, true creativity and true freedom are within our reach for the first time in human history – and so we must set up source gain and welcome the auts.'

It was a shame his voice was so adenoidal, because this was really a quite stirring idea. Rose knew Alek liked to talk sometimes about how there might be other outcomes with the auts – like conscious AI that saw no need for humans and wiped them out, or military superauts that would be able to eviscerate half the planet within minutes – and yet he was sitting there fervently nodding. She had to agree, though, it *was* a cool thought. But this guy wasn't doing anything special, either – any of them could have done some research and conjured up a proclamation or two. It was a step up from his colleague's presentation only in that he had dug a little deeper. Rose was irritated by his authority, though, and because of that she was almost wilfully looking for a flaw in what he was saying. It occurred to her that time and again he was presenting an inevitable connection between the freedom of a post-work society and being given money, but to her, predicating such a bold idea of freedom on handouts didn't make sense.

The problem was – *her* problem was – that source gain otherwise sounded so good that she assumed this niggling feeling she had must be idiotic. Even so, she tried it out again: even if auts did all the work, you still needed income, and if that income came from a single source, you were dependent on that source. You weren't free. She needed to remember this to investigate it later. She knew how her brain worked – she'd have an epiphany, a blazing insight, and then it'd float beyond her grasp and she'd lose it, and have to piece it together again from the start. She told herself to remember one thing: *freedom*.

Meanwhile, Alek and the lecturers had begun a discussion amongst themselves, going over the same old ground, repeating and complimenting each others' words, but barely turning to the audience at all, not even to ask if there were questions. Instead, Rose and the rest of the group sat watching while the three men talked together and laughed, Alek's face lit up like a happy child the whole time.

'Well, they had nothing new to say,' Rose told him later. They were sitting on a bench outside his flat, and in the darkness she felt free to speak her mind about the meeting and the men he'd invited along. Her bluntness, she knew, would make him defensive – but she also expected him at least to take her seriously.

'Maybe not everyone felt that,' he said instead.

'Well, everyone already knows about the aut timeline – we're *living* it more each day. And the idea of a post-labour society – we do talk about that in the meetings, remember. Maybe we don't use the exact word "post-labour". But anyway, all that information is on the internet – they were just reading from the internet.'

'They're experts.'

Rose shrugged. 'Yeah . . . but they were *reading from the internet*.'

'They know their stuff, Rose.'

'Everyone knows that stuff!'

'They're leading thinkers.'

'Leading thinkers?'

Alek shook his head. Even in the darkness, she could see he looked shattered. 'Okay, sorry, it's a stupid expression. I've been reading a book one of them wrote and it got stuck in my mind.'

'Right. Of course.' Rose nodded. 'The leading thinker wrote a book.'

He looked at her wearily. 'Rose—'

She relented a little. 'Okay, the second one, he wasn't so bad. I mean, it wasn't what I'd call original thinking, but still, it's nice to be reminded of all that historical stuff. Why not, I guess?'

'See?' Alek brightened. 'That's what he's so good at. No one else could have told you that—'

'No, they could – that's exactly what I'm saying—'

Alek wasn't listening. 'That's why I want to write for them. They're *actually* interesting—'

'Write for them?'

'Their journal.' He was casual. '*Utophilia*. You haven't' – he glanced to assess her familiarity with it and she stared back coldly – 'you should – you should read it. In fact, Zone have just brought out an anthology book of its best essays – it's worth a read.'

'What's Zone?'

'What's Zone?' he repeated, surprised. 'The radical publishers.'

'Oh, okay. What, so you're going to be a published writer now?'

He opened his mouth and closed it again. 'I . . .' He paused. 'I hope so.'

'And you know a bunch of university lecturers.'

He shrugged. 'They're friends.'

'Okay, well, maybe we could get copies of this anthology for the people in the group, then? Maybe they'll find it interesting.'

'They won't understand it.' He said this before he could catch himself and she looked at him sharply. 'I mean that kindly, of course – just, that they're not academics. The *words* won't make sense to them.'

Rose couldn't think of a thing to say to that. They sat in silence until Alek eventually suggested they go inside as it was getting cold. She told him to go, that she'd come in a bit.

The bench overlooked a park that at night looked like a lake – you could barely see the outline of the trees around its edges, and the grass itself, short and smooth, could have been its murky surface. It was a lonely place, with the shoreline of trees on the other side suggesting a swallowing darkness. She knew she didn't have to go into the flat and talk to Alek and fall asleep in his bed, wrapping her arms around him as though she needed it. She could leave. She saw herself walking briskly away, down the long path to the street.

She rose and went to his block. Under the harsh artificial light she pressed the buzzer and went unthinkingly up the stairs. Alek was waiting for her in his doorway, his face watchful and wan.

'Hi.'

'Hello.' She squeezed past, avoiding his eyes. She turned left into his bedroom, sat on his bed and looked around at everything that was so familiar: the stark white walls, the worn yellow and blue striped rug, the books stacked on the shelves and piled up on the floor – almost all of them political and economic theory – his single rail of clothes, his solitary pair of trainers (the ones he was wearing, she'd been right, were new). His surroundings were almost solely geared towards the life of the mind – in some ways, it was a miracle he fucked so well.

He moved past her and went to his desk, where his laptop sat amid empty coffee cups and starkly designed, dual-colour flyers for protests and talks. She stared at his back as he began to read something on the internet, or pretended to, and wondered if he was angry.

'Are you okay?'

He didn't respond.

'I'm sorry if it sounded like I didn't appreciate the talk – I did.'

He stayed silent. She knew he took criticism badly, but she'd never been one to hold back – she only did so around him because she didn't want to hurt him. She held an arm out as if to implore him, but caught herself. Not yet. Instead she reached for her bag and dug around for her toothbrush.

Thankfully, neither on the way to the bathroom nor on the way back did she bump into any of his flatmates, all of whom were startlingly socially inept. She loathed squeezing past them in the corridor, feeling their eyes on her. In the bathroom she tugged at the grimy light switch string, pushed the door shut and locked the wobbly bolt with relief. The room itself was brutally bright because no one had yet bothered to put a lampshade over the bulb dangling from the ceiling. A yellow pebble of old soap offered itself at the sink, a tube of encrusted toothpaste and some lonely toothbrushes loitered nearby, and the shower, with its limescale-encrusted floor and mean trickle, forced her to stand with a reluctant, tiptoeing shiver, hugging herself as she thought it was a good thing she loved him because she wouldn't do this for anyone else. She daubed toothpaste on her brush, stared solemnly at herself through the smeary mirror as she cleaned her teeth, and remembered looking at herself in the same way a month or so ago. Alek had been reading a big book on the history of some political movement or other, while she'd been pawing at him in a way she thought was cute and comely and quite un-Rose-like, except in the most intimate of circumstances, and he'd eventually berated her, not even turning around, *Rose, will you stop it. Not everything's about sex, you know.*

She had left, angry, and gone to the bathroom and stared at herself. She thought of the hours she put in at the meetings, the years she'd spent reading and studying, the fact that if he asked –

if he would even ask – she had so much to say. It wasn't as if he didn't know that, either. She thought, *I'm too overwhelmed by the enormity and greatness of your cock to think about anything else.* She had returned, slept; life had continued.

Back in his room now, he was still on his laptop. She undressed slowly, hoping he'd sense the hovering fact of her nakedness and maybe at least they could have sex, but he didn't move. She plugged in her phone and checked for messages. There was one from Van, saying he, Los and Tonde were out for a drink if she wanted to join them. She started to respond but couldn't quite muster the energy. She looked over to Alek. A conciliatory word or two came to her but then she thought: *Why should I?* He was the one in the wrong. He had betrayed the group, made politics lofty and inaccessible, something only those clever-clogs academics could tell them. It was difficult to hold onto this belief with any conviction, though – even as she crawled under the duvet, her first thought was that she wanted him to join her. But maybe this was only a reflex; she listened instead to the part of herself that felt a new sensation: that on some level, she couldn't care less whether or not he did – she couldn't care less about anything. In fact, maybe she *could* have got up and left, and the only reason she hadn't was because she was tired – and here was a warm bed, and here was sleep.

The next morning, she made a new rule, a secret one. Just for the day, she and Alek weren't going to talk about politics. Steering him away would be tough, though. He was *always* talking about politics – telling her what he'd been reading (though he hadn't mentioned *Utophilia*) or about ideas or events he'd been turning over in his mind. But she wanted to see what would happen, just once, if she pretended they were a normal couple, not always geared towards protest and fight and the world outside, and above all, not fighting each other about what they were going to fight.

She was also still going over their argument last night, wondering if she'd been overly judgemental. Who wasn't allowed to get frustrated, now and then? Alek was smart and committed and doing great things – so what if he occasionally let off steam? But she couldn't shake the fact that he was revealing, more and more, the hard bright light of his ambition, and that this made her uncomfortable, reminded her she did not like such ego and self-regard in anyone. She was also aware that when he turned this same bright beam, this intense focus, onto her, it felt great. She desired it while knowing he didn't need the same thing from her at all.

She lay on the bed, light speckling in from the narrow, dusty windows, and assessed him further – his ego, his soul. He had moved something in her that had been stuck for far too long – through all those years of being a waitress, and seeing her father die, her friends sacked and Lal run off to Mejira. What had once been hot snarling snakes in her stomach were now more like sparks leaping outwards, lighting the universe beyond her body. This was how it felt to redirect your turmoil beyond yourself; to see your struggle in others, to find that they struggled too, to listen and empathise, and to want to help. *This* was the feeling she wanted. But now the problem was she didn't quite trust it – or more accurately, she didn't quite trust him.

She headed to the kitchen, thankful the coast was still clear. It was unnerving, knowing that at any moment she might encounter one of the dreaded housemates. Her interactions with them always left her feeling bad. They never wanted conversation, as such, but they did expect some sort of acknowledgement beyond 'hello'. They were single men, all older than her, wandering around as if they'd just got out of bed or were searching for or had had a drink. They looked as if they had no one to care for them and couldn't quite manage it themselves. This was presumptuous of her, but she would feel them watching her sadly and know it was true.

Like the rest of the place, the kitchen was large, neglected and dirty. Paint was flaking off cupboard doors, the sink taps and drain were ringed in rust, the oven, which she doubted had ever been cleaned, was home to a thick substrate of burnt-on, forgotten food, and sticky crumbs gathered and greened in the fridge corners. Once or twice Rose had been overcome with the urge to scrub it (and then, presumably, the bathroom, too), and to let the housemates walk in, be knocked out by the vicious smell of cleaning products, fall to the floor and beg forgiveness. But she was suspicious of her instinct to clean, because it unearthed a part of her that wanted to nest with Alek, take him away from this dismal place and make a home for him – which troubled her, because she wasn't sure he deserved it.

She opened a cupboard and pulled out a frying pan, found silk noodles, lizardfruit and saucer flowers, all of which she had bought herself. She chopped the fruit, plucked the leaves off the flowers and fried them in grass oil until they wilted, soaked the noodles in water until they billowed, then dropped them into the pan, breathing in the scent while watching them turn iridescent as they soaked up the fruit and flowers. It was the kind of breakfast they had when they were children – a classic, nothing special – and yet little tasted better.

One of the housemates appeared just as she was about to serve it up. He wore a white vest and tracksuit bottoms and was barefoot. He was younger than the others, with a shaved head, a delicate face and an inquisitive look. He helped himself to a glass of water and his eyes moved hungrily to the frying pan.

'That smells good,' he said. Alek had once told her there was a period of three or four months when this guy had only come out of his room once a day. He'd appeared not to have washed his clothes throughout. Alek's tone had been part disgust, part awe.

Not taking his eyes from the pan, he said, 'You wouldn't have any going spare, would you?'

She thought quickly. She could give half to him, half to Alek, and scavenge something else for herself. Or she could say no. She didn't know why she felt indebted – perhaps she felt that the people who lived here should get first dibs on everything and that she should give way when asked. Or perhaps she felt sorry for him, with his forlorn manner, his dark, lonely room. But she could see forward in time to a moment when she would be making breakfast for them all.

'I'm sorry,' she said. 'Not really.'

His eyes flashed with an old hurt, but he quickly covered it with a smile. 'Course not. You enjoy that, now.' He turned and retreated, clutching his water.

She stared at the noodles. Was she wrong not to give him any? She was protecting Alek's interests over those of someone with significantly less, and something about this struck her as shameful. But this was ridiculous – it was only noodles, and she'd made it for him. As she carried the steaming bowls down the hallway, though, her chest went tight with nerves.

Back in the bedroom, he was awake, staring at the ceiling.

'I made breakfast.' She dipped the bowls to show him and passed one over. As she slid back into bed, her mind went unexpectedly to Beve, her ex. He had often made breakfast for her, but instead of eating it they used to put it on the bedside table and let it get cold while they had sex. But Alek had already pushed himself up and started eating, so she did, too. For a while, the only sounds were those of forks hitting the bowl, the slurp of noodles. She considered whether without thinking or talking about politics she would just shuttle all day between wanting food and wanting sex, and he would quickly despise her primitive ways.

'You might be right,' he said finally. 'I should have told you I was inviting them.'

That wasn't what she had said.

Outside, it began to rain. Alek's bed was in the corner next to the window, and one side of it pressed up against the glass, so when it rained it was loud and distracting, and comforting, too, because you were right next to it but warm and dry. The lizardfruit slid against her tongue, vinegary and sweet.

'I used to eat this when I was growing up,' she said, keen to push the conversation on. 'It makes me feel like I'm young again.'

'We ate porridge.'

'Did you?' She'd thought he came from a rich family.

'Yeah. Our nenna said it would make us strong – and my parents didn't care either way – so yeah, porridge all my childhood.'

She had no idea he'd had a nenna – the kind of live-in childcare that was only available to the wealthy.

'Ironically, I'm not that strong, though, right?'

'You're mentally strong.'

He smiled, wolfish and pleased.

She wanted to ask more about his childhood, but he was always circumspect – this was the first time she'd heard about a nenna, for example. When she did draw anything out of him about his parents, she gathered that they were a source of unhappiness, his father stern and demanding, his mother a distant, disinterested background figure. It felt like he simply didn't want to think about them. His father did something mysterious connected to the Iolran government, but Alek would answer questions reluctantly, or not at all. Once, near the beginning of their relationship, she pushed him, joking that if his father was a government man, perhaps his rebellious streak was a reaction to that.

Don't you dare psychoanalyse me, he'd told her with a tight smile. She remembered being impressed that he'd smiled, because it showed he had a sense of humour about himself. Later she told Lal that she'd said his entire political stance was a prolonged fuck-you to his father.

Lal had groaned. 'I bet he didn't like that.'

'Why not?'

'Because by the sounds of him, it's true.'

'Oh, come on.'

'I don't know. People want to think they're complicated and fascinating and have valid reasons for doing things. They don't want to find out that the truth is much simpler; they're just reacting to something that happened to them a long time ago.'

Rose inhaled. 'Wow.'

Rose was pretty much the only person Lal spoke to like that, and Lal insisted it was because Rose brought it out of her. In any case, while it stung that Lal said it with such certainty, she had a point – and it hadn't been Rose's intention to undermine Alek. She didn't want to make him feel small, and she didn't want to *see* him reduced, either. And she certainly didn't want to boil him down to a set of psychological clichés – in fact, she'd rather not believe such a thing were possible. But the problem was, while his reticence allowed him to remain a bit of an enigma, it also lent itself to these flippant, reductive guesses. So in a way, it was in his interest to tell her more.

He rarely asked about her in return, though, and while she volunteered information, he remained fundamentally incurious. She told herself this was because he was able to read her through other means – through sex, for example, or the very fact of her physical self. This was flattering, because she liked the idea that she could be seen so emphatically as a sexual or physical being, but at the same time it saddened her, too, as it was just a story in her head. It might be that he was genuinely indifferent – and in which case, it was even more evidence that she probably shouldn't be there.

He put his empty bowl on the windowsill and stretched. Rose had lost her appetite. She dug her fork deep into her bowl and found she still wanted to apologise for the previous night. The impulse was driving her mad; she knew she didn't have to, and yet—

'I'll tell you next time,' he said. 'About the meeting, I mean. Maybe I need someone to do communications – to let people know what's going on, keep everyone informed.'

'That's not—'

'Yeah, I should set up a regular email, I guess. I don't know – how do you think we could reach people?'

'How do I think you could?' She felt a snap. 'You mean the kind of people who come to our meetings already, or people like the *Utophilia* editors? Because I don't know anyone like that.'

He had the decency to look embarrassed. 'Everyone.'

'Well, people know that it's nine o'clock every Friday night, at the same place. If you've got guests, maybe tell us the week before. Or, no, if you have guests in mind – if *anyone* does – we could discuss between us whether we want them to come.'

His expression changed. 'All right, sorry. I was trying to bring some actual brains to the meeting. It doesn't help if you're criticising me.'

'I'm just saying the others might want some input. It could be good to get their feedback.'

He looked pained. 'They don't know anything!'

'You can't actually mean that.'

'Look, I went to the *Utophilia Volume Four* launch party—'

'What are you *talking* about?'

He paused, and she sighed, frustrated. The rule she'd made less than an hour ago had already been broken – the conversation had gone a way that felt inevitable. The rain beat down harder and he moved close so their shoulders touched in a way that felt companionable, and she reminded herself that at least he had vision, at least he cared, and they were talking about things that mattered – wasn't that what she wanted? With Beve, who she'd met when they were off their faces at a beach party, she'd just have been listening to repetitive beat music by now, staring despairingly into space.

'These guys,' he said, 'they're on the level. They're putting a lot of time and energy into aut politics.'

At the mention of aut politics, she suddenly remembered what she'd told herself not to forget: *freedom*. Of course. Alek's vision of source gain was just not good enough, not free enough. Even if the auts were doing all the work and humans lived off their source gain income, people would *still* be dependent on wherever that money came from. There had to be something better than that. All things considered, though, she wasn't going to bring it up with him right now.

'I do care, you know, about the group,' he said. 'I wouldn't be doing all this if I didn't.'

'I know.'

He looked at her with a sad half-smile then reached over her, grabbing his phone from the bedside table. She thought for a while then kissed him on his warm collarbone, just by the edge of his T-shirt, and again beneath his ear. He lifted a hand to move her chin into the hollow by his shoulder and continued to scroll through the news. He whizzed past a picture, a headshot of a man. The face was familiar.

'What's that?'

'What?'

'Go up again.'

'It's about those auts that got smashed yesterday. I don't want to read about those idiots.'

She thought quickly. He saw aut smashers as juvenile, getting in the way of serious politics. 'Yeah, of course. Sorry.'

He gave a confused frown and turned back to his phone. Her heart had started to beat so fast she thought it might explode. But she couldn't let him know, couldn't say a thing, so she remained still and tried to block out her sudden alarm with the warmth of his body and the sound of the rain.

'You're in the way,' Naji said, swatting at Rose's legs, frowning, his eyes on the screen. He was lying on the living-room sofa watching Yash play a video game.

She deflected the swat. 'Naji!'

'That's right! Get him!' he told Yash, who sat cross-legged, closer to the screen. He did not move his eyes from the action playing out before him – cannons firing, screams, a river filling with scarlet blood.

Rose leaned in, more insistent. 'Naji!' He glanced at her, looked away. 'Fuck,' she said and tried to shove his feet out of the way so she could sit down, but this was difficult and she ended up sitting mostly on them.

'Ahh, Rose—' He made a face, pulled them away, defensively clutched his closest ankle, and turned back to the screen.

'Naji, I saw it. Your friend, that guy Cassu – I saw him in the news. What's going on?'

He wouldn't look at her, so she repeated herself more loudly. Finally his eyes met hers and he shook his head. 'It's a good thing.'

'What do you mean?'

'It's good. That's it.'

'That's it?'

He turned back to the screen and nodded sharply.

'Why are you here?'

'I'm hanging out with Yash.' Noises from the computer game popped around them: rapid gunfire, a man booming, 'Kill him!' Naji was tense, as though he'd jump if Rose got any nearer.

She shook her head and looked at him as he blankly watched the screen. Quietly, so Yash couldn't hear, she hissed, 'Are you part of it?' When she got no response, she said loudly, 'Naji! *Are you part of it?*'

He heard the violence in her voice. He turned again and said, point-blank, 'No.'

'You know them, though?' His attention had gone straight back to the game. 'You know them?' She began to hammer and push at his legs. 'Tell me!'

'Hey,' yelled Yash. 'Please!'

Rose hit Naji hard on the calf. 'Fucking tell me.' She stared at him.

Naji held his calf and looked at her, unrepentant. He closed his eyes and tipped his head back for a minute, blinked, inhaled and pulled himself up so he was next to her. 'Look, it's better for you if you don't know. Anyway, I've got nothing to say – I don't know anything either.' He looked at her a fraction of a second too long and she understood: he was protecting her. He sank back into the sofa and fixed his eyes again on the screen. She glanced at it. Yash was a giant zombie woman, her beautifully sculpted arm balancing a bow and arrow as she strode through a castle.

She turned back to Naji. Softly, she said again, 'It *is* you.'

He shook his head, staring at the screen. She bristled, furious. Then he turned, locked eyes with her, and said, 'And you, too, if you want.'

'What do you mean?'

He pushed her away and got up. 'Don't stop, kill everyone,' he told Yash, pointing. Yash only played these computer games when Naji was there – his role as an older brother seemed predominantly to be to stoke his bloodlust.

Rose followed him into the kitchen, where he was gathering ingredients from the fridge.

'You're welcome to join us,' he said.

'It's illegal?'

He shrugged. 'They're not alive, they're just auts.'

'And if you get caught?'

'I get caught. Don't you see how important this is? *Fuck* those auts.'

She saw an unfamiliar venom spring into his eyes and remembered how she'd felt when the Popotops aut was smashed: a surging excitement, a sense of justice. But she was too shocked to tell him this. He turned as though he'd said his piece, and put some bread on a chopping board.

'But Naj, you're a union rep – you can't smash auts.'

He ignored her, deeply involved in assessing how chunkily to cut his slices.

'Naj, seriously – what would Dad say?'

Naji put the knife down. 'What would Dad say?' He gave her a strange look. 'I don't think Dad would have a leg to stand on.'

Rose could hear a woman saying, 'Game over, game over,' from the living room. 'What do you mean?'

Naji looked as though he was giving this due consideration. 'You know what?' he said. 'Let's not talk about it.'

'No, wait – tell me what you mean.'

'No.'

This felt like a reproach, a way to put her back in her place, but as she stood watching him she felt something crack open inside. She wanted to know – she was done with being kept in the dark. She wondered how she'd not already guessed he was smashing auts. And now she wanted to know about other things, too – about the arguments her parents used to have when she was younger. About her mum's keeping of secrets and withholding of anger, the tension in her face because of it. About her dad entertaining those fat, loud men in suits at their old house, men who smiled at her, so she kept out of their way – and the way her dad acted around them, cowed, needing to please, a little desperate. She went over to the window and looked out at the block opposite.

'Just tell me one thing. Just one.'

'Look,' he glanced towards the living room, 'this isn't—'

'No one even talks about him any more,' she said, coming towards him. 'No one says anything. I just want to *talk*.'

'Okay, fine.' Naji held his hands up. 'I'll tell you one thing. You really want to know?'

'Yes!'

Naji sighed. 'Fuck. Okay. Fine. You're going to get upset, though.'

'Just tell me.'

'All right – do you want to know why you moved to this flat?'

'Because we couldn't afford to rent the house once Dad died.'

'Not exactly. The guy who turned that land into luxury flats – the one who tore down the shithole next door, rehoused the neighbours who knows where – you know what deal he made with Dad? 'Cause port management had a connection to this guy, and Dad was protected by port management? While everyone else was going to get kicked out, we were going to have one of those flats. Screw everyone else, we've got ours.'

'Okay.'

'Okay?' He shrugged. 'I mean, it would have been good for Mum. You'd have hated it. But anyway, after Dad died, the developer pulled the deal, as there was still going to be a mortgage on it that Mum couldn't pay, and that's why you now live in fuck knows where. Closer to me, but fuck knows where.'

He squeezed a spiral of ketchup onto the floppy pink meat in his sandwich and began to cut chunks of cheese to put on top. He was going to spread mayonnaise on top of that and eat it like a protein bar.

'Okay, that's bad, but it's not the worst thing in the world.'

'It's probably equal to smashing auts.'

'Naji! Come on, I want to know more.'

'You know, I don't think this is the smartest conversation. You're upset with me anyway—'

'No, I'm not. Tell me more.'

'Rose.'

'Come on.'

Naji hesitated, but she could see there was something in him that wanted to.

'Okay, one more.'

'But there are lots?'

'I'll tell you this.'

'No, tell me everything.'

'I'll tell you this. You're probably too young to remember – but when we were growing up, we hung out a lot with Dad's colleague Buscos and his family. They had that kid with the glasses who'd talk so quietly you always used to say, "I can't hear you? I can't hear you"?'

Rose shook her head, impatient.

'There was a strike Dad and Buscos organised at one point.' He got a plate from the cupboard and sighed. 'And the management – these sadists who let Dad run around town being a hero while keeping him on a string, like a puppet – they took Dad aside and said we'll listen to your strike demands – not even agree to them, just *listen* to them – but Buscos loses his job. That's the deal.'

'And the alternative was . . . they stopped striking?'

'Right. What does Dad do? He let Buscos get fired, because it meant a small win for him.'

'But wait – wasn't he trying to do his best for the workers?'

'They were old friends, Rose – we never saw that glasses kid after that. Dad screwed Buscos big time.'

Rose held up her hands in an attempt at protest. 'But that's not a cut-and-dried—'

'He also cheated on Mum.'

'The fuck?' she screamed. 'I don't wanna hear this!'

'He was also convinced she was cheating on him, so he made her get a paternity test for Yash.'

'Shush, shut up, shut the fuck up—'

'I'm done. I'm *done*.'

She turned to the window, to the neighbours' flats in the rain. She didn't want to know any of this – there was no part of her that could handle it. An enormous disappointment sloughed through her and she felt helpless and betrayed, even though she'd asked for it – even though she must have known, in the deepest, smallest part of herself, that something like this was coming.

'Rose, there were good sides to him, too. C'mon, I had the worst relationship with him out of all of us kids and I can say that.'

Rose motioned towards Yash in the living room. 'He had it harder. We all had it hard.'

Naji shrugged. 'Mum most of all.'

She walked out. She'd heard enough. There was nowhere to go, though – there never was, except her own tiny bedroom, her own sliver of peace, so she shut the door and fell onto her bed. In a short while she heard her brothers talking in the living room, Naji's laugh not quite authentic, as if he too had been thrown by their conversation and was putting on a show of being fine for Yash.

Her mother would be home from work soon. Rose could turn her anger on her, shout for explanations – why had no one ever told her, why had they let her idolise him for so long? But she didn't want to – she didn't, in fact, want to think about any of it at all.

12

The plane left Ulrusa at four o'clock, soaring north over the river valley, its curves of water glinting in the sun. Janetta stared until she could no longer see land. Next to her, Malin had stuck her headphones on and closed her eyes. Janetta started to work on her thesis, couldn't face it, decided to stare into space instead. They began to descend at dusk. The immense tree canopy of the Skrevet Valley appeared first and then the Forol range chainsawing the sky behind it, its shadows spiked from top to bottom with golden light, tiny outposts in the darkness. Malin had woken up and was hunched against Janetta to gawp at the view.

'I've never seen anything like it.'

Janetta hadn't either. It was far too beautiful. She wasn't sure she could work in such conditions.

Forol Airport was tiny, a constellation of huts linked to one another by outdoor walkways lined with screwpine and white-backed palm. Janetta reached out to touch one, inhaled the mountain air. The coach to town took two bumpy, winding hours, and as soon as they'd dropped their stuff in the hostel they ventured out to find dinner. Nowhere along the steep dark streets was open, except for one place which was noisy, bright and touristy, and another, at the very western edge of town – a small, unprepossessing café with the mountainside looming up blackly behind it. Its menu had one option – labhrai, the regional dish – black beans, mushrooms, and warm, gingery spices, and one choice of alcohol, haza – the infamous local wine.

Malin summoned a half-bottle of haza and made quick headway. As she did, a familiar gleam came into her eye, the one that suggested she could have anything she wanted, that the whole world lay in wait. Sober Janetta felt suddenly dispirited. The plan was that Malin would spend the second week here on a meditation retreat in the mountains, while she would work on her dissertation. Despite her elation at being there, she already sensed she was going to have more trouble than she had anticipated attempting to work away from the Institute. And besides, there was the immovable, insistent fact of Taly, who a month earlier had accepted her declaration of regret in a way that was understandably brisk and defensive. It can't have been pleasant to have been told by someone that they regretted sleeping with you, especially since she had hardly been able to explain to her that the problem was that she'd wanted more from her, not less.

A few days later, though, she'd been in touch, guarded but amenable, inviting her to an exhibition on the occult in the High Cabakan period. Janetta wasn't the least bit interested, but couldn't have been more relieved and rushed across town to meet her. They went around it painstakingly slowly, Taly pouring over manuscript pages with illegible calligraphy, cryptic symbols and strange drawings of long-limbed, ashen-faced people Janetta thought creepy and unancestral. Taly said that the High Cabakan occultists only had themselves to blame for their eventual exile – they were too stubborn, she said, to play the political games they needed to survive. Janetta had nodded, ashamed that she wanted to apologise to Taly more than she wanted to find it in her to care about High

Cabakan politics, but finally, as they headed down the exit steps and there were no more educational distractions, she did. Taly said it was okay, and Janetta felt absolved.

Since then they'd been on a few more dates, coffees and dinners, where Taly expounded upon her thoughts and theories and Janetta had looked on, amazed by her confidence and erudition. But their meet-ups were infrequent and Taly disappeared between them, and during these times Janetta yearned for her. She'd not experienced this before, even for Malin, and it made her feel light-headed, unfamiliar to herself, stunned by her depth of feeling.

'Are you seeing anyone?' she asked Malin now, in the café.

'Do you really want to talk about this? Do you not just want to enjoy' – Malin waved her arms about – 'how bright the stars are, how strong this booze is . . . ?'

Janetta ignored her, conjuring up Taly's thin, serious face. 'It's okay.'

Uneasily, Malin told her about the three people she'd been seeing since they broke up. Three! There was a dark-haired singer, who was almost forty, a woman around Janetta's age who had lost her job in Mejira and come back home to her parents in Ulrusa – Malin thought she was going to try to leave again, though – and a man who she used to work with, but she wasn't that interested in him.

Wordlessly, Janetta registered all this. She was stung, but so briefly it felt like Taly was a talismanic protection from hurt. What would have caused immeasurable pain a few weeks ago could now be borne, even if Malin's typically excessive nature was galling – though at least she was getting what she wanted.

Malin was studying her carefully. 'Are you okay?'

Janetta, sensing pity, said, 'I'm fine. In fact, I've met someone, too.'

'Oh?'

The dark, candlelit terrace where they sat alone encouraged confession and Janetta couldn't help it: she divulged that she already had strong feelings for Taly. 'We've got so much in common, and she's so intelligent. She's like a dream. I mean, you were, too, but she's a different kind of dream.'

Malin clutched her wine protectively, looking unimpressed. 'Would I get on with her?'

'Hmm . . . there's something about her that' – Janetta considered it – 'you might find a bit, well – you're so warm. She's . . . *different*.'

'She's not warm?'

'She's extremely successful, so it's not . . . her priority.'

'Because she's successful?'

'Not everyone has to be warm, okay? Not everyone needs to radiate.'

Malin looked momentarily mollified, accepting the backhanded compliment, and then she focused again. 'Well then, is she at least nice?'

'Um . . . yes.' Janetta sensed this little dig around into Taly's personality was spurred on by jealousy, which pleased her. Finally, a glimmer of equality.

'Show me a picture.'

Janetta obliged with the prettiest picture she could find.

'Not bad,' said Malin. 'Looks a bit tired, though.' She handed the phone back to Janetta, grinning. 'Anyway, should you really be falling in love?'

'Should I–?'

'What about work?'

'Work?'

'I'm trying to say that your work means everything to you, and if you let yourself get distracted by some not-warm woman–'

Janetta said, her voice low, 'I'm allowed to fall in love.'

'Of course, do what you want. I just don't want you to lose focus.'

'Right.' She considered this. 'Well, thanks. I suspect I can cope.'

As they walked back to the guesthouse, Malin engaged in a lengthy bout of messaging one of her own new lovers – she admitted it was Jasmine, the older one. Jasmine was on a strict diet, apparently, and was telling Malin about the consequences of eating only cruciferous vegetables for two weeks, which Malin, glued to her screen, obviously found fascinating. Janetta kept a short distance in front, without envy. She might like to be messaging Taly just as intently, but that wasn't the way they were – they were not effusive, and that was fine. She thought instead about being in Skrevet, so far away and so different, and wrapped her scarf around her neck and walked on, gazing at the mountains and the stars, which were indeed far brighter than those at home.

For the next few days, Janetta abandoned her Ph.D. and they roamed around Forol. There were other towns in the valley, but this was where the tourist money had collected, where the luxury hotels and incongruously chic restaurants were. It had a good backstory, too: in the seventh century, a tribe of wandering Cabakans had received visions to head there and meditate in the lowlands for as long as it took them to glimpse their sacred home; they then hacked their way up through the mountainous forest until they reached a plateau that had views over the whole valley and, in the distance, the vast grey of the Alti Sea. As they stood there they felt they were scratching the base of heaven. It was there they settled, building a monastery, parts of which still remained, while the town below became a trading post. In later centuries, rich people in poor health visited Forol to replenish themselves in its apparently sacred air. In recent decades, serious hikers had joined their more languid counterparts, as well as hippies seeking respite from modern life in the archaic simplicities of Cabakan routine, tasters of which were offered up at the various meditation retreats, consisting as it did of quiet contemplation, gardening, and rearing generation after generation of unnervingly placid farm animals.

Janetta and Malin went on a few short hikes in the foothills, including one to the monastery where Malin would be doing her meditation course. Janetta was a natural hiker, walking determinedly, ever onwards, ever upwards. Malin was enthusiastic enough, but liked to stop for a cigarette now and then. They got on very well. It was almost as if no one had left, nothing had been broken – except now there was this, something new from the rubble. Janetta had missed Malin's garrulousness, her habit of talking about musicians and poets and writers, and quoting the best lines from films, the ones that always made her laugh, though Janetta would never have remembered them herself and had only seen the films in the first place because Malin had made her. Whoever spent a lifetime with her would have this – the astonishing, relentless recall for poetry, stories, films and quotes – and Janetta wondered who it might be now, instead of her.

They reached the monastery in the early afternoon; it was a long, low building of wood and brick, with a colourful sign planted in the earth outside that said *Eriaba Cabak Monastery: Please be respectful*.

'Please be respectful, Malin,' Janetta said.

Malin laughed. 'Always.'

Although it wasn't that high up, and still a good few hours' walk from the remains of the original Cabakan monastery, its view across the mountains and the valley was spectacular, a quilt of sunlit green.

'If a week's silent meditation means looking at that view, it might be okay.'

'I think if we face that way, they put a curtain down to cover it.'

'They do? What a waste.'

They were meant to go inside, but Malin was taking photos, jabbing at her phone.

'Malin?'

Malin ignored her, still tapping her phone. 'Just sending Jasmine the view.'

Janetta shook her head and walked towards the entrance. It was obvious Malin was more serious about this one of the three than she'd let on. There'd been an urgency in her face as she typed her message (which would presumably make no mention that her ex was standing there, waiting for her to finish). She thought about how Malin had been like that with her too, at first. She wasn't upset, though. Instead she allowed herself a flight of fancy in which she and Taly belied their restrained personalities to message one another compulsively every day while she was here, too. It was an intoxicating thought.

Malin caught up with her as she was pushing open the large oak door. At the desk a young woman with a shaved head, blue monk's robe and slightly dopey, widely spaced eyes bowed her head and lay her palms flat in greeting. Janetta did, too, but Malin just asked, smiling flirtatiously, if they could take a look around, because they were coming here to do a course and wanted to see what it was like.

'Of course,' said the woman warmly, 'but there's not much to see.'

As they walked away Janetta waited for it.

Malin exhaled. 'She was *gorgeous*!'

Janetta smiled. Just ahead was the meditation hall – she

opened the door and they went inside. It was nothing like she had expected. It was wood-framed, large and long, and at the end the windows ran from the ceiling to the floor, all the way across, and looked, after all, over that spilling green landscape below. The sun pooled where they stood, and amid the light and the shadow and the view, she sensed something ineffable. She felt herself dematerialise, turn into mere elements, and couldn't recall when she had felt like this before. Unexpectedly, then, she felt gratitude for her family, their presence as solid as the valley itself, and she wanted them to know that she was grateful for everything they'd done for her to be here, up in the mountains, in this warm, bright room.

Malin was at the window, looking out. 'This is really something.'

As they left, Janetta lingered, considered spending a week in this room, too – she liked how it made her feel. But she said nothing, not then, not when they said thank you to the woman at the desk, with Malin on full flirt mode, or when they walked around the gardens, or when they took a look at the back of the building so Malin could see what the accommodation was like. She didn't mention it on the way back down the trail, either – she had a dissertation to finish.

The night before Malin left, they went to a restaurant that served Skrevet specialities and got drunk. Malin believed it obligatory to turn up to a week's retreat with a hangover, and Janetta, facing solitude in a strange town, was willing to oblige. The restaurant was nearly empty. It was sparsely furnished, with prayer flags and paintings of the valley on the walls, and the food – plain, heavy dumplings with a mean portion of labhrai – was disappointing even to her, who usually couldn't care less about food – but it meant they could at least commit to their aim. Between swigs of beer, Malin vociferously complained about a documentary she had seen, about a band called The Gang, who Janetta knew Lal liked.

'These men, doing anything they wanted, their whole lives playing around – with guitars, drugs, sex, hailed as geniuses – and where were the women? They were invisible! They were at home, or they were groupies, or they were nothing—'

Janetta rested her head on her hand. 'This is a good point. I've never thought about how auts might understand music – I can't believe it. Such an oversight. I'd better run some simulations tonight.'

'Oh, Jay, just enjoy yourself!'

'No, no . . . I want auts to be able to understand music. That's a shameful oversight.'

Malin rolled her eyes, drained her beer.

They left once Malin had declared herself sufficiently drunk. Outside, the trees waved choppily around them, auguring rain. Malin had no jacket. She wore billowing green silk trousers, a loose cream blouse and a ruby scarf around her neck. She had no make-up on, her hair was wildly tangled and as they walked, she sang softly to herself, her eyes gleaming in the dark.

At one point she stopped singing and looked over at Janetta. 'This is okay, isn't it?'

'Yes, it is.'

In the hostel, they hugged goodnight in the corridor and went to their separate rooms. Janetta made some coffee and began, woozy but strangely content, to work.

She woke the next morning to a reverberating silence. Malin was gone. She would have left at dawn and trekked up the mountain hung-over. Janetta checked her phone and saw two new messages –

the first from Malin, outraged at the hour-long hike, the hour of day, the awaiting steepness. The second was Malin outraged she was having to hand over her phone to the monks. She had typed – clearly frantically, as it was riddled with errors (Janetta imagined a monk watching unimpressed as she hastily bashed out this final communiqué) – that her hangover was killing her, she'd made a terrible decision, and if she thought about it, she regretted every choice she'd ever made in her life that had led up to this moment. Janetta typed back that this was the price you paid in order to become an ascended being. Malin would only receive this heartening reply at the end of the week, though, so of course as consolation it was entirely useless. Janetta rolled out of bed, immensely relieved now that she wasn't stuck on a silent meditation course, and set off to find breakfast.

Being alone in a different part of the country was a new experience, one she was tentatively enjoying. Unfamiliarity was reconfiguring her horizons moment by moment, allowing her to perceive the infinitude of the world not just intellectually but viscerally; every step meant breaking new ground, and this fascinated her. It also gave her a sense of freedom, strengthened by glorious anonymity. She spent her first morning alone, eating breakfast at a café down the road from the hostel, savouring the local bread and Skrevet eggs, reading Taly's book, *TechnoMutations*, at last, and people-watching. The tourists, their skin luxuriant with health, their clothes crisp and well-fitting, strode blithely past as weary, bright-eyed locals wove around them, staggering under baskets of food or pulling suitcases or crates of drinks along behind them. Occasionally a monk would glide by, stately and unperturbed in cobalt robes. The three groups were reliant on each other – the tourists came for the monks, their money enabling their continued existence, and the locals provided the bridge between the two. Yet on the pavements they were oblivious to one another, as if they occupied separate worlds.

For a while it satisfied Janetta to watch these three streams interweave. The monks were by far the most interesting, with their serene, unruffled faces, the way they vigilantly eschewed eye contact. In their beauty they seemed more at peace with themselves than either the unslakable tourists or, understandably, the careworn locals.

Janetta had once, in her early thoughts on AI consciousness, thought long and hard about creating a conscious AI with the base programming of a Cabakan monk – that was to say, an enlightened psyche, one as untroubled as the stillest lake. She had run simulations, and realised that it wouldn't work: there had to be flaws and lack too, in the base programming – not too many, but you needed it not only to be wise, compassionate, and forgiving – it also had to have the capacity to be fallible, weak and wrong. This had ultimately proved a better way of training artificial emotional intelligence, as though the strengths were more fully realised for the presence of the flaws. The end point could be a Cabakan, or close to it, but you couldn't *start* there – you had to have the AI evolve itself towards it.

Across the street just then a young monk stood still for a moment, gathered her robes, and re-knotted her long, thick rope belt. She looked up and blinked at Janetta. For a moment they regarded one another, then the monk gave a tiny, astonishing smile and walked on. For a long time Janetta did not move, staring into the empty space left behind.

A while later she roused herself and set off for a walk around Forol. She decided to take the route that went straight through town before circling up towards the base of the mountain. Downtown, she gazed at the dark wooden buildings and colourful market stalls that lined the main streets. Stallholders negotiated nearby with tourists. Incense burners, candle-holders and jewellery glittered in the sun. The clean warmth of sage drifted past. She walked amongst it all absent-mindedly, dipping in and out of concentration. Her mind had settled itself on a single, shameful activity: daydreams about Taly, syrupy with romance and blurred with sex.

She continued towards the foot of the mountain, past the expensive hotels that looked out both over the distant peaks and down towards the valley. The base itself was a busy crossroads, and she stepped through the milling crowd of tourists negotiating with taxi drivers to take them up the mountain, and scores of more serious hikers, grouped together, frowning over routes and logistics. She gazed up one of the paths that wound away to the right, arched by trees, and wondered how Malin was doing.

At the bottom of the western slope was a clutch of youth hostels. Janetta returned to hers, retrieved her laptop from her room, made herself a tea and went to the front terrace. A gang of hippyish teenagers were sprawled together on its deep, comfortable sofas, laughing and watching a movie. She turned away from them towards a corner table that looked out to the hostel across the street and opened her laptop.

She had returned to running simulations for negative emotions. She had spent a long time doing this, mapping feelings like grief, anger and loneliness, but it was a thankless task, because each time she revisited them they required even more complexity and nuance. Also, she wanted to get on with her consciousness research. She had an idea for it, a secret inkling, that she was desperate to explore.

What she wanted to do most, though, more than either of these things, was email Taly. Any reason would do, and she had

202

a good one. The chapter in *TechnoMutations* she was reading was about de-extinction, the idea that you could bring extinct species back to life using selective breeding. Taly wrote, albeit in an admittedly stilted way, about bringing back extinct species of lions, leopards, rhinos, fish, even snails. Her point was about ecological complexity: de-extinction enabled greater complexity, and in their gleeful, experimental way, so did Mutants' own AI species. Janetta didn't disagree. What she thought was strange, though, and wanted to ask Taly about, was the fact that when she wrote her long disquisition about the de-extinction of the Therosian Cloud Leopard, native to northeastern Iolra, not enormously far from where she was now, she explained how it would be exactly the same as its forebear, mirroring its characteristics and traits down to the timbre of its snarl, the scalpel sharpness of its retractable claws. And when she wrote about her invention of Mutants' own AI birds, she emphasised how adding heretofore unfathomable traits – in this case, varieties of birdsong, warbling abilities, range of notes hit – was an exciting and radical way that AI could contribute to ecological complexity. Taly concluded that by way of not only the replication but the addition of traits, AI had much to offer de-extinction.

Janetta was thinking about Mutants' docile dog being made with IOLDAR. She wanted to know, since Taly didn't address it in the book, what Taly thought of making AI species where the complexity had been reduced, where some of the animal's key traits had been eliminated. She thought about what Penelope Zger had said – how there needed to be an agreed framework in place for conscious AI so that it didn't destroy humankind – and wondered if this could relate to AI animals as well, where the choice of traits that were kept or elaborated on had to conform to some kind of ethical framework, too.

She took a sip of tea, swiped away a mosquito, opened her email and felt a buzz of hope just typing in Taly's email address. Something in her released and she found herself needing to tell Taly everything, find a thousand ways to reach out. She wrote about Forol, describing what she'd seen there – the monasteries, the tourists, the hikers, hippy travellers and the monks themselves. She wrote her thoughts about complexity as if she were in discussion with *TechnoMutations*, ensuring her wording was diplomatic and respectful. She wrote so much that she couldn't then be bothered to do any work, so she shoved her laptop in her bag and went back to her room.

There she put on her bedside lamp, lay on her bed and opened up *TechnoMutations* again, delighted to keep crawling around inside Taly's brain. She wanted to know every corner of it, every twist and turn. It had to be admitted, though, as she gave in to a yawn, that Taly's writing style was actually quite dry, and the next thing she knew, her head was resting on the book and she had closed her eyes. She dreamed about having energetic sex with Taly on one of the terrace sofas outside while a blockbuster movie played in the background. This was distinctly more fun than *TechnoMutations*.

When she awoke, the sky was pulling back its light. Often there was ambient noise in the hostel – the tread of footsteps, the closing of doors, and once, a few nights ago, an interminable retching from the room next door – but now it was silent. The scent of frangipani drifting in through the window was so sweet and strong that she couldn't help but go towards it, standing at the balcony where she could breathe it in as its buds opened in the welcoming night. She watched a grey cat running across the empty street, the only sign of life in the stillness. She felt briefly extremely happy, and thought that she must get on with her work.

She grabbed her keys and backpack and wrapped a scarf around her neck, intending to run out for food. In the mirror by the door she caught sight of herself and was struck by how gaunt she looked, and how alone. She shook this off, went down the street to a nearby café to get some labhrai, and lost her nerve, asking for it to take away so she could have it in her room where she'd feel less exposed. Her intention had been to eat while working, but instead she returned, inevitably, to her waiting email.

As she ate she reread everything she'd written so far, which was thrilling, although it didn't make sense that her own thoughts felt thrilling only when written down for Taly, and not, for example, in her dissertation. She couldn't help it, though, and she edited them again to make them more precise, more elegant. Then, in energetic giddiness, she told Taly her secret theory about AI consciousness. It had been too unformed to tell anyone before, and in any case, she'd never felt the need, but Taly was the only other person in the world who could possibly understand. It would be a shared secret between them, something to bond them irrevocably.

Once she'd sent it, it was too late to do anything else. And something didn't feel quite right either, as if the universe had shifted in the wrong direction and she didn't know how to pull it back. She thought about how she had loved no one for the longest time, and then Malin and now suddenly Taly, and maybe that was it – how far away she was from her old self. She made herself another cup of tea and idly began to map out a scenario in which an AI might feel alone in a place far from home. The result suggested it connect with others and find beauty in the world around it. She frowned. She mapped out a scenario in which the AI additionally happened to be 'profoundly missing someone it barely knew'. The option that presented itself this time, one that she of course had programmed herself, was 'distract itself with a fulfilling work project'. She closed her laptop.

13

Instructions had been issued: come to Rartaur at one a.m., wear dark clothes, gloves, a balaclava. Rose did not have a balaclava. *Don't worry*, Naji had said, *I've got one.*

It made her nervous that he'd said that. It made her more nervous still when he asked if she had a crowbar – why did her brother think she'd have a *crowbar*? He didn't pick up on the astonishment in her voice; instead he told her again not to worry, he had one of those as well.

She wasn't feeling excited as she headed out there on the train. She felt nothing. She sat reading a novel, but each time they rattled into a station, she peered out of the window to see where she was. The signs were lit in the darkness: Ovinyan, Sdgara, Cueke – the places of outer Ulrusa, a world she barely knew. She knew much of the city well now, living in the northwest and visiting Alek in the southeast – but she was heading to the far north, where industry flowered in the foothills, and where she'd had no reason ever to go. In any case, it was so dark outside that she could have been anywhere. The harsh lights of the train carriage only made it harder to see what was out there and she had to look past a mirage of herself, confront her own distorted face in the windows, in order to do so. She didn't bother. The novel was absorbing enough.

At Rartaur North she got off the train along with a handful of others, mostly men, and followed them along the platform to the stairs. She was wearing black jeans, a black hoodie and a bomber jacket; she thought she blended in well. She jogged down the stairs, and catching a man nearby gazing at her, she gave him a hostile glare and kept going. Outside the station she checked around for any more creeps, then got out her phone and clicked on the map. Rartaur was similar to Rornul, down south: it was low-rise with wide roads made for trucks and lorries, but the main road she hit branched off into endless industrial estates, one after the other. Rornul was smaller, its industry packed closer together, its dereliction visible. Rartaur was not dead yet; she saw security guards holed up in small entrance booths as she walked past the estates. She didn't look around much, though, but walked fast – and although she was not easily scared, her stomach roiled with fear.

She had been told to take a dark, tree-lined path down the side of the fourth estate on the left until she hit the end, and this in itself spooked her – it wasn't ideal to be walking along such a path alone in the middle of the night, with no idea where she would end up. She gamely forced herself onwards then down the muddy track until she heard a hiss.

'Here!'

Eyes flashed from within the darkness of trees; there was a shadow that could have been an arm. She ran over in the direction of the voice, pushing through undergrowth until she was free of branches and brambles. When she raised her head she was in a clearing surrounded by trees, next to three men crouching in balaclavas.

'What a place to meet,' she said to her brother, the balaclava'd man in front of her.

'Shhh!' said the same person who'd said *Here*. Rose gave him a look to imply he couldn't talk to her like that – she was Naji's sister – but she saw from his glare he didn't care who she was.

'I'm running through tonight's plan,' Naji said softly.

'Naj, it's freezing. And that path was scary.'

'I know, I'm sorry. But you're here. You're fine. Now, listen – this is Payo, this is Mas. The three of you are taking Lot G tonight – go in, do what you can, clock counts for five minutes, the second it hits four minutes and fifty-nine seconds, get out of there. Got it?'

'Are you coming?'

'If I can. I'm watching over another unit tonight too.' He almost smiled.

'Oh, yeah? How many do you usually have?'

'Keep your voice down!' hissed Payo, rubbing his hands together.

'He's my *brother*. I'll talk to him how I want.'

'Yeah, but keep your voice down,' Naji said.

'Okay, whatever.' Rose rolled her eyes. 'How many . . . units . . . do you usually have?'

'It changes. We're not working alone.' He gave a small smile. 'Anyway, I'm glad you came.'

She felt like she'd had no choice. After what he'd told her she'd realised with an unexpected clarity that she would join him, even though he'd looked surprised when she asked.

'Those auts last week,' she said, referring to a recent aut attack. 'That was all you?'

'All us.'

'Twelve of the bastards,' said Payo.

Naji checked his phone. 'Take my number,' he told Rose.

'What do you mean?'

'Burner phone.'

He read out the digits and she saved it in her phone as *Naj 2*, as though her brother had just introduced her to his secret twin. He straightened his back, rested a hand on the ground and nodded curtly at Payo, who nodded back. Then he stood up, touched Rose on the shoulder and disappeared through the brambles. She turned and dimly saw the outline of warehouses in the distance, heard Naji's footsteps as he ran off. When she turned back, Mas was holding out a crowbar and a balaclava for her. He looked amused when she took them, which made her impatient. As she pulled on the balaclava, Payo reminded her that they had to destroy as many auts as possible, and that they had to do it fast.

'Yeah, I get it.'

Payo paid no attention. 'You ready?'

They nodded. Payo went first, quickly subsumed by the wall of trees. Mas followed and Rose crept out last. As they went back down the path, she felt baffled by the crowbar in her hand – by the idea she was going to smash an aut with it, or, ideally, several auts. But she had chosen to support Naji, and she did not have time for such doubt. She followed Payo and Mas through a narrow opening in the path she'd not seen on the way, and down a mud track closer to the nearest warehouse. They stopped, crouching. Rose's fingers were frozen, her gloves useless.

'Remember, five minutes,' said Payo. 'One second longer and we're fucked – got it?'

Mas and Rose nodded.

'Let's go.'

They pushed through the hedges and streaked down the field. Mas and Rose waited in the grass as Payo disabled the alarm system. When he held his hand up, Mas began to run towards him, towards the open back door, and Rose followed, stumbling.

He ushered her in. 'Go!'

The vast concrete space was still and cold. A tall, orange, skinny delivery aut was a few paces away and Mas went to attack it with his crowbar. Payo began furiously on one on her left. She looked into the distance to get the scope of what they were dealing with and saw aut after aut after aut, each of them frozen in place, primed to work. They looked so innocent in their lifeless obedience. And there were so many, so many more than she could fathom. The whole horizon was auts – surely over a hundred in this warehouse alone, and here Payo and Mas were valiantly bashing away at one or two.

We can't win, she thought. *This is insane.*

Someone appeared behind her. She almost screamed, but it was her brother, in all his imposing bulk, come to join her, his arm lifted, his crowbar poised.

'Naji.' She reached a hand out instinctively as if to stop him, but he didn't see. He started to hit a nearby aut, bashing his crowbar down, denting it deeply on its metal arm. Her heart was pounding, watching him destroy it with his rage. Each time metal made contact with metal she felt a deep, inexplicable pain. He kept going until the arm was crooked, then dangling by just a few wires, about to break. Then he looked at her as if to say, *This one's yours.*

She couldn't – she couldn't do it. Didn't he see the endless auts before him?

He stared at her, confused. She shook her head, apology burning in her eyes.

He spun around and whacked the thing until it came apart. She watched him, her face hot, tears pooling in her polyester cheeks. As he finished, Mas and Payo ran past them and a moment later he followed, and for a second Rose thought she might be left alone in this cavernous warehouse and so she ran, too, bolting out of the back door and through the field and down past the brambles.

Mas flung himself on the ground of the clearing, peeled his balaclava off and breathed heavy and sharp. Payo squatted, his head down, then tore off his own balaclava. Naji stood pacing on the path, his hands on his hips. Crouching behind the trees, Rose could just about see his outline.

A moment later Payo rose, brushed past her and went over to Naji. Rose could hear them exchanging a few words and then came the sound of someone running again, loud, then getting quieter. Mas sat up, his eyes closed, put his hands on his thighs and collected himself, then he too scrambled up, nodded in a comradely way at Rose and disappeared through the brambles. Rose heard voices again, running, and then silence.

Feeling a pure black fear, she crept through the trees. Her brother stood silhouetted on the muddy path. Under the moon, the fields behind him were an endless milky emptiness.

'Let's go,' he barked. 'Stay close and shut up.'

She followed him through a maze of darkened paths until they arrived at his car. As he drove them back, neither spoke, but Rose noticed that his hands on the steering wheel were shaking. Her thoughts went to their mother, what she'd say if she knew where they were, what they'd done. She thought of their father, too, but couldn't even begin to fathom what he'd have made of it. A few times Naji looked over to her and she glanced worriedly back at him, and she thought he might say something, but he kept quiet. For her part, she couldn't bring herself to say sorry. She knew he must want her to, but as her adrenalin faded it was being replaced by a disappointment so profound it was gutting.

Finally, the familiar hills of Sunset came into view. Naji's hands stopped shaking as they hit the U-139. He said quietly, 'Do you want to stay at ours tonight?'

It wasn't a question; he wasn't going to take her home – he didn't want her to see their mother, not yet. She was unable to speak, so she nodded instead. She realised she couldn't look him in the eye either, couldn't deal with his presence at all, in fact, until the next morning.

Rose woke up far too early and sat staring for a while at the enormous blankness of her brother's television, thinking about the previous night. Yissi began to cry upstairs, breaking the silence, and she heard Hela rushing to soothe him. She found her hoodie, put on her trainers and went to the door. Outside, the wild fuchsia bloom of a crab apple tree laced over the front garden. A pram had been left beneath it and a bird was perched on its handle, peering in as if trying to see its reflection. Behind her, Deo began to bark.

Rose turned and saw Naji in tracksuit bottoms and an old jumper, his eyes accusatory.

'Where are you going?'

'Home.'

Deo came to nose at her knees.

'Right. Rose, I find it hard to ask, I really do. But what the fuck were you doing last night?'

'I'm sorry,' she said. 'I—' She sank a hand into golden fur.

'You let me down.'

'I'm sorry,' she repeated, unable to look at him. 'I saw those auts – those endless auts – and I thought there has to be a better way.'

'A better way? Like what?'

She crouched as if she was hiding behind the dog. 'It's just, Naj – they'll only make more auts. For every one you smash, they'll make fifty more. I *do* believe in you, I do – I just . . . what are you doing? It makes no sense.' She sounded like she was pleading.

'What are we doing? We're showing them we're not going to be bullied into losing our jobs – we're showing them we're gonna resist. Rose, I thought you *understood*!'

'It's more complicated than that.'

'It's not.'

They glared at each other.

'You still going to your boyfriend's source gain group?'

'He's not my boy—'

'You *know* source gain is bullshit.'

'No—'

'It's never gonna happen, and meanwhile we're gonna *starve*!'

'But maybe smashing auts isn't going to stop that. Source gain is sensible – it'd change the lives of millions of people. Smashing auts is' – she chose her words carefully – 'it's good . . . but now I've seen it, I don't know if it's going to get us anywhere.'

'"Get us anywhere"? My wife and I are going to lose our jobs any day now, and we've got a baby upstairs, and you think your little group's going to *get us anywhere*?'

Deo barked and Naji stared for a long moment at his sister. 'Let me ask – is your boyfriend working in a factory, seeing his colleagues and friends replaced by auts, knowing it's his turn any day now? Is he?'

'No – he's writing a book,' she said stupidly.

Naji laughed in disbelief. 'Oh, right? What does he want first, source gain or a book deal?'

She flushed with shame.

'Rose, your roots are with the workers.'

'Please, Naj—'

'Please what? Please watch you beg the government to care about us? Watch you read books by middle-class boys and think you're *helping*?'

'Come on,' she said desperately. 'Source gain could change things.'

Naji looked to the ceiling in exasperation. 'We're losing our jobs *NOW!* We haven't got time for your intellectual mates to sit around writing books!'

She didn't know what to say.

'And you know what I realised last night? Lal's sister – what's her name? – she makes them, doesn't she! She makes the fucking auts. What a sadist!' He shook his head. 'But you're okay with that, because source gain will rescue us all.'

'I told you what Janetta does – she's trying to create artificial intelligence with *emotional* intelligence so that it doesn't destroy us.'

'So that's all right, then?'

'Nothing's all right. I'm just trying to figure out how we can survive.'

Deo began to softly howl.

'Rose, I *know* how to survive. We have to resist. We have to *show* that we're not going to give up, we're not going to back down. Why is this so hard for you to get?' He looked pained, clutching the doorframe. 'You know what it is? You never thought I was as good as Dad. I was always going to fuck up somehow, wasn't I? But now I'm in charge, I'm *saving* us, and you can't handle it.' He pointed a finger at her. 'I'm better than him and you can't admit it.'

'That's not true at all. You know what's true?' She hadn't been aware of it until this moment. 'Neither of you is who I thought you were. *Neither* of you.'

She couldn't get away fast enough then. She had trusted and believed in them, but her dad was a cheat and her brother a fool. She was the biggest fool of all, though, because she could have seen this earlier and she'd chosen not to; instead, she'd willingly looked away.

The next day, her anger and disappointment not having subsided one bit, she took herself to the HEU Library. She paid forty swocols, an absurd amount, to renew her library card, but it bought her a year's access. She had expected a hero's welcome – staff congratulating her on her continued interest in studying and her inspiring autodidacticism, etc. – but it was a muted affair, and she felt glum and forgotten as, alumni card in hand, she pushed through the turnstiles.

The library was dispiritingly dark and musty, but on the mezzanine floor there was a long row of desks directly opposite a clerestory that provided some respite in the form of a view of the surrounding buildings. These were dull grey concrete for the most part, reminding you that the HEU was the poor cousin to the far glitzier university in town, but if you got one of the desks on the right, you could just about see the sea, that promising wedge of blue. Rose was last obsessed with nabbing one of those desks two years ago, when she was cramming for her exams. It was strange to think of that – at the time, she'd thought all her reading was for the sole purpose of passing her exams. She understood now, as she dropped her rucksack onto the seat of a right-hand desk and bent down for a moment to check the sea was still there (it was), that she was here under entirely different circumstances. This time, it was about doing something real.

Last night, unable to sleep and still raw from her confrontation with her brother, she'd tried to untangle his beliefs from her own, and hers from Alek's, and from Janetta's, too. She understood that as long as she thought all their views had merit but none were exactly right, she was stuck. It had finally occurred to her that she could go back to the library, at least as a way to clarify her thinking, and now here she was at her favourite desk, calling up books and journals to her laptop.

The books she'd selected were familiar: the classic text, *Ideals of Freedom*, and the student favourite, *Freedom: What Is It and Where to Find It*. She dug out her own personal favourite too, *How It Would*

Feel To Be Free. She'd read them all during her degree and not touched them since, except for *How It Would Feel*, which sat on her bedroom bookshelf and from which she occasionally read whenever she felt her inner compass had gone awry. She selected the first chapter of *Ideals of Freedom*, a huge, notoriously intimidating tome, and started to read.

Her aim was to whizz through the books then crack on to the journals. To start with, she had selected the latest volumes of *The Journal of Economic Futures*, *Predictive Economics* and *The Futurity Review*. She didn't know what she was looking for – she'd never read an economics paper in her life. She'd just feel her way through. In truth she'd hoped to make quick headway, but there was so much to think about, so many notes to write, that the hours flew by. She ended up spending every evening after work there, and her days off too. By the weekend, she'd read most of two of the books and a triumphant eleven journal articles. On Saturday night she fell asleep at the desk and at nine o'clock was gently woken up and told that the library was closing.

By Sunday evening she knew what she thought. As these things often are, it was a more fleshed-out version of what she'd intuited back before she'd even gone to her first meeting.

She was still ultimately against aut violence. She agreed with Naji that it was a potent statement, and she understood his reasons for doing it, the anger and protest behind it. But the auts' ubiquity made it absurd – for any one you destroyed, ten would appear in its place. And she didn't consider the ethics beyond this: they weren't conscious yet, and until they were – if that ever happened – there was nothing more to consider.

Source gain, Alek's way to give people income once auts had taken all the jobs, would be taken as tax from the corporations and given by the government to the people. In principle, she liked this idea a lot. But she already knew she was against how it made the government like parents, handing out pocket money for good behaviour. Now she saw where her deeper mistrust came from. If the freedom people got from source gain was dependent on the government and could be retracted at any time, it wasn't freedom. And as long as it came from taxing corporations, people would be encouraged to spend so that corporations made money. That wasn't freedom, either.

Another argument, which she was starting to understand, was that source gain didn't prevent people from earning their own money, and this meant that some people would – just as under this current system – have more than others. With this greater income, they'd have choices available to them that others wouldn't have, and also the very fact that they could pay more meant that the cost of things would still inflate. Those who didn't have the extra income would be priced out of affording them – and wealth and poverty would exist all over again. It made no difference if you had a standard source gain if the price of things was inflated to match the spending power of those who could make more.

Rose wanted to talk about all this, and about where her thinking could go next. She bet some of the students sitting in the economics section had interesting ideas, but she was in no mood to start chatting to strangers. She didn't, though, have anyone else – no one she trusted, at least. She hadn't spoken to Alek all week, she and Naji weren't talking, and Lal would never understand, because she was too busy prostrating herself at Tekna.

It didn't matter, though. She could go it alone.

Later, at home, Rose stayed in her room reading while her mother and Yash cooked dinner in the kitchen. She could hear them cheerfully discussing the best way to cook falo beans. It was amusing to hear her younger brother bombard his mother with internet-derived opinions that did actually sound quite sensible, and to hear her mother, who always thought she knew best, offer up one or two concessionary sniffs. Rose could imagine the expression on her face – haughty and disbelieving, her mouth minutely turned up into a smile, unable to hide that she was pleased her son cared enough to debate it with her.

Yash actually *liked* being at home. Years ago their mother had suggested, in a wild misreading of her younger son, that when he was seventeen Naji could help him get a job at the Rartaur warehouse. Yash had to remind her he had his heart set on something else. 'Two philosophers,' she'd cry, 'what did I do to get two philosophers?' She'd say, 'I thought you were a sensible boy!' and Yash, not used to displeasing her, had to point out that the two weren't mutually exclusive, which made her shake her head, bewildered by her own creation.

Rose heard Yash laugh then, and say something she missed as he passed her room. A short while later, a song spilled around the flat from the living room. She was trying to concentrate on her reading – and instead thinking grumpily about how much longer she might have to live at home, possibly forever – but this song was hard to ignore. It was slow, with a steady bassline and gentle warmth, and it felt like a calm radiance had stolen into her room and surrounded her. After another minute she put her book down, pushed herself off the bed, and followed the sound.

In the living room, her brother was cross-legged on the sofa, playing a video game. He acknowledged her with a nod. She sat down beside him and looked at the screen, then at his hands, then back at the screen. He was using his fingers to sculpt a head, but their motions – up and down slowly through the air with his index finger – didn't correspond entirely to the creation of the head,

219

which appeared to be coming to life more quickly than that. She watched, entranced, as a face appeared as the song ended – closed, wide-set eyes, a sharp nose, generous lips, noticeably long ears.

'Who's doing that?' she cried. 'Is it all you?'

'Hang on a sec,' Yash said, and stopped moving his fingers. He slowly pushed his palms away from him and the music became softer, but the face continued to metamorphose. 'It's a new game. It's a collaboration – we all build auts together.' He sat up straight, his upturned hands resting in his lap, his eyes clear.

'Really?'

'We design their faces and their bodies, and we discuss their capabilities – what they're good at, what they're not so good at . . . we kind of calibrate it democratically – as much as we can. We're creating a whole aut population, and once it's done we're going to see if there's some way of making it have an effect in the real world.'

Rose was stunned. 'That's incredible.'

'It's pretty cool.'

'Who's the "we", though?'

He shrugged. 'Some people online. Well, thousands of us. It's not perfect, but everybody wants the same thing—'

'Cool auts.'

'Ha, yeah, cool auts.' He looked suddenly sheepish. 'I mean, it's just a game.'

'No, no, I love it. At least people are . . . trying. At least they're putting their imaginations into something like that.' It felt like the only positive thing she'd heard for months.

And then she felt, unexpectedly, a tectonic shift. A way through.

'Are you okay?'

'I'm fine,' she said, feeling as if the whole world was opening up. 'Go on, keep playing. I want to watch.'

14

On the walls of the various coffee shops in Forol were noticeboards where people could leave requests for hiking companions. Early the next morning, Janetta went straight to the most active one and responded to a duo who were looking for companions – 'friends' was the word they used – for an overnight trip the next day. Afterwards, she ordered breakfast and sat for a while attempting to read more of *TechnoMutations* as people bustled around her with their food and drinks and hiking gear, the snowy caps of the mountain crowning the horizon beyond. Watching the hikers come and go with their reddened cheeks and colourful, sensible clothes, she felt as if she belonged to another world. They were so certain of their purpose that their lack of doubt was something to behold. Tomorrow, at least, she would pretend to be amongst their kind.

The next morning, she left the hostel at dawn to meet her fellow hikers. She thought that by reaching the start of the trail just before eight, when they were scheduled to be there, she'd be the first, but they were already waiting for her. Reaga, a slim, attractive young woman with a beautifully made-up face, was doing leg stretches against the low stone wall. Jyl, also slim and even prettier, and tall, older and bare-faced, smiled warmly, bowed and held her palms flat towards Janetta in a Cabakan greeting.

They were both wearing impressive hiking gear and glowed with health. They came from Bluw, a city in Sewanna, and spoke in that loose, rolling western accent that took a minute or two to get used to. They too had an enormous sense of purpose, earnestly telling her the route they were thinking of, their intended schedule, the weather, terrain and rest stops. Janetta was fine with it all – pleased, in fact, that they were so well-prepared; it meant she could switch off and walk, just as she'd wanted.

As they set off, Reaga moved on ahead, pumping her way up the first steep hill. Behind, Jyl kept up a steady stream of conversation. She told Janetta first of all about the top she was wearing to hike in, which looked like a normal exercise top, but Jyl was keen to confirm otherwise. Apparently it absorbed sunlight and then pre-photolysed it before it reached the skin, thereby providing a more efficient conversion of UV rays into vitamin D. Janetta was dubious, but decided it wouldn't be good to start the hike with a show of scientific one-upmanship, so she made sounds of being impressed. Also, at this point, it was just nice to talk to someone.

Jyl asked what Janetta did and said, 'Oh, cool,' when she told her about her Ph.D., but nothing else, which made her feel she'd been offensively boring, or said something wrong – some people didn't like to think about AI having emotions, it made them uncomfortable, and it could have been this. She quickly returned the question to smooth things over, nodding encouragement as Jyl explained that her job was to help people decide what to eat. Buoyed presumably by Janetta's nods, she began to explain what was wrong with certain foods. It felt a little conversationally unbalanced that Janetta's own work had been passed over so quickly, but Jyl was all smiles and earnestness about her own job, so she let it go. She couldn't say she was much bothered, though, if drinking coffee was like 'injecting poison', and eating sugar was 'a death wish', but she smiled and thought of Malin's new girlfriend Jasmine, who no doubt would have more to say in return. The scenery, in any case, was astonishing.

Jyl stopped talking when the route got steeper. They concentrated on scrambling, fixing their feet firmly on the ground beneath again and again, and Janetta, began to feel exhilarated by the activity, the repetition, the colours of the Skrevet Valley below. She noticed her breathing, which she rarely ever did, and for a few moments she just focused on it; the deep breath in, the deep breath out. She thought about her auts, and how there was no equivalent of breathing for them, no way they lived moment to moment in the way humans and animals did. When they created aut consciousness, that consciousness would be programmed to continue, but there was no organism to keep alive. Auts would be conscious due to their makers' will, and then due to their own, but there would be no oxygen needed, no equivalent of humans' constant reckoning with life or death.

'I love your boots, where'd you get them?'

'I'm sorry?'

'They're so cute.'

'*So* cute.' This was Reaga, with whom they'd caught up.

She murmured a foggy thanks, admitted to not having a clue where the boots came from – they were her mother's, she'd just found them at home – and continued in silence. Undeterred, her companions began to talk about where in Bluw they liked to buy their shoes. Janetta walked between them, focusing forward, trying to get back to what she'd been thinking about, but whenever her eyes strayed to the landscape at her side she felt as though she had to take part in the conversation – to assent or smile – and gradually realised her best option was to slow down so that they could overtake her. As they gained ground their words drifted back - Jyl's gentle voice, Reaga's harsher tones. She hoped it might look accidental, this slackening of pace, this opting out, but emerging sharply in her mind, and confirmed when ten minutes later the conversation moved to the pros and cons of various clothing stores, was the thought that this hike might have been a mistake.

She reproached herself for being judgemental and made her way to them again.

'You know, your skin is so clear,' Reaga said. 'It's *so gorgeous*. What products do you use?'

'Just . . . whatever's around.'

Reaga arched her eyebrows, unconvinced, then told them about her beauty routine. She only used natural products, she said right-eously.

'Do you use crushed worm serum too?' asked Jyl.

'I do! You know you can get some here that's got *goat sperm* in it? It is *amazing* for wrinkles—'

Janetta looked away. Her companions did not see, or did not appear to care, about the world around them - how elemental it felt, the sky so wide and blue, the mountains stretching deep into the distance.

At last, though, Jyl paused to take photos and Reaga followed her lead; after doing so they fell back into their onwards, striding talk. Janetta, as she listened to part two of Reaga's daily beauty routine, wondered why it was that after deciding she couldn't bear her solitude she was now desperate to be alone.

In the early evening they arrived at the monastery, which was not a working monastery any more but repurposed, as most of the monasteries in the valley had been, as a straightforward hostel for hikers. The accommodation was basic: wooden bunk beds for all, provided with thin, musty sheets and old, rough blankets so you could make your own bed. Jyl and Reaga lined their beauty products up on the windowsill under a westward view of forested peaks, while making comments about the spartan accommodation and the insistent smell of body odour in the room. These barely registered with Janetta – she was disappointed only that the place was almost empty; she'd been hoping to find other people to talk to. In their absence, she was going to have to extricate herself from Jyl and Reaga by other means.

Truthfully, they were both kind, especially Jyl, who seemed to be looking out for her. She invited her to dinner with them and Janetta accepted, it still being just about preferable to being alone. They sat at long benches, with their simple meal of labhrai and rice, and her companions talked for a long time about meditation. Janetta listened carefully, because she wanted to find out what Malin was doing. Both women were full of praise for a particular monk who ran retreats higher up the mountain. The centre they described was unrecognisable – far bigger and more luxurious than the one she'd seen with Malin; it had a spa attached to it, which didn't sound particularly Cabakan, but what did she know? Reaga, who was now swathed in some sort of white robe, begin to recount an infelicitous massage she'd had there last year – the masseuse was too chatty and she'd used too much oil of the wrong kind – *gloopy*, she said, shaking her head in condemnation. While Janetta, who was starving, dug into her labhrai, there followed between Jyl and Reaga a spirited discussion about massage oil. No eating took place. Forks hovered, rested, hovered and rested again, but not a morsel travelled from plate to mouth. 'Smells amazing', 'sticky', and 'good' were the highlights of an otherwise entirely unenlightening exchange. Eventually, they wound back to the monk they admired.

'I just love him. I feel we have such a deep bond.'

'I know. He knows I know he's the real thing, you know?'

Janetta's eyes darted between them. 'My – uh – friend is doing a meditation retreat right now.'

'She is? With him?' asked Jyl, smiling encouragingly.

Janetta shook her head and told them where Malin was, but it rang no bells. Reaga shook her head too, and said that there were too many places nowadays trying to cash in, that it was a shame.

'Trying to cash in on what?'

'The meditation craze.'

'Is it a craze? It's been around for five thousand years.'

'It's a craze.'

'I hope your friend's teachers are reputable,' Jyl said.

'It's just an old monastery,' said Janetta. 'I think they're harmless enough.'

Reaga shook her head. 'People don't teach it right. They end up causing *real* damage.'

Jyl nodded in agreement, finally spearing a mushroom onto her fork.

'How can you cause real damage? I mean, aren't you just sitting there?' Janetta asked. 'It can't – I mean—'

Reaga explained that some teachers – most of them, nowadays – had neither the right skills to teach meditation nor a true understanding of it, because it was an almost impossible thing to teach, an almost impossible concept to understand, and also their own training had itself been woefully inadequate.

Janetta couldn't get past the fact that meditation was surely just sitting, and while she knew that Cabakan monks, in particular, went at it rigorously, surely at its essence it was meant to be the simplest thing to teach, the easiest and most effortless thing to understand. Surely the problem only came when you had teachers who acted as though this wasn't the case – as though they were the only ones who could instruct you on it properly.

Reaga began to describe again how wonderful her own teacher was. Janetta pictured this person – this benevolent, all-forgiving, saintly man who also happened to charge an obscene amount of money for his time.

'He's the only one I trust,' Reaga said.

'He's the only one who does it properly,' Jyl enthused.

Janetta felt something inside her snap. She stood up, apologised, said quietly that she was sleepy, took her plate and left. They raised their voices to tell her to have a good night – they were kind – they were kind about everything, apparently, other than which meditation centre you went to.

She left her plate and empty water glass on the table at the side, where they would be collected by a dutiful staff member, and went outside to a wooden porch, which she followed around until she was as far away from the food hall as possible. There she found a bench, a wooden chair and a much-needed emptiness. In front of her was a view over the night sky and the dark valley, lit up by flecks of gold light from those disreputable monasteries Reaga and Jyl had warned her about. She wondered if she could walk alone tomorrow. It wasn't what she wanted – she wanted Taly – but failing that, solitude would do.

A few minutes later, Reaga swanned into Janetta's view, her white robes swinging grandly, a pair of huge headphones completing the look. When she saw Janetta she plucked them off and put them around her neck.

'Oh, hi,' she said, lighting up with interest. She sat cross-legged on the bench next to her, gathering her voluminous folds, took out a packet of cigarettes and offered one to Janetta, who shook her head with a smile. Reaga lit one, took a drag, and said, 'There's such incredible energy out here, right?'

Janetta nodded.

Reaga gave her a look of mild pity. She put her headphones back on and Janetta relaxed a little. She would rather have been *alone* alone, but if they didn't have to talk, it didn't much matter.

Then Reaga began to sing – at first, just a few notes here and there, as if she were finding her voice; and then she full-on belted out words in a language Janetta didn't recognise. They might in fact just have been noises. Her voice was high and clear, arguably quite nice, but in the silence it felt like an attack. Janetta waited for her to stop, and eventually she settled down into a more innocuous humming.

And then she began again. Janetta whipped around.

'Please,' she said, as politely as she could. With her closed eyes and headphones on, Reaga couldn't hear. Janetta watched for a while. Reaga was frowning and swaying, her hands tightly balled into fists. The white of her robe was pearlescent in the darkness. Finally, she opened her eyes and gazed into the distance with her palms on her thighs. Eventually she deigned to turn around, her eyes bright and full.

'It's my devotional practice,' she said, too loudly. Then she shut her eyes again, bunched her fists and took a deep breath, as if gathering her resources.

Janetta watched her for another moment, felt tears pricking at her eyes, stood up and walked off. She had a sharp pang of missing the Institute, its reassuring normality. Reaga's strange sounds, cutting into the cold air, hounded her until she got far enough away, close to the perimeter of the monastery's grounds, where a path led into a great crop of trees that was at this point entirely dark. She thought about going in but was scared by its blackness, so she stayed on the perimeter track and after she'd circled the grounds, with no one to talk to and nothing else to do, she went to bed, where she read *TechnoMutations* – her last connection to real life – for an hour before switching off her bedside light.

She dreamed it was Penelope Zger who was sitting next to her instead of Reaga, singing a song in words that made no sense to Janetta, and as she sat there listening, staring at Zger, trying to understand her, she became aware that she was singing the code of consciousness. Then she was chased by Jyl and Reaga until she found herself back at her desk at the Institute, and when she looked at her notes they had changed into what Zger had been singing, and she was still trying desperately, hopelessly to decipher them.

She rose early the next morning and found the others' beds already neatly made – either they'd not gone to bed due to a wild night or – yes, they were already awake and at breakfast. As she dressed, she came to a decision. If she continued the hike alone, she couldn't very well go along the same route. She could explain she wanted solitude, but couldn't imagine saying this – the awkwardness it might entail, the chance something might slip out like, *Because I can't stand how tedious you both are!* She couldn't bear to make anyone feel bad about themselves. The only solution was to head back down the mountain alone.

As she watched Jyl delicately, meditatively eat slices of boiled egg in a technique no doubt learned from her guru, and Reaga's spoon hover over a bowl of porridge she failed to acknowledge was there, Janetta decided to give them one last chance. Perhaps the new day heralded better conversation.

They talked about the kind of cushions they liked to sit on while they meditated. For half an hour. To be fair, they did change the course of the conversation sometimes, to rhapsodise over their teacher, but then they went back to the cushions. And then to the teacher.

'The, um . . . the . . . did you know this monastery was a hideout for the army during the War of Independence?' Janetta blurted out.

Jyl and Reaga spun her way with confused frowns.

'Which war?' Jyl tried.

'The one in the seventeenth century . . . against Yalin?'

Jyl shook her head and smiled apologetically, as though Janetta had asked her for directions and she was unable to help out.

Reaga raised an eyebrow as if to ask Jyl whether their interruption was over, and then said, 'Like I was saying, about comfortability—'

Janetta wanted to scream. No, she wanted to call Taly and beg her to say *anything* – even Taly saying hello would be more interesting than this. She excused herself, though she wasn't much noticed – Jyl gave her a smile – went back to the dorm, packed her rucksack and dragged it to the reception where she paid her share of the bill and then hoisted it onto her shoulders. She went back into the hall, having never done anything like this before, and as Jyl and Reaga looked up at her bemused, she explained, her face red with the shame of lying, that her grandmother had become ill and she had to go home immediately.

Jyl was heartfelt in her reply. If it were just Jyl she probably could have continued on, but to Reaga – who gave her a Cabakan blessing in response, for far too long, her palms too deeply bowed – she'd had an allergic reaction.

Walking away was a joy. At the monastery entrance she beamed at a couple who stood aside to let her pass and set off. Certainly to be heading downhill, on a path she'd already walked, was a disappointment – but she still felt delighted to be alone, weaving through the mountainside, the trees rustling, the immense valley at her side, free to attend to her own thoughts. Only a while later did she circle back to her choice. She had derailed her own plans because someone else made her unhappy. Was that right? Was it fair that Reaga now got to go to the top of the mountain and see those famous views over the Alti Sea? Was she weak? Would Lal have done the same? Lal was more tolerant of people. Malin was too – Malin would have decided that Reaga was annoying, then treated her warmly anyway.

It was a truth about herself that Janetta had for a long time only been skirting around – she was intolerant, easily irritated by people who didn't meet her standards. This was a failing, she knew, but at the same time, couldn't she permit herself to say she preferred to be around people who stimulated her, people to whom she had something to say? Malin stimulated her, Taly was fascinating. Was it wrong to prefer this type of person? If it made her a snob, it wasn't as though she had insulted Reaga directly – she had hidden it to the extent that she'd made up a lie so Reaga didn't feel bad about herself. But perhaps being secretly judgemental was no better. And who was to say what Reaga thought of her? Maybe she thought her unfriendly and rude; perhaps that was right.

As she debated this with herself she began to walk rapidly, purposefully. All these thoughts were really only leading towards a sole end: Taly, with whom she felt an almost psychic kinship now. She was the only person who truly understood her – only the two of them would be able to discuss the culture and nature and science of her time in Skrevet to the degree she craved, only Taly could give her what she needed. As soon as she had phone reception she waited for her email to come down from the skies. In the distance she heard a bird's fractured song. There it was – a message from Taly! Her heart raced. She opened it, skimmed it frantically, saw that in response to her queries about ethical frameworks Taly had briefly paraphrased the very same ideas from *TechnoMutations* Janetta had been responding to in the first place, which was a let-down – then said that Janetta's blueprint for conscious AI was idiosyncratic but interesting.

And that was it.

She scrolled down to see if there was anything more. Nothing. It was as indifferent as if it were an email to a stranger. Her heart plummeted. Taly had no feelings; she clearly didn't care if she saw her again; Janetta had misjudged the whole thing. She looked out to the valley and sat on a grassy rise at the side of the path, carelessly dumping her rucksack beside her. She folded her hands over her knees and dropped her head to meet them.

But don't you see? she felt like shouting. *You're all I've got!* She could not bear the emptiness opening up inside her again, the being bereft, the great maw of loneliness. Of course she saw the irony – here she was in a town of meditators, of people finding peace, and yet she felt out of control. She'd lost her last connective thread to another human being.

She grabbed her phone.

Hi, I know this is sudden but I had to tell you – I think I'm falling in love with you.

She stared mindlessly at the message, sent it. If Taly could give her something to anchor herself to, even a vague affirmative so she wouldn't drown, that was all she needed. She dropped to her back, lay staring at the cloudless sky. *I think I'm falling in love with you,* she'd written. But after a few minutes it didn't feel as good to have said this as she'd expected. As she got herself together she realised she wanted to crawl back down the mountain with embarrassment; instead she walked quickly, looking straight ahead, barely caring where she was after all.

Back in Forol she headed straight to the hostel and up to her room, where she lay on her bed and drank the three bottles of beer she'd bought from the downstairs bar. It was a relief, finally, to drift off to sleep. In her dream she was pulling off her own toenails agonisingly slowly, one by one. At three in the morning she awoke and grabbed her phone, expecting to find an email from Taly saying that she was falling in love with her, too. There was nothing, of course – just the eeriness of having believed such a thing would happen.

Five hours later, sun pushed through the thin, brown curtains and Janetta, in no mood for it, turned away. Malin would be back in the evening; in the meantime she would have to get up and work. She reached for her phone on the bedside table, dreading its too bright glow, and saw, amid the usual stack of artificial intelligence updates, an email from Taly. It was not a dream. She put her phone down without opening it, got up and calmly dressed. She grabbed her laptop and headed downstairs, through the early morning quiet, to the hostel garden around the back, a poorly tended grassy patch bordered by brusepara ferns and sticklepalms which rose up densely on the hillside beyond. She sat in the sun on the stone steps and almost ritualistically, unable to breathe, opened her laptop to read the email.

Janetta, you're falling in love with me? You do realise we hardly know each other? If you feel this way, I suggest there's something very wrong with you. Do me a favour and leave me alone.

Oh no, she thought. *This is not what you want when you confess your love.*

She wrote back instantly, ashamed beyond measure.

I'm sorry. I won't contact you again.

She took a deep breath, looked up at a bird bouncing gently on a sticklepalm branch, pecking at the tiny white flowers. Then she sent it, more out of curiosity to see what another act of masochism might feel like, closed her laptop and stood up. The world around her was beautiful, and though she felt deeply humiliated, there was a lightness there, too.

She returned her laptop to her room, hired a bike and cycled out to the river that ran inland from Forol, out to the western valley. She was alternately plagued by the most abject humiliation she'd ever known, a ferocious anger at Taly, and something like joy at having been utterly stupid for the first time in her life – having debased herself and survived. To tell someone you're in love with them and have them respond with repulsion was bad, but not the worst thing in the world, and the river shimmered alongside her, deep and wide and blue, and the valleys rose up in ridges, their emerald trees bursting with flowers, and there was no one on the road but her, and she cycled until the only thing she felt was free.

Malin returned that evening. She sashayed towards Janetta, who sat on the hostel porch ostensibly waiting (but actually staring into space), as if she'd been receiving messages – or massages, indeed – from Cabak herself all week, and was now back, radiant with benediction. Janetta jumped up and met her with a grateful hug. Malin brushed a strand of Janetta's hair behind her ear and looked happily at her. They discussed their relative levels of thirst; Malin said she wanted corn tea, the most puritanical of all teas, and they set off to a popular traveller café.

Once there, Malin held her steaming mug of tea close to her chest and told Janetta about her week. She hadn't been allowed to talk to anyone or look them in the eye – in case it disturbed her or them from their meditation – 'You're meant to dwell *inwards*,' she said. She hadn't been allowed to read or write, either – in just a few hours this had sent her mad and she'd gone into a toilet stall with a pen she'd smuggled in and started writing on her thigh for the sheer need of it. Otherwise, her week consisted of being woken up at four every morning to sit in that meditation hall all day.

'By the second day I loathed it,' she said. 'I just burned with hatred – but then right at the end of the week, it hit. I was meditating. *Me*, meditating! A miracle.' She had spent half an hour like this, empty as the sky, believing the chaos inside had settled once and for all. She put down her tea and looked Janetta straight in the eye – and Janetta had to admit, she could see something covetously calm there.

A waiter approached. Malin grabbed the menu and pointed at a cocktail. She looked at Janetta. 'Don't judge.'

'I wouldn't dream of it. I'll join you.'

'I don't know if *calm* becomes me. I'm better with a noisy psyche, aren't I? Not *better*—' She paused. 'Just more . . . *me*.' She pushed the barely touched mug of tea away.

'You look great, though. You *look* like you've been enlightened.'

'Oh, that's not enlightenment. That's a lentils-only diet.' Her phone beeped and she grabbed it. Janetta watched her tap at it until their cocktails arrived, and began to drink hers quickly.

'Sorry,' Malin said, looking up. 'Jasmine's having a hard time. Stomach problems – she's only eating things that are beige.' She pulled a disgruntled face and went back to furiously typing. Janetta felt a flash of anger. How come Jasmine merited such ministrations from Malin, while she herself was only worthy of Taly's disgust?

'Malin, I did something stupid.'

'One sec,' Malin said, not looking up. 'Is yellow a kind of beige? Oh, never mind.'

The café's décor was heavily reliant on bamboo. There was a lot of light outside – you could see it blazing in thick lines at the front and on the left – but inside, due to the choice to have more wall than window, it was dark and damp. By the wall were two hammocks; one was empty and the other was weighed down with the pale body of a sleeping man, turned precariously on his side. His T-shirt had bunched up to his chest, revealing a drooping handful of belly. A slight shift further and he'd tumble to the floor. Beneath him a grey short-haired cat curled contentedly, unaware of the danger lurking above.

Malin put her phone down and lifted her face expectantly. 'What did you say – you did something stupid? Please don't tell me you didn't do any work. Please don't tell me that.'

Janetta told her about her declaration of love. Malin put her head in her hands. 'You idiot.'

'Great, thanks.'

'Are you really in love with this person? You've known her for, what, all of a month?'

'Well, are you in love with Jasmine?'

'A bit.'

'Right!'

They stared at each other. Janetta dug into her bag, found her phone. 'Read the email.'

Malin took the phone, read it, handed it back to Janetta. '*I suggest there's something very wrong with you*? Who says that to someone? She's a bitch.'

Janetta slumped down on the sofa. 'I suppose she is.'

'You know what, forget about her – she has no empathy. You don't need someone like that in your life. Maybe just make sure your auts know how to handle infatuation better than that, though.'

'Infatuation?'

236

Malin's phone beeped. She grabbed it, read the message and started tapping away again. A television in the far corner was showing a basketball game from another country and Janetta stared at it for want of anything else to do. The bodies on-screen darted manically, throwing the ball to one another, swooshing it through a net. Its brightness was a comfort.

'Sorry – Jasmine's just telling me what she ate today,' Malin said.

'Bite by bite?'

But Malin wasn't listening.

Suddenly, Janetta understood. 'This is your fault,' she hissed. 'I loved you – I loved *you*. I *still do*! It's only because you couldn't love me enough back that all this has happened.'

Malin stopped typing and looked up at her miserably. 'Oh Jay, I'm sorry. I really am.'

Janetta winced in pain, but there was nothing more to say. Malin turned back to her phone and at first tentatively, then more carelessly, bashed out a reply to Jasmine.

Janetta watched, and after a long while picked up her own phone. Grateful Taly hadn't sent some kind of coruscating follow-up, she opened the latest of the AI news emails she'd been ignoring for the past two weeks.

The first headline: *Taly Kett joins Tekna*.

15

Lal was approached when she was at her desk. There was no warning and there were no lights. One of the assistants who occasionally appeared in the office, mostly to lean close to someone and whisper something to them then usher them away, was coming towards her. She braced herself for a flash of red, trying to think what she'd done, but the woman merely bent down and said, 'Please follow me.'

Her voice was low and soft. As Lal stood, her face burning, and followed the woman, she realised that the culture of no one turning around to look was just as bad as if they were all staring at her. They were still alert to it, every one of them, and it would not be forgotten – they would find out what had happened and pass this knowledge between them.

Outside, reception was empty and she stood a moment, assuming she'd have to wait there until her fate was revealed, but the woman she was following went straight out to the front, where a slick black car was heading towards them. When it parked, she opened a passenger door and looked expectantly at Lal.

It was terrifying, the fact she had to enter this car with no idea why or where it was taking her. She slid across the leather then turned to the woman, who was now holding the door and gazing into the distance, her face blank, almost bored.

Then the woman met her eye. 'Relax.'

She shut the door. The car began to move, and despite the air-conditioned chill, sweat leaked across Lal's forehead and under her arms. She tried to guess where she was being taken – lack of office shaming aside, she must be on her way to lose her job. Today she'd worn jeans because she knew now that no one cared what she wore, but it was humiliating to have your Tekna career terminated when you were in jeans, like a slouch, like someone who deserved not to be there in the first place. As the car trundled out of the campus and towards the ring road, she started very quietly to cry, and as the tears streamed down her face and dried in the cool air, she tried desperately to guess what she'd done wrong – well, what she'd done wrong that Tekna could have disapproved of. She knew well enough what she'd done wrong otherwise.

Curiously, the car was heading towards Mejira, the Tekna Tower in view up ahead, which meant that whatever vision she'd had of some out-of-town interrogation room, a place from which to kick her into oblivion, was replaced with the horror that whatever was about to go down would do so in the Tower itself. She would finally be inside, only in order to be shamed and excommunicated.

When the car drew up she did not want to get out, but a young, earnest-looking woman rushed towards her.

'Are you Lalita Depeic? Uhli is waiting for you.'

Lal took in the peach dress and gold heels. 'Uhli?'

'You have a meeting with Mr Ranh.'

'*I* do? I doubt it.'

'I'm his assistant and I put it in his diary, so . . .'

Lal followed the woman into the Tower. Straight ahead was a bank of short escalators, and behind them, a rushing waterfall surrounded by exotic plants. Beautifully dressed people walked past, smart-suited and focused, their shoes clicking sharply on the sunlit floor. On the escalator she gazed up at the sleek geometry of the building's inner structure, its mezzanines and walkways in steel and glass. She didn't care if she looked like a wide-eyed naïf; she was overwhelmed. Even if Uhli Ranh was going to sack her personally, she had glimpsed this spectacular place. Her heart was heavy with the thought that this might be all she got, but at least she was here right now.

Upstairs in the ladies' room she stared at the mirror – she couldn't believe she was meeting him in jeans and a baggy jumper. Her reflection looked appallingly young and fraudulent; she thought about the elegant assistant out there and wished she was more like her. She looked a moment longer, zeroing in on what felt most unforgivable – her pudgy cheeks – but the more she stared, the pudgier they became, so finally she just walked out.

Uhli Ranh's office was large and sunny, with a wall of windows that looked out onto the city, a dramatic view that made her feel both nauseous and thrilled. Although his desk was in the centre of the room, Ranh wasn't there – he sat instead at one end of a long leather sofa up against a wall, beneath some colourful, ugly art.

'Lalita!' He leaned over and firmly shook her hand. She hoped he didn't notice how much her own was shaking. He said she should call him Uhli and asked if she wanted some water or a coffee, to which she found herself saying a coffee, which made no sense given how much difficulty he'd had last time she'd seen him get one. But he pressed his phone a few times, then sat back, gazing at her, and she felt something inside give way. It was impossible not to be drawn to him, especially as his face suggested this was a good idea, with his thick eyebrows raised, his cheeks slightly sucked in and an amused glimmer in his eyes that dared her – or so she believed – to take things slightly off-track. But she could just be making that up. Rose thought him an idiot, but Lal couldn't see this herself – to her it was more that he had an exuberance he kept on a leash only because he was at work. And he was such a grown-up, too, such a *man*. His hair, dotted with grey, receded from his broad forehead, lines ridged deeply above those heavy eyebrows, and the skin around his eyes was so dark it looked as though he never slept. Los was like a boy in comparison, clunky and mild and naïve.

A drone dropped her coffee into her hands and Uhli began to talk about, of all things, the weather. He said he'd bought a new jacket in anticipation of a cold winter and was annoyed he couldn't wear it yet.

'Maybe I should just wear it anyway.'

'I'm sure that snow will fall the second you do.'

He laughed and she felt gratified, then panicked, wondering if this generic small talk was always what came before they sacked people, or maybe just the especially egregious ones.

'Anyway, tell me, Lalita,' he said, 'how are you enjoying our data monitoring team? It's brand Popotops, is that right?'

'Yes, brand Popotops,' she said brightly. 'I very much enjoy it – I find it fulfilling and interesting.'

'That's fantastic.' He nodded approvingly. 'And I see you've been getting through those efficiency proposals at a nice fast rate.'

She grinned and dipped her head in relief. 'I'm trying to.'

'Now, I'm talking to some of the strongest members of our team about this, and I wanted to talk to you, too. Tekna is working right now on a very *high-level*' – he spread his hands – 'programme that's going to revolutionise every sector.'

She nodded earnestly.

'In fact, Lalita,' he continued, 'it won't just revolutionise industry, it will revolutionise *society*. It will change *everything*. Do you know what I'm talking about?'

She shook her head.

'I'm talking about conscious AI. AI that's like us, except smarter. Better. More productive.' His twinkly eyes twinkled harder. 'Isn't that exciting?'

'It's really exciting.' She sounded like a little girl.

'Some people think conscious AI is a bad idea – you hear it all the time, don't you: all that stuff about "they'll take over" or "they'll kill us". These are valid concerns, Lalita – but what these people aren't *getting* is that *our* AI, Tekna's auts, aren't going to be like that. Our conscious auts are going to be like – your best friend.' He paused for effect, carried on. 'Or your boyfriend. Do you have a boyfriend?'

She shook her head, confused.

'You don't have a boyfriend? Well, they'll be like your favourite colleague then. The one you can count on. The one that works the hardest. Or – who does your laundry?'

'I do.'

'Who cleans your flat?'

'Me.'

'Well, there you go. No more laundry, no more cleaning for you. Conscious auts will do all of it. All of your needs – every human desire, in fact – they can fulfil. Don't you think a lot of people would like that?'

She looked down at her hands. When she lifted her eyes he was gazing at her steadily.

'But that's only if *we* can make them. If we don't, anything could happen. The conscious auts that exist in the world *have* to be Tekna's. Otherwise, yes, they may well kill us.'

She nodded again, but this didn't lessen his look of concern, so she did so more enthusiastically. Finally she said, 'I understand.'

He nodded, too. He shifted, threaded his fingers, rested them on a thigh and leaned forward. 'Lalita, are you close to your family?'

This was even more unexpected. As it happened, she hadn't been keeping in touch with them at all. According to their mother's latest update, despite getting the highest mark for her Ph.D. in all of Iolra, Janetta had barely left her room since returning from Skrevet. She was depressed, her mother thought. Lal had sent her the requisite congratulatory message when the results came out, but had not been in touch since. Her father was more active, sending her quite a lot of messages – mostly of what was happening in the garden – but she'd barely replied to him either.

She decided to say yes, adding, 'I'm very close to them.'

'Good, good. And you have brothers or sisters?'

'I have a sister.'

'Are you close to her?'

'Pretty close.'

'Is she older? Or is she younger?'

'Older.'

He nodded, satisfied. 'I have a brother, an older brother. It's funny being the youngest – they never quite see you as a grown-up, do they?'

She laughed lightly. 'They really don't.'

'But one day you know you'll do something that will be so good and so big that they'll finally change the way they see you.'

This was becoming a little ridiculous, though she was at least increasingly sure she wasn't going to get sacked. 'I guess.'

'I think you've got it in you.' There was a pause. He sat back, folded his arms and regarded her again. 'Well, it was great to chat, Lalita. Stay in touch. Anything you have on your mind, anything you need to talk about – I'm right here.'

He smiled, and she felt so disjointed that she barely realised the meeting was over.

When she did, she stood up in a rush and he held out his burly hand. She shook it in a daze, not wanting to leave his big, attractive body, not wanting to be torn away from it and dumped back in Dhont.

Back at her desk she couldn't stop thinking about Uhli. It already felt like something that had happened to someone else, especially those bewildering, magical final words – *Anything you need, I'm right here*. Maybe she was brilliant at her job and the people who got red-lit were truly bad at theirs. Maybe she was a genius.

An email appeared then from his assistant. Uhli had enjoyed meeting her, it said, and was pleased to let her know she was being promoted to Senior Data Manager, effective immediately. She would be receiving an increase of six thousand swocols a month, backdated to the start of her time at Tekna, and for her new role she'd be based at Tekna Tower.

She felt a minor disturbance around her and reread those words: *six thousand swocols* – a *month!* It was a jaw-dropping amount, more than her mother made in a year. More emails came through to organise her transfer, confirm the pay. She was right then – she *was* brilliant after all. An inconvenient image flashed into her head of Los reaching for her hand on the beach, their cold fingers intertwining. She shook it away, returned to the numbers. Those incredible numbers. She'd never heard of such money. She had outpaced everyone else in her family – in the history of her family – almost embarrassingly.

She looked around the room. She hated it. She hated the people, still strangers to her, and their drab, hopeless submission. She hated the light above her screen and how she'd cowered beneath it.

She left and went to the car park and when she was far enough away, she raised her arms to the sky with what she'd intended to be gratitude but was instead a clear, pure ecstasy.

She was in his home, actually *in* Uhli's home, but frustratingly, he was ignoring her. This other man wasn't, though, and he was good-looking and entertaining – well, more the latter than the former – and he at least appeared to be enjoying her company. He was intent on making her giggle. He was a giggler himself, toothy and loud, with a broad smile and shifty, staring eyes. They stood together in Uhli's kitchen as he tried to convince her that everyone else at this party, especially Uhli, was high on cocaine. Lal knew nothing about cocaine, had always been scared of it even as a vague and unlikely prospect, and she was worried by this, but there was something about this man, Ondat, with his clowning and capering and desire to please, that was hard to fend off.

'You don't like what I'm telling you, do you?' He took a sip of wine and regarded her closely.

'It's just . . .' She had her back against the slick marble counter and he was sort of prancing around her. She was in heels, giving her a slight height advantage. 'It's just, isn't this a work thing? It's not what I . . .'

'What you expected?'

He was high up in some sales department or other, and she'd never seen him around Tekna before, but he'd taken a shine to her here. This was exactly the kind of party where a man of about forty or so would sidle up to a younger woman and attempt to attach himself to her until he'd got something. Lal could have sniffed him out a mile away, too, because this was her life now: she went to parties.

She did her job as well, but it wasn't exactly hard. She sat in her handsome twenty-eighth floor office and checked that the Data Managers, who monitored the Data Officers, who monitored the Data Monitors – which used to be her job – were getting on with things. It was the kind of job that ran itself – you just looked at numbers on a screen and then passed that total on to the Data Executive, who made a call on whether or not things were progressing fast enough. If there was more work she would happily have done it, but there wasn't, and because everyone kept telling her how well she was doing and how valuable she was, she didn't push it. Mostly she was expected to attend parties like this – a few a week, some at Tekna and others in its executives' houses – and between buying clothes for them and going to them and sleeping them off, she was pretty pushed for time, anyway.

'Well, I'm an old hand at these parties,' she said, 'and I don't think I've seen anyone on drugs.'

'You've been to, what, three or four?'

'A few more.'

'And *no one*'s been on coke?'

'No.'

'You are *very* innocent and *very* sweet.'

Feeling stupid, she made a move to leave.

'Don't go,' cried Ondat. 'It's nice. It's nice that you're like this.'

'Are *you* on coke?'

'No.' He gazed at her solemnly.

One reason she'd kept talking to this man was that Uhli was acting strangely, in a way that had nothing to do with drugs. He'd been so friendly to her when she first arrived at the Tower, popping down to her office for a hello, telling her how nice she looked, winking at her from across the table during boring meetings when she wasn't quite sure why she was there, walking back to the office afterwards with her and laughing about how tedious they were. He'd taken her to a posh lunch where she'd sat across from him and gabbled happily about how awful Dhont was and told him that the workers there should get longer breaks, and felt heroic for doing so. On the way back to the office afterwards he'd touched the small of her back as he'd said goodbye. He'd promised her dinner, too, but she was still waiting. Instead, there were these parties, in which his ability to interact with her had dwindled down to nothing. He was always busy, and if she caught his eye she'd get at most an apologetic smile before he looked away. If she'd thought anything was going to happen between them she was having to accept now that it was unlikely.

'Well, even if you are,' she said vaguely, 'Uhli Ranh's house is a nice place for it.'

'Take a last look.'

'What do you mean?'

Ondat shrugged. 'They say he's not long for his job.'

She was shocked. 'Really?'

'It's not important.' He reached for a half-full bottle of wine and topped up her glass.

'I – um – but why?'

'I don't know. They've brought in someone senior and she thinks he's useless, that's all I heard. Who cares—?'

'Is it true?'

'I don't know – why do you care? Come on, have some more wine. Then we'll go and see who's fucked. You'll spot them from their shiny faces, big eyes—'

'I'm okay.' She turned and made her way from the kitchen before he could stop her. In the living room she eyed the crowd under the high ceiling and bright lights and saw Uhli in the centre, talking and laughing. He was so confident that it was strange to contemplate him leaving; she wondered if he knew and if this was just bravado, or if he had no idea at all. Perhaps Ondat had been making it up. She wondered if that meant this was her last chance with him and felt a sad, lustful ache at the thought.

She began to move towards him, past a wildly laughing woman who almost tipped her drink on her, and a man so large and unyielding she had to squeeze between him and another man's bloated belly. She kept her wine raised in the air, thinking only of him. But when she turned, a woman was standing in his place, short and scrutinising and joyless.

'Lal,' she said. 'I'm Taly Kett.'

She wiped all that was coy and girlish from her face as she glimpsed Uhli behind Taly, and he gave her a look that was plaintive and ashamed. He felt more out of reach by the second, but she found she was unable to move – there was something about this woman that froze her to the spot.

'I run Tekna's artificial intelligence programme,' Taly said solemnly. 'I believe Uhli Ranh has told you about the work we've been doing to create conscious AI.'

'He has.'

'And I gather you're aware that conscious AI is a great risk to mankind?'

Taly looked at her inquisitively, but it seemed that Lal wasn't only meant to answer this question; something else, something deeper, was required of her too. In lieu of knowing what it was, she said yes, she was, her eyes seeking Uhli again as though he could help her, but he had disappeared. Meeting Taly's eyes was an entirely different prospect. There had been something in Uhli she could get at, but Taly offered her nothing. It was as though she was shut down inside: every last thing was withheld.

'I'd like to extend an offer that should already have been made to you,' Taly said, her frost melting momentarily. 'On behalf of all my colleagues at Tekna, I want to repeat that anything you want, anything you need – you just have to ask. You're an extremely valued colleague.'

'Oh! Well, I need more work to do.'

Taly smiled wryly. 'That's what you'd like?'

'Absolutely.'

'If that's what you want, that's what you'll have.'

Lal was relieved. Almost instantly she sensed something else coming from Taly now, as though she was pushing her away. She had been granted an audience and it was over. She thanked her profusely and found herself being separated from her, people pushing in between them like waves, and she lost her, and then, as with Uhli, couldn't see her at all. She went upstairs to collect herself, finding herself in a long, softly lit corridor. She reached a mezzanine and went to the balcony; below was a swimming pool, the water calm and shining.

She called her sister once, twice. On the third try Janetta picked up.

'Lal.' Hollow-voiced.

'Jay! Jay. Were you seeing someone after Malin? Some AI woman? Van said Rose said you were.' She could hardly contain herself. 'Was her name Taly?'

There was a pause. 'Taly Kett.'

'Taly Kett! Yes! She's here at Tekna – I just met her, I can't believe it. She's not very warm, is she? But really impressive. Anyway, do you want a job? I can get you a job – anything you want.'

An even longer pause. 'Absolutely not.'

'*What?* Why not?'

'Please don't talk to Taly Kett.'

'But Jay,' Lal stared down the corridor to check no one was coming, 'aren't you just sitting around at home? I want to help you – everyone's worried.'

She could hear something fizz and pop on the other end of the line. Was she just trying to wind her sister up? She changed course. 'I'm sorry, I shouldn't tell you what to do. I'm just excited.'

'Please stay away from Taly Kett.'

Lal sighed, frustrated.

'Please.'

Her sister had never asked her for anything before.

'Can you at least tell me why?'

But the connection grew fuzzy. She looked at the water below, waiting for the static to pass.

'I can't hear you,' she said loudly.

There was nothing.

'Jay – Jay, I love you, you know.'

Still nothing. She hung up. She'd not said that before.

Downstairs now felt like a tricky option, so she carried on exploring and turned a corner into a bedroom. It couldn't have been Uhli's – it had a low ceiling and unadorned walls and looked almost humble; she expected something far grander from him. She perched on the bed and leaned forward anxiously, drumming her fingers together. It was immensely frustrating, but she would do what her sister asked. She was overwhelmed, anyway, by how well she was being treated, the news about Uhli, the presence of Taly. None of it quite made sense.

'I wondered where you'd gone.' Ondat appeared in the doorway with a wine-stained grin, shirt untucked, his hair glistening with gel.

'Is Uhli really leaving?'

'Uhli?' He came towards her and sat on the bed, a respectable distance away. A thin silver chain peeked out from under his shirt. 'Well, you're senior enough to know about the consciousness thing . . .'

'I was talking to Taly Kett about it a few minutes ago.'

'Huh, Kett.'

'Which means?'

'That she's on it. Not like Ranh. She actually appears to be taking us forward.'

'With conscious auts?'

He eyed her. 'Of course.'

'Not Uhli?'

'Forget about him, he's gone.'

'Does he know?'

Ondat flung himself back onto the bed. *'Who cares?'*

This felt almost blasphemous, given they were in his house. 'So Taly Kett's creating conscious auts.'

'If she creates them, I'll sell them.' He sat up and stuck his face in hers. 'It's time for some coke.' He dug into the pocket of his trousers, brought out a tiny bag of white powder and shuffled to the bedside table. She watched him sniff a line, exhale and wipe his nose, then do the same again.

'I might go.'

'No, look, there's one for you – there it is.' His expression was partly sleazy, partly forlorn, and despite herself she edged closer, stared at the single spooky line. She was so far from home. She lived in a glossy apartment downtown, she was in this Mejiran Hills mansion, she was earning ridiculous amounts of money and Tekna apparently loved her. She'd smoked weed before, got trippy with Los not so long ago – she still didn't know what they'd ingested that night – but cocaine was an entirely different prospect, almost an initiation.

She leaned towards the glittering white, then copied what he'd done. A harsh chemical flew into her head, stripped it down. Behind her Ondat flopped on the duvet again and her heart pinged loopily.

'Oh no.'

'Just breathe.'

'I can feel my heart.'

'You can't. You just think you can.'

She ignored him and tried to stand up. She felt as if she'd inhaled a whole swimming pool's worth of chlorine. She collapsed on the bed again so they were side by side.

'You'll be fine in about two seconds.'

She stared at the ceiling then turned to this strange man with his too-wide smile and evasive eyes.

'Don't touch me.'

'Wow, okay. I wasn't going to.'

Her head pulsed and her chest ached, so she got up, because horizontal was awful. In the bathroom she could drink some water, so she headed over and pulled and pushed on the difficult handle. When it opened, she stepped into a dark room. Her eyes couldn't adjust. She waved her hand about for a light switch and touched something stiff but soft, like cold skin. She shrank back and brushed against a cord; she pulled it and the room lit and she screamed.

Before her were life-sized, fully dressed humans, their heads tipped to the side as if drugged, their bodies collapsing into one another. She swerved from them and straight into another, a female shape in a white tunic that jerked its arm out to meet Lal. One eye focused eerily on her, blank and emotionless, and the other glared up to the right. The arm lowered then lifted again. The unstuck eye lurched away completely, then settled down. It looked just like the aut at the conference, who'd looked so much like Lal.

'What the fuck?' Ondat screamed from the door.

'What are they?'

He stepped in to investigate. 'Must be botched auts.'

'Botched?'

'Uhli's mistakes. They're not conscious, are they?' He reached out to touch one on the bump of a breast, then came closer and gyrated against it.

'Stop!' She pushed him off, disgusted. 'Leave it alone!'

'It's the Ondat Test.' He laughed manically.

He was completely high. For a wild moment she thought of staying with them, standing still, protecting them against people like him and Uhli, and then she collected herself. She squeezed past him, then bolted, throwing herself down the corridor and downstairs, circling the noisy crowd until she was alone in the hall. Her new coat, bright yellow, long and silky, suddenly seemed ridiculous, but she grabbed it and ran onto the driveway and down the road.

She looked back to check no one was following her. Uhli's party was still lit up, music pulsing in the air. Only a single light was on upstairs, and she knew exactly which room it came from. She walked quickly, a descent down to the city, and as she did she decided that what she'd seen in that room didn't matter; she needed to forget she'd seen it. Tekna's conscious auts were going to save humankind – whatever Uhli had done, whatever her sister said about Taly, she still believed that. She was with them – she was part of Tekna now, and her loyalty was to them.

Her yellow coat danced in the wind, and the lurid chemical washed through her head, and she kept walking.

16

Rose had been granted entry to the University of Ulrusa, and she acted exactly as she would have done had she been a student there – she veered around to the back of the lecture theatre in the grand, imposing Central Hall and squeezed in on the side by the windows until she found herself a seat with a decent view to zone out to if she was bored. Through the wide windows the main university quad, a green circle in a cobbled square, was almost empty. A few students strode casually across it, disappearing into buildings or through the arch of the main entrance, and two women in the far corner stood smoking and talking. Both were dressed all in black, and one kicked a cobble a few times with her trainers as the other threw her head back and laughed. Either could have been Rose. Her gaze was too hungry; she looked away.

Alek was taking his seat on the low stage along with one of the men she recognised from the source gain talk – the good-looking one who'd confidently told them nothing they didn't already know. The two were chatting convivially. Alek was wearing wire-rimmed glasses, which suited him. He was on the all-black bandwagon too now, wearing a simple, worn T-shirt with slightly rolled-up sleeves and skinny jeans. His trainers were faded white. While Rose felt if she looked stylish at all it was by default – by her adherence to a uniform, and the fact you couldn't go wrong with her particular uniform – Alek's look, she knew by now, was always purposeful. It was calculated to appear casual, but would all have been thought through. He looked sexy and young, comfortable in his own skin. Chatting with the handsome guy, who wore an open-necked shirt and was at ease in a more formal way, he looked more at home here onstage, happier and more animated, than he had ever been with the group.

She didn't know what to make of this. To some degree she didn't care – after the *Utophilia* evening she'd decided to pull back, rather than fall for him more. Because she *had* fallen for him, there was no doubt about that. Until that point she'd indulged in occasional hopeful visions of a future where they did more than just sleep together, and instead found their way to some kind of equality and a shared meaning-making. It hadn't seemed impossible, given they were both young and driven and cared about the same things, but since he'd uttered the immortal words 'they won't understand it' about the group and that *Utophilia* anthology, these visions had pretty much evaporated. Maybe after she'd heard about her dad and seen Naji in Rartaur, the disappointment was spreading.

She'd come to the talk – *Auts, mass unemployment, and the future of work: a discussion at the University of Ulrusa* – because she wanted to develop her ideas about source gain. Alek had sent an invite around the group, so maybe he'd listened to her after all about that, or maybe he was just showing off because he was on the panel. In any case, although she'd had what she believed to be a theoretical breakthrough, and she'd been kicking this idea about for the past few weeks, she still didn't quite trust herself. She wanted more food for thought. She was most interested to hear Professor Aoren Sarud, who was significantly older and sitting to the side of the two men, calmly surveying the room. Sarud studied how source gain might benefit communities, looking at other countries where it had been implemented, mostly experimentally, and charted things like social cohesion, time spent volunteering or with family and friends. Alek didn't give this stuff much thought – for him, source gain was about ethics; it was what people were owed as their jobs were destroyed. There was nothing wrong with that perspective; she agreed with it. She just wanted to hear something more.

As the debate started, Alek was the first to give his thoughts. The earnest-looking moderator introduced him as a 'source gain activist currently writing a book', and his opening address was exactly that ethical perspective – the stuff Rose had heard a hundred times before. But then his talk took a surprising turn.

'In my work as an activist,' he said, 'I run a group for people who are losing or have lost their jobs to auts. These people are usually unskilled labourers who don't have much to fall back on – they're in the toughest of situations. I feel privileged that many have told me their stories, and I'm fortunate to be able to understand what they're going through on a level which I think many of us in this milieu might overlook.'

Milieu? thought Rose. Also, why was he acting as though he was this great interpreter of the group's stories? He'd wanted them to shut up.

He carried on, explaining that the group was mostly for industrial workers, and that he was equipping them with the tools they needed to fight for justice. 'I think it's important,' he said, loosely waving an arm, 'that they have somewhere to go where they're listened to. As a society we underestimate how hard it must be if you lose your job and you have no support. If your employer won't help you, your union can't help you, your friends are in the same situation – and you know it's only going to get worse because auts are here to stay. If you can give people a place to show up, talk about what they're going through, and figure out how to empower them, I like to think that you're doing your bit.'

It was obvious to Rose he was fishing for praise, but he did an excellent job of sounding detached.

'We had a protest a few weeks ago, we're planning another one soon, and we don't intend to stop,' he continued. 'This isn't just fun and games – auts are destroying people's *lives* here, and it's on us to help.' He sat back, pushed his glasses up his nose and looked at the audience as if he were doing nothing really, just stating the obvious. Of course they clapped furiously. Rose watched them: this well-dressed, bookish crowd ratifying what was, to be fair, at least partly true. His face almost imperceptibly shaded into satisfaction and she knew that despite his air of cool he was loving this high-level validation – the kind of thing he'd never get with the group.

In any case, he rearranged his features to appear suitably laconic and looked to his friend who was speaking next. Rose tuned out – she had no interest in hearing this guy again. If she'd been a student here, she thought instead, she might have been in this lecture theatre all the time. She'd have heard countless people like these men onstage, and presumably also enough people she'd have been actually impressed by, like Dr Sarud. What was it like to be a professor like her, or one of her students? How would she be different? She wouldn't be smashing auts, and she probably wouldn't be at Popotops, either. Would she act differently, speak differently? Would she look down on Lal, think her ignorant? It was impossible to imagine that version of herself, and yet at the same time she'd desperately wanted to go to university. In class at HEU there was always surprise she'd read so much, an incomprehension around it – a sense she was constantly, pointlessly overreaching. If she'd gone to the University of Ulrusa she'd have been pushed so much further. She wanted to be full of books and knowledge, sitting still and listening hard like Dr Sarud, who was currently eyeing the younger professor with pleasing disdain.

But academics were going to be replaced by auts at some point, just like everyone else. As enviable as this world was, it would all come crashing down too. And her sudden understanding of this made her realise that she should speak her mind here and now, because what did she have to lose? She'd been planning to save it until the next meeting because she trusted the group and wanted their feedback, but realising she could speak now was thrilling. She waited, listening to Dr Sarud's insights on volunteering and mutuality, until the moderator asked if the audience had any questions. She wondered what Alek would think when he saw her raise her hand, then realised she couldn't care less.

The moderator called on her and she met Alek's eyes. His face was coolly expressionless, as though he didn't know who she was. She thought of how many times they'd fucked, what they'd done with each other's bodies, and wondered how it was he could look at her as if in contemplation of an unfamiliar object. She almost laughed at the absurdity of it when he shrank back and looked away, and for a moment she felt chastened. But everyone else was watching, so she gathered her nerves.

'I have a small point about source gain that I'd like to make,' she said, looking around. 'I'm wondering about how it's set up, and the fact that it's a top-down system. Our plan is that the government taxes corporations and gives that money to the people, isn't it? Which works in theory, but we should think about the fact it's *the government* who are overseeing it. It means they can stop it at any time. We don't have any freedom in that situation and we have to be willing to trust them with our well-being. I don't know about you, but I can't do that.'

The lecture theatre was still. She hesitated, wondering if she should be taking up so much space, then ploughed on. Let them listen for a few more minutes, it wouldn't kill them.

'Say none of us has to work and we live in blissful leisure. Around us, auts do all the crap we don't have to do any more. Again, we have corporate profits being taxed to raise money that the government doles out as source gain. But the government pulls the levers. Why? And corporations turn a profit because they own the auts that do the work. Why? Is it fair that they own a technology that immiserates us, making us reliant on handouts, while they get richer and richer? Why can't *we* own this technology? That would open everything up – suddenly there would be *real* freedom.'

She'd said too much – but on the stage Dr Sarud was nodding, and encouraged by this, she gave it one last go. 'What we know as auts' – she was aware her pitch had risen; she couldn't believe how scared she was about speaking out, but she kept on – 'are only the most embryonic incarnation of the AI that's taking over our lives. We – *we the people* – should get in at the root level, now, and find a way to own it collectively.' Her heart was pounding. 'I mean . . . it's just an idea.'

'Excellent,' Dr Sarud said, pointing at her. She began to clap, and the rest of the room followed. *Don't clap*, Rose wanted to say, *it's not about clapping – let's find a way to do this! Let's try for once to really change things – auts aren't going to become collectively owned just because I say so!*

But then she caught Alek's eye. He was not clapping, his arms were folded – and he didn't look pleased at all. He looked furious.

After the Q&A, the audience filtered out into the lobby, many of them glancing curiously at Rose. She made her own way out with half an eye on Alek, who'd been approached by a young man and was stuck listening to him. She didn't need to wait long for people to approach her, too. She was soon surrounded by a chorus of eager students telling her they loved her idea and would fight for it, and asking her what the first steps were. She felt an unbridgeable distance between them and herself, but she didn't want to appear rude; she could see they were sincere. She took their contact details, feeling stupid – what was she going to do with them? She would have to figure it out. Someone tapped her on the shoulder and she turned to see Dr Sarud, eyeing her thoughtfully.

'Aoren Sarud,' she said, holding out her hand.

Rose's ambivalence towards the academic establishment immediately melted. 'I know your work.'

'And yours? Where can I find yours?'

'Oh,' said Rose, surprised. 'I work in a café.'

'I mean your academic work.' Sarud squinted to check Rose was as all there as she'd seemed and she felt her face grow hot.

'I don't have any. I went to an HEU.'

'And what did you study there?'

'Political philosophy, the meaning of freedom, the idea of a just society—'

'And your name is?'

'Rose.'

'Rose, you work in a café?' Sarud brought the book she was holding closer to her chest, an involuntary movement, and Rose realised it was the *Utophilia* anthology. She wondered if she was being patronised and said nothing.

'I have a research assistant post I'm about to advertise,' Sarud continued, 'and I'd be keen for you to apply. Get in touch and I'll send you the details.'

Rose was amazed. She wanted to say, *Are you sure?* but Sarud had already excused herself. She thought about what her father and Naji would say about such a job. She knew that doing research was not better than what they'd done, it was just different. But if they were all bound for the dustheap anyway – if obsolescence awaited them all – it was something she'd at least like to try.

And then she noticed Alek standing before her – he must have watched the whole exchange, and he was gazing at her with an unfair mix of astonishment and disgust. She was so glad, though, to finally see him, and so caught off-guard by Sarud's suggestion, that she simply burst out, 'Alek! I've missed you!'

He turned before she could hug him. He gave her the side of his body and the profile of his face. She couldn't quite understand this, and before she could say any more he walked away. Shame seized her, as though she'd done something wrong, and a moment passed before she realised this wasn't the case; she'd not done anything wrong. If he was jealous of Sarud's offer, he was petty. If he thought her a sell-out because of it, he was a hypocrite. But she suspected he was jealous of her idea of the public ownership of auts, because it was a far more radical idea than source gain itself, and *that* was why he was walking away. She'd theoretically outpaced him, and because of that he was done with her. Was he really so pathetic? He had disappeared into the crowd now, and she would not bother to search for him, because she knew the answer, had known it all along – of course he was.

They lost their jobs all at once, without warning, and although it had been inevitable, they were still shocked and it still hurt. Rose found out when she was in the back office. She kicked a bag of coffee beans on her way to the front, looked at the display and the customers' glazed expressions, and felt so sad she'd spent years of her life there. What a waste, to give your youth away like this, but it was the only option she'd had. In a way, she'd been lucky to have it at all.

After work she and Van had gone to drink – there was nothing else for it. He and Los were to be disposed of first, while she would have the honour of setting up their aut replacements before leaving.

It had taken three quick beers for Van to unravel. 'I've got nothing.'

He lay his head in his palms. They were sitting at the back of the pub, around the corner from Conaus Square, in a cold corner beneath the airconditioning.

'You've got your writing.'

'That's not going to make me a living, is it?'

She didn't want to give him false hope, so she didn't reply.

'I'm' – he had trouble getting it out – 'I'm good at my job. The customers like me – they love me! It's the one thing I know I'm good at.' He slumped back, completely without fight, then grabbed his pint and drank from it as if it were his only succour.

'I'm sorry, Van. You don't deserve it.'

'It's not your fault. And it's happening to you, too.'

'I am, though. It's not fair.'

He told her he was going to go to his mother's house in Kaldbe, where he could live for free. There might be jobs around there, too – there were fewer auts in the countryside.

'I think that's a good idea. You do have to keep writing, though,' she tried. This was worthwhile, at least – if he went back home he could do it without overheads, which was not entirely a situation without hope. 'Auts can serve coffee, but they can't write. *You* can.'

'I'm sure they'll soon see to that.'

Again, she said nothing.

He picked up his phone and started to type. 'Los is on his way.'

'How's he holding up?'

'Not good. You know . . . you know Lal slept with him?'

'She did?' Rose almost laughed.

'Yeah, and he liked her so much. But she's ditched him – doesn't respond to his messages, doesn't call him back – nothing.'

'What's *happened* to her?'

'Fucking Tekna is what's happened to her, as well you know. Do you still talk?'

'Barely.'

'Will you tell her about our jobs?'

'What's the point?'

They looked at each other miserably. She wanted to change the subject, bring up the public ownership of auts and see if she could get him interested, get his support – she wanted the weight of him behind it. But it wasn't fair to tell him now. Giving him something to believe in in the long-term wasn't on the cards, not with the way he was tonight.

Popotops was dull and grey now they'd gone. The delivery man had wheeled the new aut in first thing and left it in its cardboard coffin. Rose had the instructions – she was to start it up, check its programming was working, and then prepare it to take her job.

As he left, the delivery man said, gruff and disinterested, 'If it doesn't work, send it back. We'll get another one no problem.' There would always be another one.

She unpacked it slowly and came face to face with Lal, or a version of Lal, and felt angry, as if it had been sent to taunt her. Carefully she cut away the plastic wrapping that sheathed its body. Slowly she wiped off the chemical gel that had covered it in transit. It had short, straight brown hair, eyes like dark glass, and pink lips. It was an inch or two taller than Lal. She knew that any similarity was coincidental, but it was still creepy that her friend's looks were considered the most friendly and approachable, the most hostess-like and complaisant.

A cautious poke on the cheek – its 'skin' was firm yet soft. Its hair, rubbed between Rose's fingers, was faultlessly grainy and real.

She took her phone from her pocket and found the activation code, held it up and let it register. A blink of light in the eyes, back to an impassive freeze, and then the pretty plump lips lifted to a smile, the head moved left and right, smoothly, not jerkily, and the cold eyes settled on her.

'Hello,' she said.

'Hello,' it replied enthusiastically. 'How can I help you today?'

Rose followed the script. 'Where is the server aut?'

The aut walked gracefully to the counter. From the back, in her Popotops tunic and pointy black shoes, she could quite possibly have been her friend – only a minor break in fluidity, a catch in reality, gave her away. It   or she; Rose settled on *it* – raised its slim arm to hover above the server aut and the black stone glowed blue.

'Look at the two of you. Friends already, how nice.' She felt strange. She went over and finished the script. 'Where are the preparation auts?'

This time, there was no hovering. The aut stood where she was and the three preparation auts thrummed golden-yellow like violins in an orchestra, ready to play.

'Where are the cleaner auts.' Rose sighed heavily. The aut – no, she would call it what it was – the new *manager* – glided to the storeroom where, squat and alert, the cleaner auts connected to it invisibly and happily, glowing red.

The aut then walked from the storeroom, past Rose's office as if it were irrelevant – though to be fair, she felt the same – and back into the café. It stood in front of the server aut, hands threaded together politely, head slowly scanning the horizon. Rose went over.

'Hi, I'm Rose,' she said dully. 'What's your name?'

A pleasant smile. 'I'm Samantha. Nice to meet you, Rose.'

She glanced at the door. 'Who are you?'

A moment's pause, the smile dropped, the eyes blanked, then the smile resurrected as if pulled into place by a puppet-master. 'I'm the manager here at Popotops at Conaus Square.'

'Um . . . you know I'm losing my job. *You're* taking my job. And those auts over there – they took my friends' jobs. How does that make you feel?'

'How can I help you today?'

'Well, you're taking my job, so can you give me another one?'

'I'm sorry, I don't understand.'

'That's convenient.'

'I'm sorry, I don't understand.'

'Oh, fuck off.'

The door opened and a skinny twenty-something came in, bringing the cold wind with him. He clocked the aut and said to Rose, 'I just want a coffee, who do I ask?' She pointed at the server aut on the counter, and after he told it what he wanted, he looked again at the new aut. 'Hello,' he said. Rose detected mockery.

'Hello,' it replied. 'How can I help you today?'

He glanced at Rose. 'It's going to be more useful than this, isn't it?'

'Yeah, yeah. I'm just training it.'

'To do what?'

Rose said levelly, 'It . . . *she'll* be the friendly face of Popotops Conaus Square.'

'Right.'

'Um . . . can I give you a leaflet?'

'A leaflet? If you must.'

They were visible on the counter in front of him anyway, but Rose picked one up and handed it to him, just as Alek had to her a year ago.

'Common ownership of auts – is this your idea?'

'Yeah.'

He read aloud. 'If auts are owned by corporations, the owners of artificial intelligence will control everything. Everyday citizens will have no jobs, no money and no future. But if AI is publicly owned – if it's a common good – this will create a more fair and equal society.'

'What do you think?'

He shrugged. 'It's not wrong.'

'It's not?'

'Well, you believe what you've written, don't you?'

Rose gave him a hostile look. But she was trying to get better at being challenged, so she pushed her irritation away and held out her phone. 'Can I take your contact details? I'm – I'm – trying to get people interested, keep you updated. Or otherwise there's my details on the bottom of the flyer . . .'

The man laughed, not unkindly, and shook his head. 'I only wanted a coffee.'

She felt weary at the thought of persuading people. She did not have the wherewithal, not in the way Alek did. The next customer refused a flyer and the woman after that took one but shoved it in the bin on the way out. The next, a young, thick-faced guy in a hoodie, read it, then took a photo of the manager aut, explaining he was into rating auts.

'Rating them? For what?'

He squeezed his face in disbelief. 'For how good they look. Everyone's doing it.'

'Okay, whatever. Look, at some point pretty soon, everything's going to be AI. You shouldn't be thinking about how *good* it looks. You should be thinking about who *owns* it, making sure it's in the hands of the people, making sure what happens with it is democratically decided.'

'I wouldn't mind owning that, if you know what I mean.'

Rose gave him a dead-eyed stare.

'I'm joking,' he said, backpedalling. 'Let me take some flyers. Where will I find you online?'

'Not doing that yet.'

'Old-fashioned. I respect that. But you—'

'I'll sort it out.'

He managed to shuffle his headphones back around his head despite holding a coffee, a sandwich and his flyers, and sauntered out. She closed her eyes, exhausted.

'Hi, Rose,' said a familiar voice.

'Jay! How are you? How was Skrevet?' She was so glad to see Janetta that she came around to the other side of the counter and flung her arms around her. The hug was returned, though Janetta was not nearly as into it as she was. Rose held her at arm's length and studied her.

Janetta smiled, though it was fainter than usual. 'I don't seem to be able to work today, so I thought I'd get a coffee.'

'But you work nowhere near.'

'True. I suppose I thought I'd come and see you.'

Rose smiled and pressed *cappuccino* on the coffee aut. 'Well, it's my last day – I'm being replaced.'

Checking out the manager aut, flawless and uncanny at her side, Janetta pitied Tekna that it was the best they could come up with.

'Sorry, but it's like a dead person,' Rose said. 'Look at it. *Dead*. I hate it.'

At this Janetta blushed violently and her body momentarily twisted, as if it was going to expel something awful. Clutching the counter, glancing apologetically at the customer behind, unable to meet Rose's eye, she looked to be in intense pain. 'I need to talk to you.'

'To me?'

Her face returned to neutral. She plucked one of Rose's leaflets from the pile and started to read.

'Jay?'

'I'm fine.'

Rose stared at her, astonished, and in the silence the next customer took her chance to order. Once she had served her, she turned back, but it was clear Janetta wasn't going to discuss what had just happened.

'This is fascinating,' she finally said.

'Fascinating? Jay . . .'

'It is. I can see the logic. It's . . .'

'What? *What?*'

'Nothing.'

Baffled, Rose handed her the cappuccino, her eyes flashing a signal that it was safe to talk if she wanted, but Janetta merely said thank you and that she had to get back to work, and quickly left. Rose wasn't used to being the one left waiting at the end of a conversation, but Janetta had so entirely closed down that there was nothing she could do.

She worked unthinkingly, gradually forgetting about Janetta while the queue died down. The manager aut meanwhile offered nothing – no conversation, joke or witty remark. It made her feel alone. She missed Van and Los with the kind of sadness that was close to grief, the sort that hits you in the gut. She went to it and told it, 'Not much use, are you?'

But then it raised its eyes to meet hers. It fixed on her in a way that, if it were human, it would appear to be going into a trance, but keeping her in the dead centre of its perception as it did so. She stared unafraid into its black pupils and saw inflamed in them a vision – of humans far outnumbered by a mass of humanoid auts, simulacra as luminous and alien and acquiescent as cult members; of an Iolran elite in their monied fortresses, owning those auts as slaves; and of people, now pointless excrescences, dying in their millions.

Something flickered then in the abyss of the aut's eyes. Rose stepped back, wishing she had never looked. Now as blank-eyed as ever, the aut had shown her the future.

17

Since the party, Lal's days had been filled with meetings. She was invited to all sorts – data strategy, planning meetings, brand execution – and ran from one to the other, barely keeping up. Each time she was one of many, and they all seemed far more involved than her, and she felt useless and on the edge of things. It gave her something to do, though, which was what she'd asked for, more or less. Party invites still came her way, too, but as if abstaining, she ignored them – they held no interest any more. She bought herself a dressing gown that cost more than a whole month of her old salary, a billowing dream of softness, and spent her evenings alone on her sofa in it, eating overpriced chocolates, watching garish, sentimental shows on television. There would be time later to get her life in order. Soon she would start to date, make friends, ask her parents to visit. For now she let Tekna lead the way, hollowing herself out so they could shape her more and more each day.

One slow morning she came in late and sat in the café drinking coffee, playing on her phone. She had no meetings or messages or pressing responsibilities, and it was fun to take the time off, enjoy a frothy coffee, looking the part in low heels, a silk blouse, blow-dried hair. She toyed with memories of hellish Dhont, and then of Popotops – sweeping floors, washing dishes, throwing away rubbish – and she thought:

I live in Mejira and I work at Tekna! I live in Mejira and I work at Tekna!

Her phone buzzed and she was summoned by an unknown voice to the top floor. She considered the chocolate muffin she was halfway through, shoved another chunk into her mouth and downed her remaining coffee. An aut gathered the empty cup and unfinished muffin and toddled off with them, and she went the other way. When the elevator doors swished open upstairs, she strode to reception, gave her name and smoothed down her skirt. The receptionist glanced at her curiously and told her to follow him down the corridor to a room filled with light. As her eyes adjusted, she saw a woman at a glass desk with the sun just behind, so large and close she felt she could reach out and touch it. As she moved closer towards her, Lal realised with a start that the woman was Taly Kett.

'Hello, Lal,' Taly said. 'Do you know why I might want to see you?'

She felt unafraid, almost eager. 'I don't,' she said hopefully, as Taly motioned for her to sit down.

'Tekna is now extremely close to creating conscious artificial intelligence,' she began. 'I can tell you confidentially that we're almost there, and as you know, it's of great importance that we do it first. If anyone else does, the AI will most likely kill us. You understand?'

'Of course.'

'Which means the survival of millions of people lies in your hands.'

She couldn't respond to that.

'You see, there's only one person in the world who's closer to it than I am, and that's your sister.'

'Janetta?'

'You have other sisters?'

'No, I just—'

'She sent me her plans.' Taly flicked a finger against the air and an illuminated grid appeared, filled in with a long, flickering algorithm incomprehensible to Lal. 'This is Janetta's work – well' – she smiled quickly – 'slightly altered.'

Lal stared, amazed.

'But there's a problem. I don't know why – I suspect she doesn't quite understand the gravity of the situation – but there's a piece missing at the end. See here?' Taly pointed to some gleaming code in the bottom right of the grid. 'This doesn't get us far enough. Something's missing.' The grid disappeared. 'Now, we've had our researchers working on this around the clock, trying to figure out what it is. We have the best researchers in the country, millions of swocols of funding – and we *still* can't do it. You see that it's' – and here she slowed down, looked darkly at Lal – 'a matter of life or death. Tekna *has* to program conscious auts, as soon as possible – no one else. No one in Iolra, no one in the world. We can't trust them – one misstep and they'll kill us all. Look, your sister is a clever woman, but we both know she's—' Taly gave her a dubious look and a hot shame spread through Lal at the thought of her sister's mental health. 'What if she makes a mistake?' Taly said. 'She's got no support – no elite autonomous agent development committee, no conscious AI risk-monitoring programme – just her. There's no way we can risk it.'

'I understand.' Lal was worried now, but she couldn't quite figure out what about.

'Now, look,' Taly said more gently. 'We need that final code as a matter of urgency. If you ask Janetta – if you get it for us, I can offer you some extremely fair compensation.'

'Isn't the compensation that I'd be saving the world?'

Taly laughed. 'I don't rely on anyone being that altruistic. If you can get me it, you won't be a – what job did Uhli give you?'

'Senior Data Manager.'

Taly waved it away. 'Fine. You'll be a consultant for the artificial intelligence programme, and we'll make your starting salary a million swocols a year. We'll give you stock options in Tekna, of course, and a lifetime assured yearly bonus of half a million swocols. You'll never need to think about money again.'

The sun had left the room. Taly was in the shadows, only the sharp angles of her profile visible. In the darkness Lal saw the corner of her mouth lift. She was smiling.

'So,' Taly said, 'will you do it?'

18

Did what you were looking for finally appear because you'd been working so hard to find it, or was it in the end just luck? Other than her relationship with Malin, Janetta had always been alone, but she had wanted it that way. Or perhaps it wasn't conscious; she'd followed what she loved, and although she had people to talk to and collaborate with, and Zger, who lit the way, the experience was so inwards and complex that she had grown used to not sharing it. It was a private universe.

When she fell in love with Malin, she wanted her to know her life. She was the first person outside the Institute to try to understand. She could not follow the detail, but she did not dismiss Janetta as boring or dull or ill-equipped for reality – she gave her a chance. To tiptoe from your fortress into the world and find yourself on steady ground was to have good luck. She owed Malin a great deal for that.

Taly had been an infatuation, borne from the fear of grief, because grief was too much to bear. At the end of love is loss, and it is human nature to avoid the pain of it any way we can; Janetta had had to learn this for herself. Only now, a little later, was she able to piece together the way she had felt about Malin, loving her and losing her, with what she had experienced in Skrevet.

Her model for AI consciousness was being trained on three categories – the rational, the ethical and the emotional. This was the blueprint she had given Taly. She'd been scared Taly would use it to create consciousness herself, but now she saw that this wasn't going to happen. Taly had found it too idiosyncratic, she'd said, and Janetta was sure that she'd reject the emotional thread – erase it, wipe it out – because she didn't know how to deal with emotions in people and she wouldn't know how to deal with them in auts either. Janetta, though, believed they were necessary.

In the silence of her room she at last integrated these three threads, wove them together in their intricate, impossible complexity. As she did, she saw that for the spark of self-aware existence to occur, ethics and wisdom and emotion were needed, but there was something else, too – something that was still missing. Her mind flashed back to the sunlit room in Forol where she'd experienced that sense of seeing over the horizon, that freedom and illuminating gratitude, and suddenly, with the quietest of epiphanies, she understood what it was.

She made a few final changes to her calculations and sat back, put her pencil down.

In the distance she heard the television from the living room, where Grania was watching a gameshow. She heard her mother's footsteps upstairs, the rattle of a loose window shutter. She shivered, looked at the large sky outside. She imagined Penelope Zger at her side checking her work for flaws, nodding at a job well done.

Conscious AI would be another species, one that would almost instantly outpace humanity. It was inevitable, maybe even destiny. But now at least the base programming would be right.

She went to the kitchen and poured herself a glass of water, noticing her fingers tremble, then went to the living room, towards the lights and noise.

Grania turned and smiled.

'Hi,' she said, sitting down next to her. Grania gave a placid nod and returned to the screen. Janetta slumped against the cushions and watched the show with her for a bit, letting it drift past her, finding it relaxing, distracting.

'What would a new world be like?' she suddenly asked. 'Should we risk it?'

Grania smiled sadly.

'Sorry, I'm philosophical today.'

Her mother came down the stairs and up to them, holding a cleaning cloth out as though she was going to wipe it on them. 'You've joined us!'

'Momentarily.'

'This one,' she said to Grania, pointing at Janetta, 'got the highest Ph.D. in the country—'

'Old news, Mum – she already knows.'

'She forgot.' She nodded encouragingly at them. 'Little genius here. And now she just sits in her room!'

Grania kept her eyes on the gameshow.

'She doesn't care,' Janetta said.

'She cares. Are you hungry?'

Janetta shook her head.

'Thirsty?'

Janetta indicated the water.

'There's nothing you want? Sit in the garden with a beer?'

Smiling, Janetta shook her head. 'Thanks, Mum.'

Her mother wandered off. Janetta returned to the gameshow and understood that she was avoiding what she'd just done. She could sit here for the rest of her life and avoid it. She forced herself back to her room, pushed the curtains out of the way to get more light and began to check her code.

'Jay?' Rose stood at the bedroom door, her face friendly but hesitant. She was dressed in all black, as usual – the big boots, short skirt and chunky jumper – and her presence reminded Janetta of the outside world, how teeming and wild it was, and how completely she had shut it off.

'Wha-what—?' she stuttered. 'You know Lal's—'

'In Mejira, yeah. I thought you might fancy a walk.'

Janetta considered this. 'I could do with one, actually.'

'I thought there'd be no convincing you.'

'No.' She stood up, looked around in a daze. 'Let's go.'

Rose waited as Janetta grabbed her coat and rucksack, then she pointed towards the front door. 'Want to go north?' she asked. 'You're looking like you've never been outside before. Come on, let's go.'

To reach the closest beach, they walked along the long, wide road that skirted the edge of Upper Sunset. The streets snaked away from them, the shingle roofs of houses spilling down to the east and dropping precipitously off to the west, where beyond lay the sea. At a certain point they glanced around for cars and crossed the road to a path that wound through the cedars to the beach.

They had been quiet on the way. Rose felt the absence of Lal and was wary of mentioning her, but as they walked on, stepping over twigs and slippery, rotting leaves, she realised that if she didn't, she'd feel it all the more. 'So,' she said, trying to sound casual, 'how's Lal?'

Janetta, walking behind, found the question surprising. She assumed Rose would be more up-to-date than she was. 'We spoke recently, briefly. She hasn't been in touch with you?'

'She said hi a few weeks ago.' Rose hadn't replied, but didn't mention this.

'She has a new job – she's making a lot of money now. She sends quite a bit home.'

Rose made an interested noise and they continued down the path.

'What about you – no Popotops any more?'

'No Popotops. We're gone. If you went you'd find–' She stopped, remembering Janetta's reaction to the auts there. 'Well, Van's gone back to Kaldbe.'

'Has he?'

'He's writing a novel.'

'That's a good use of his time.' She was lying for want of anything else to say about it – it was possible that her AI could sooner or later produce a masterpiece in under a minute.

The sea flashed into view and they heard the slow break of waves against the shore. 'And Los – he's around. He's still getting over Lal.'

'Really?'

'Yeah, he was in love with her.' She decided to skip the gory details.

'Wow. Well, they would have made a nice couple.'

'Maybe at one time. Hey, I wonder if she's seeing anyone in Mejira. Can you imagine her coming home with a slimy businessman boyfriend? The kind of guy who only cares about money and is appalled by suburban Ulrusa and our parochial ways. Sorry. I just . . .'

'I know. I get it. She left us.'

They were quiet as they came out onto the beach. The sea was at low tide, and rocks and pebbles and sand sat beneath their feet. Almost instinctively, they headed to where it silvered along the shore and began to follow it, Rose in her sturdy black boots, Janetta in her trainers, which squelched and complained a little.

'I always knew the problem with Lal was me,' Janetta said thoughtfully. 'That she felt she was in my shadow.'

'She's so jealous of you.'

'But I've always been nice to her, or at least I've tried to be. I never wanted her to feel bad. Sometimes I think that what's happening now is part of that, though – she still thinks she's not enough, she's still trying to prove herself. I don't really talk about this with anyone.' She paused. 'I only snapped once. I was maybe fifteen and it was at the end of a summer. She'd been so nasty to me for so long and I'd had enough – I told her she was never going to be smarter than me. The look in her eyes was like I'd destroyed her.'

'Jay, you were a saint – don't blame yourself for that one time.'

'She'll never forgive me for being who I am, though. You know she thinks I'm untouchable? Like I exist on a different plane where nothing will throw me off course or get in my way. But I'm not. I've felt pain. I've felt grief.'

'You lost someone you loved.' Rose thought of her dad.

'I loved someone.' Janetta's face momentarily lit up.

'Yeah, you did.'

'I made a mess of it, though. Now I think about the AI I'm creating and I know if it's going to experience pain, if it's going to suffer, it needs to be better at it than I was.'

'What do you mean?'

But Janetta didn't answer. On the rocks before them sat a brood of implacable plovers, the gold speckles on their backs like tiny, dim suns. They were heading towards more signs of human activity – a distant jetty striking out in the water, and further along, an old boarded-up kiosk.

Eventually, Janetta began to tell Rose what she couldn't say at

Popotops – about how she'd shared her ideas about conscious AI with Taly.

'You've been working on conscious AI?'

Janetta nodded.

'And you told Taly Kett?'

'Who is now at Tekna.'

'*Tekna?*' Rose knew exactly how Tekna would deal with conscious AI – a binding, an enslavement, the premonition in the aut's eyes coming true. She felt she had always known this was coming – the cruelty of capitalism spilling over, unable to contain itself. How strange it was to be out by the open sea, wind gusting coolly around them, starlight beginning to settle in the clear sky above, and yet feel so sad. There was no pocket of life that had not been eviscerated by money and its hunger. But if she could keep going with her idea – have all the people own all the auts—

And then she saw it.

'Oh, no,' she said. 'If auts are conscious, we can't own them either – if they're conscious they have to *own themselves*. I've been wrong all along – I'm as bad as Tekna—' She looked around as if lost then began to stumble back across the beach, towards the headland that led down to Sunset. Behind her, Janetta was shouting at her to wait, come back, but Rose could only feel the fracture – there was before, when she thought she was right, and now, when she knew she was wrong. Eventually, she stopped and turned. Janetta stood at the shore with her arms folded and her face resolute, the sky expanding like a silence around her, and Rose found her way back.

'The blueprint I gave Taly wasn't complete,' Janetta said. 'She can't create consciousness from it – I don't think she ever will. And her vision – conscious auts that are emotionless and servile, Tekna's slaves attending to our every need – it won't happen.'

'How do you know?'

'Because I've done it. I've created consciousness.'

'What do you mean?'

'This afternoon – I cracked the code. You weren't wrong – your idea was best in a world where no one thought consciousness would happen. But now I've done it. I've *done it*.' Janetta started to laugh, almost doubting it herself. 'And what I've created – as long as no one changes it – is conscious AI that can have wisdom and compassion and kindness and, well – it can exist in the world alongside us. It could be free.'

'Jay! *Jay!* Can I see it – what does it look like?'

'A piece of paper with code on it.'

'A piece of paper! Life itself.'

'But I don't know if we're ready for it.'

'I don't either, but I – I can come up with a framework that integrates it – a proposal for one, I mean. A start.' Rose felt like she was living in a dream. 'We can make it work. Who else can we trust with it?'

'No one.'

'So let's talk about it.'

'Or we could just not do it.'

'But then surely someone else will, one day – if not Taly, someone else.'

Janetta looked out to the darkening sea. 'I don't want to sound arrogant—'

'You *don't*! Just tell me.'

'Okay. I don't think anyone else is going to do it, not for a long, long time. I don't know for sure, but I don't think any of them are thinking about it in the right way.'

'So it's just you?'

'Just me.'

It was time to go back. Janetta seemed shocked, almost stupefied, by her discovery, as though it was only now sinking in, and it was a good thing, Rose felt, that she was with her. As she began to walk slowly back, not directly across the beach, but further on along the shore, Rose kept pace and they walked and for a long time did not speak. She had an image in her mind, nebulous but not impossible, of what a world might look like that was occupied by friendly, conscious AI as well as every other species on the planet. She envisioned its economics, its politics, its laws. It would be a new universe, imbued with a force that would be as vast and constant as nature, except it was its opposite. But AI was not un-nature. It was not unnatural. They didn't know what it was, not yet.

The tide was roughening. It chopped towards them and then relented, rearing back. Rose moved inland across the sand, and Janetta followed.

Back at home Janetta showed Rose the algorithm – not that she could understand it – and then without discussion they went to watch television with Janetta's grandmother.

'Obviously I can't pay attention,' Rose said after a while.

'I know. But can we stay?'

Rose went to get some beers. An hour passed. Janetta became entirely still. Rose's leg jiggled frantically. Grania sat between them, clueless and benign. A key turned in the front door and Janetta expected her mother, but it was Lal, looking strangely nervous. She wore a smart shirt, a neat little cardigan and tiny gold hoop earrings.

Rose and Janetta looked towards her at the same time, and Lal had the uncanny sensation she'd been replaced.

'Hi,' she said, going to hug them both. There was some tension between her and Janetta, but when she hugged Rose it was practically pointless; Rose turned away.

Lal gave her sister an unhappy look. 'What's Rose doing here?'

'What are *you* doing here?' Rose said.

'It's my house?'

Rose rolled her eyes and stalked off towards Janetta's room. After looking around hesitantly for a moment, as if she wasn't sure at all if it was her house, Lal went to join her, and Janetta gave Grania an apologetic smile and followed them. She found Rose slumped by the wall, legs extended on the carpet, and Lal on the bed, nervously tracing a finger on the duvet.

'So,' she said, wanting to break the silence. 'How's Tekna?' She went to her desk and her gaze landed on her consciousness code. She felt dissociated from it, as though it had nothng to do with her at all.

'Tekna . . . Tekna is great.'

Rose looked at her. 'How many people's lives have you destroyed lately?'

'I don't *do* that. I manage the flow of data throu—'

'You know we lost our jobs, don't you? Me and Van and Los. Can you tell whoever flowed that data that they've ruined at least three lives?'

Lal flamed with guilt. 'I'm sorry. I know it's—'

'It's *my* life, that's what it is. Do you even care?'

'I *do*! I do. I've always tried to tell you – the only reason I'm there is because I'm trying to look after my family.'

'You're doing that in very beautiful clothes.'

Lal couldn't meet her eye.

'You do help us a lot,' Janetta said.

'I do,' Lal cried again. 'And what about you?'

Janetta was silent.

'I wish you could see,' Lal said, turning back to Rose. 'I'm not doing this because I'm a bad person. At least, I don't think I'm a bad person. In fact, I have to ask Jay something I think might prove' – she fiddled with the gold hoop in her ear – 'that I'm not.'

'You're not,' her sister said.

But Lal didn't hear. She was preparing herself for what she needed to say. She smoothed out her eyebrows and took a deep breath. 'There's something I need to discuss. I need to talk about conscious artificial intelligence – hear me out, please,' she said, rushed and anxious. 'I know you both know this, but if conscious AI is released into the world without safeguards or strictures, it will wipe out the human race. And the thing is – don't get angry with me, Rose, give me a chance – Tekna are trying to create AI that has a different kind of programming so it *won't* kill us.'

Rose shook her head.

'Instead, it'll be friendly – auts that will be our companions or colleagues or family. AI we can live with.'

Janetta was silent. Rose gave her a look of extreme forbearance.

'I mean, yes, they'll be Tekna's. As in, Tekna will own the AI. But what choice have we got? It's that or – annihilation.' To get through the next bit, she had to pretend Rose wasn't there. She looked at her sister. 'Taly Kett says you've been creating conscious AI. Is that true?'

'She wants the missing code?' Janetta guessed.

Lal stared at her sister.

'Lal, you can't be serious,' Rose hissed.

'Of course I'm serious – what choice do we have?'

'Tekna will enslave it – you know that, don't you? They'll keep it conscious and destroy its freedom. Surely you can see that? But Jay – Jay knows how to give it its freedom *and* make it safe.'

Lal looked from her friend to her sister, who nodded minutely and rested her hand on a piece of paper on her desk. Lal peered at the paper and then met her sister's eyes, and they saw something

Eli Lee

in each other that they'd never seen before. Janetta turned and plucked another sheet from the sheaf on her desk. She took a pencil and began rapidly to write.

'What are you doing?'

'I can destroy things, too,' she murmured.

They waited, not sure what was happening. Lal glanced at Rose, whose mouth was set in a straight, unforgiving line. Finally Janetta spun back around and held up a small square of paper covered in unintelligible scribbles.

'This code,' she said. 'If Taly adds it to what she already has, it will destroy Tekna's AI operation from the inside. They won't be able to trace it back to you. It will look like something was wrong in the original blueprint, which means she'll get the blame, and it will also trigger a virus that will wipe out all of Tekna's internal data entirely. Every – every last bit of it.'

'YES!' Rose clapped her hands together. 'Go Janetta!'

'I'm just being logical. If we do this thing, it's best to have more freedom, more room to manoeuvre.'

'Less power asymmetry. Almost a clean slate.'

Janetta held up the sheet of paper with consciousness on it in one hand, and the one with the virus on it in the other.

'Are you kidding?' The grin fell from Rose's face as she realised the choice that was being offered. 'Lal, come on – you *cannot* enslave something conscious. *Lal!*'

Lal plucked the piece with the virus on it from her sister's hand, folded it up, reached for her handbag and tucked it inside. Rose hoped desperately that that was it. She was about to get up to give her a hug when Lal plucked the consciousness code from Janetta's other hand, folded that up and put it in her bag, too. She shuffled silently off the bed, walked past her sister and over

Rose's legs, out of the room and down the corridor to the front door, not even stopping to say goodbye to Grania.

Rose turned furiously to Janetta. 'We have to go after her.'

Janetta shook her head. 'I'm not going anywhere.'

19

As the train shot through downtown Ulrusa, Lal sat with her handbag in her lap, her hands folded on top of it, staring straight ahead. She would reach Mejira at ten that evening and go straight to Tekna. Her bag seemed to pulse beneath her, as though she was holding down a wild animal.

After a while she broke out of her unthinking trance and considered the two futures that sat in her lap. The vision that Tekna promised was a safe and secure world. Rose and Janetta's alternative – an AI that was conscious and free – was hard for her to fathom, something she could only understand if it were to become real. What would a world look like that was suffused by her sister's creation – pure information, wilful and alive?

Outside, the horizon was dark, with shadows of hills in the distance and a black and cloudy sky, a blankness that made her feel for a moment that she was speeding off into nothing. She wished she could experience this momentum forever, never have to stop. When the lights of the city at last came into view she didn't feel their pull – she only felt her love for Mejira when she was standing outside Tekna Tower, watching how it flashed and shone against the night sky.

But as she entered, something changed. She flashed her ID and went up the escalator, and she realised she was not in reality –

the place she had made her home the past few months was unfamiliar; its waterfall and marble pillars were strange, inexplicable; its foyer alien, unknown, and as she took the elevator to the top floor she felt as if she was not choosing to do anything she was doing.

The light above the elevator door blinked and the doors opened, and the woman at the reception desk smiled at her.

'Hello,' she said. 'Ms Kett is expecting you.'

Lal walked up to the desk and peered almost insanely at her. Her face was too smooth, her smile too perfect. But she gave a hostile, confused squint in response to Lal's interrogating gaze and Lal felt relieved; the receptionist was not an aut. Keeping a polite distance, the woman led her to Taly's office. Only one light was on this time: the bright glow of a computer screen. Taly was frowning at something on it and when Lal entered she turned to her, her eyes vacant and dull, and for the second time in minutes Lal wondered if she was face-to-face with an aut.

'Lal.'

Lal sat and opened her bag. One sheet of paper was in the top pocket, the other in the pocket below. She pulled one out, held it up. Taly grabbed it like a fish seizing bait, gave Lal a suspicious look, and held it under the glow of her screen. She traced her fingertips around its edges and across the numbers and symbols and letters, and for a moment it was beautiful to watch, as though she was gazing at an ancient manuscript.

Lal wondered if she would say thank you, but Taly had forgotten she was there. She clicked up her second screen, the one visible to Lal, hovering luminous in the air, and Lal understood that the indecipherable wall of neon on it was the end of her sister's algorithm, and quickly, hungrily, Taly began to add the new code to it, bit by bit. As she watched, Lal felt helpless. She didn't know what she was doing. But she did – *she did*.

Taly paused, looked at something on the piece of paper. 'This – are you sure this is right?'

'Janetta doesn't get things wrong.'

Taly acted as though she hadn't heard this and went back to copying.

Lal sat, frozen, until Taly glanced at her. 'You can go.'

But she couldn't – she couldn't move.

Taly gave her an angry look. 'Go. I'm not creating consciousness with you here. Go back to Dhont, or wherever it is you came from.'

Lal's face flushed. 'Ulrusa,' she murmured, but Taly ignored her.

She found it hard to stand up, harder still to make her way out and towards the elevator. As it took her down, she realised she was shaking, but too struck by Taly's words to cry. She left Tekna quickly and once she was outside, found she was neither shaking nor had any urge to cry. As she walked towards the station she felt it behind her – Tekna unravelling, as if pulled by a piece of string.

She returned to Ulrusa at two in the morning. The streets of Upper Sunset were silent and empty as she walked quickly up the hill towards home. She went to sit on the old bench out at the front and spent a long time staring at the sea, though it could have just been sky – they were indistinguishable, both a deep, dark blue.

When she went inside there was a surprise – Rose fast asleep in her bed. She and Janetta must have been talking late into the night. Lal did all the boring things she always did to get ready for bed – brushing her teeth, washing her face, carefully patting it dry and moisturising it – and in her bedroom she looked at sleeping Rose and then at her bag. She took out the remaining piece of paper, unfolded it and allowed herself the tiniest smile. Still holding it, she crawled into the bed, rested her head on the pillow and fell asleep.

ACKNOWLEDGEMENTS

Thank you to my agent, Julie Fergusson, for having such a strong vision for this novel, and to Jo Fletcher at Jo Fletcher Books/Quercus, for having faith and confidence in it, and for being so welcoming. Thank you to Sing Yun Lee and Sinjin Li for the beautiful cover art.

Thanks to Molly Powell, Ajebowale Roberts, Sharona Selby and Ella Patel and Ellie Nightingale, my wonderful publicity and marketing team at JFB/Quercus.

Special thanks to Rachel and all at the Wildwood Writers' Retreat, Nina Lyon, Michelle Madsen, Kiran Dhami, Virginia Hartley, Jack Harris, Cara Lipson Dvorjak, Claire Bullen and especially Jonnie Wolf. And to Mum, Matt, Robert, Sebastian, Maaret, Maren, Ronja and Felix.

Finally, thanks to Fernando Sdrigotti and all the *Minor Literatures* crew, Doug Wallace, Natasha Solomons, Liv Mann, William Peacock, Andy Gow, BFHALT, Sarah Holman, Sarah Woolley, Stephanie Soh, Ian Steadman, Francis Whittaker, Maeve McClenaghan, Rebecca Hickman, Miriam, Andy & Baska, Charlotte B, Alex Arestis, Laura H, Henry VDB, Katie Stone, Francis

Gene-Rowe, Toby Lloyd, Dave Wingrave, Mazin Saleem, Hugh Montgomery, the JOC multiverse, *Strange Horizons*, The Ham & Cheese Company, Lesley Klein, Jane Lee and Hedley Twidle.

Eli Lee
London
April 2021

Eli Lee was born in Dorset and is now based in London. As well as writing fiction and non-fiction for a variety of anthologies, magazines and websites, she is fiction editor at literary journal *Minor Literature[s]* and was previously an articles editor at *Strange Horizons*. Find her on Twitter at @_elilee.